Elim Henry D'Avigdor

Hunt-Room Stories and Yachting Yarns

Elim Henry D'Avigdor

Hunt-Room Stories and Yachting Yarns

ISBN/EAN: 9783337403300

Printed in Europe, USA, Canada, Australia, Japan

Cover: Foto ©Andreas Hilbeck / pixelio.de

More available books at **www.hansebooks.com**

HUNT-ROOM STORIES

AND

YACHTING YARNS.

BY

THE AUTHOR OF "ACROSS COUNTRY,"

"FAIR DIANA," Etc.

WITH ILLUSTRATIONS BY EDGAR GIBERNE.

LONDON: CHAPMAN AND HALL,

LIMITED.

1884.

LONDON :
R. CLAY, SONS, AND TAYLOR,
BREAD STREET HILL

TO

ARTHUR LONGMAN, ESQ.,

Of Shendish, Herts,

M.F.H. AND YACHTSMAN,

THIS LITTLE VOLUME

Is Affectionately Dedicated,

IN REMEMBRANCE OF THE MANY PLEASANT DAYS

I HAVE SPENT WITH HIS HOUNDS.

April, 1884.

PREFACE.

Some of the Tales in the present volume have appeared in the columns of the *County Gentleman*. To the Editor of that newspaper I beg to tender my sincere thanks for his kind permission to reprint them. I have also to thank the Proprietors of the *Court Circular* for the same favour.

THE AUTHOR.

April, 1884.

CONTENTS.

b

LIST OF ILLUSTRATIONS.

HUNT-ROOM STORIES

B

HUNT-ROOM STORIES.

THE COLONEL'S BOOTS.

"HERE comes the Colonel," said pretty Mrs. Rainer, as they were waiting in the lane below Harbury Wood. "I hope he won't stick close by me all day as he did last week at Crowsford."

"I will relieve you of him with pleasure," cried Lord Audrey Fantail, a small youth on a game-looking thorough-bred, whose legs showed signs of work, though her heart would probably carry her through many a severe run when cocktails might be unwilling to face more fences.

"No," exclaimed Mr. Pottinger; "getting rid of bores is my special province. Leave him to me, Mrs. Rainer—*I* will settle him." At the same time he turned the head of his handsome weight-carrier as if to cut off the Colonel's advance.

"You will just be good enough to leave the Colonel alone," said Mrs. Rainer. "I admit that he is rather a nuisance sometimes, but he is a good fellow and I won't have him bullied. I like him very much."

B 2

Before Pottinger and Lord Audrey could reply, the gentleman in question had joined the group. "A fine morning, Mrs. Rainer," said he; "a very fine hunting morning. Delighted to see you looking more beautiful than ever, upon my word as an officer and gentleman. And the mare, why she's quite the pink of perfection. I believe we shall get a run, don't you, Mrs. Rainer? And," added he, lowering his voice, "I hope you will let me pilot you as you did last Tuesday from Crowsford." Then looking round as if he had only just perceived the other two, "Morning, my lord; morning, Pottinger," said he, in a somewhat condescending manner.

He got his horse close to Mrs. Rainer's, with the evident intention of stopping there. Both the other men curled their lower lips, and returned his greeting with silent nods. Even the most superficial spectator would have noticed that they were rivals. While the hounds are drawing Harbury it may therefore be as well to enlighten the reader.

Mrs. Rainer is a charming widow whose years no book of reference states, but who can certainly not yet have reached thirty summers. After two years' marriage with a man twice her age she was left with a very large fortune entirely at her own disposal, and without what the servants call encumbrances, and what are termed children in other classes of society. The late Mr. Rainer, who had been M.P. for a Scotch burgh, had lived much in London, and had introduced his country wife to many of the best houses; but shortly after his death his widow took up her abode with her father—a man of moderate but independent fortune living near Crampleton, the county town of Crampshire—and had only paid a few short visits to the metropolis in the three years which had since elapsed. Mrs. Rainer preferred a country life. Her very considerable income enabled her to add a new wing to her father's house and to build new stables, and she appeared perfectly contented to console the old gentleman's declining years by her cheerful society, to receive a few friends during the hunting and shooting season, and to join in the Crampleton festivities, few and far between as they were. It was no secret in Crampshire that she did not spend a quarter of her revenue, and that her capital was large enough to enable any second husband she might accept, to keep a very good house, with well-filled cellars and stables, on his wife's money. And Mrs. Rainer was a desirable *parti* for other reasons. A brunette on a small scale, her dark complexion was animated by the healthy blood which coursed through her veins. She had black eyes, rather deep-set, and they were occasionally so piercing and so strange in their glance that it was not quite pleasant to have them levelled at you. But then, on the other hand, they were often full of soft languor and dreaminess, or, again, sparkling with fun and mischief. At such moments a smile, which illumined the whole face, displayed a row of teeth which might be a little larger than the strict classical critic would approve, but were white and regular. And when this by no means unfrequent smile appeared it brought with it a dimple which made her look young as a schoolgirl, and seemed to remove all the respect which a previous keen glance from those deep-set eyes might have inspired. In figure Mrs. Rainer was plump without being fat, and it was open to one prophet to declare that she would be dumpy before she was forty, and to another to forecast that she would become sinewy and tough, like so many riding women. Meanwhile critic and prophets all agreed that she was charming, and knew how to dress and how to ride. Under the circumstances it was scarcely surprising that Mr. Pottinger, the wealthy Crampleton brewer, whose father had made the fortune which the young man had only to spend, or Lord Audrey Fantail, the second son of the great house of Paon, *the* people of all others in Crampshire, should both be paying much attention to the lovely widow.

Nor must the Colonel be forgotten ; in fact the Colonel deserves special notice. He was now on half-pay, but had served Her Majesty with distinction in the 50th Dragoons. It was his boast that he had never got into any scrapes, never played any practical jokes, never as a subaltern had disagreeable interviews with his commanding officer, and had never spent more money than he could afford. The

Colonel was nothing if not methodical. He was the only representative of a good old Crampshire family, and had come to live on the small family estate when his elder brother had died without children. He then left the army, and devoted his attention and his method to the raising of wonderful crops of mangolds and the thorough drainage of neglected lands.

Though his moustache was black, and his hair showed no traces of changing its hue—thanks to the aid of sundry patent dyes, as his enemies asserted—no one could take the Colonel for a young man. Crows'-feet were too numerous and too distinct on his temples, while the deep furrows between nose and cheeks were caused rather by years than by hard service. But, notwithstanding the undoubted fact that he was rapidly approaching at least middle age, the Colonel affected all the ways and manners of extreme youth. He was an indefatigable dancer at the Crampleton balls, the first to come and the last to go. He filled up his card weeks beforehand by riding about and engaging partners at the various houses. He never missed a meet if hounds were anywhere within reasonable distance, and he occasionally even attempted to show the way across country; but, failing in this, fell back on his really excellent topographical knowledge and his extended experience of foxes and their ways, to be "there or thereabouts" as often as anybody.

After the Colonel had talked for a few minutes with

Mrs. Rainer, during which she showed some signs of impatience, Mr. Pottinger suddenly held up his hand.

"A fox, I believe!" cried Lord Audrey.

"This way, this way!" called out the Colonel, hustling his somewhat heavy-topped underbred horse towards a gap in the fence. "He is sure to break on the lower side."

"Come with us," almost whispered Lord Audrey, "and we shall get rid of the old bore."

And away went the three precisely in the opposite direction. When the Colonel got into the ploughed field and looked back, he found himself alone. The others had turned through a bridle-gate and galloped along a drive in the wood. Lord Audrey, who was nearest the fair widow, seized the opportunity to remark, "What a horrid nuisance that old Colonel is! Never knows when he is not wanted."

"But perhaps I *did* want him," suggested Mrs. Rainer.

"I don't believe you did," replied his lordship. "Why, the old fellow runs after you in the most barefaced manner! If you encouraged him a little bit, I believe he'd propose directly."

"Well, perhaps I should not object," answered the widow, looking her companion straight in the face. "I might do worse."

"It is cruel to talk like that," exclaimed Lord Audrey, his face flushing up, "when you know that I——"

What he would have said can only be guessed, for at that moment Pottinger called out, "To the left, Mrs. Rainer; you can't get over that fence, and hounds are running left-handed," ranging up alongside of them as he spoke. For a quarter of an hour or so there was no talk. They were galloping over a good country, grass alternating with plough or stubble, and there was nothing formidable to stop any decently mounted sportsman; but then occurred a check. The hounds spread out doubtfully, then a few straggled still wider, then they collected round a spot in the hedge, almost tumbling over each other in their eagerness. "Hold hard, please," was shouted by the huntsman, and re-echoed from a dozen mouths, though those who called "hold hard" had been just as willing to override hounds as the rest. But long before the "tail" had come up they were off again in full cry, the fox having doubled up the hedge and then turned sharp to the right. On his new line there were several nasty places to negotiate, and both Lord Audrey and Mr. Pottinger had enough to do to keep their places, Mrs. Rainer going well, thanks to her good horse and her light weight. Soon even the leaders were glad of another check, and this time the scent was not picked up quite so quickly. They were behind a cunning old fox, who was evidently up to every trick of his race. As hounds seemed to make nothing of it, the huntsman lifted them, and making a wide cast the scent was hit off near a ruined barn, when away they tore again in full cry, pointing for Finch Wood. Would they get there before the fox, or would the fox beat them ? That was the question, for Finch Wood was a great straggling place, broken up by many deep dells and pits, where a fox of any talent could easily baffle his pursuers, and at the worst indeed induce a fresh colleague to run instead of himself. The last mile over the pastures which bordered this refuge was covered at a great pace, and Mr. Pottinger's steed was outpaced. Yet hounds were too late ; they had lost valuable time at the barn. Soon they were hunting slowly up and down the gorse and thick undergrowth, while the field gradually closed up outside. Pottinger came up on his panting horse to where Lord Audrey and Mrs. Rainer were standing, their heads turned to the wind ; and as he rode towards them from one side up came the Colonel from the other, his appearance a marked contrast to theirs. Lord Audrey had covered himself with mud and glory by rolling over at a post and rails. Mr. Pottinger had scratched his face severely in jumping through a blackthorn hedge, and both were attempting to remove the traces of their mishaps with pocket-handkerchiefs, which were quite insufficient for the task set them. Even Mrs. Rainer looked somewhat excited, her face flushed, her hair partly down, and the neck of her mare white with foam. The Colonel might have been on his way to parade, if parade there were in white breeches and pink tops. There was scarcely a spot on either, his hat was smooth and redolent of the iron, his moustache pointed as stiffly as usual, and his hair not even out of curl. "There is nothing like method," quoth he, as he joined the party. "Look at my horse! Not even turned a hair. And yet I have seen all the fun, even to the check at Price's barn. There's nothing like knowing the country and method! Better trust me another time, Mrs. Rainer."

"Where is Captain Bradbourne?" asked the widow. "He showed me the way for ever so long."

"In the ditch close to the barn," answered Lord Audrey. "I saw him fall in, but had not time to help him out."

"Serve the young man right," exclaimed the Colonel, who was as jealous of Captain Bradbourne as of every man whom he suspected of admiring the widow. "He is a very reprehensible young man."

"Reprehensible! What do you mean?" asked Pottinger.

"A most irregular person," continued the Colonel; "a man whom *I* would request to exchange if *I* were his commanding officer."

"Indeed! What has he done?" asked young Snider of the Guards, who had joined the group while hounds were hunting in the inaccessible cover.

"You would scarcely believe it," replied the Colonel, "and I don't like to abuse a man behind his back. But the fact is, that when I was last in Crampleton Barracks

Captain Bradbourne asked me into his room.   His servants brought in some letters.   I could see that they were bills. Now, what do you think ?   He actually threw them into the fire without opening them !   A young man of most irregular habits ! "

There was a roar of laughter, in which even Pottinger joined, though he had probably never known what it was not to be able to pay his bills.

" Is that all, Colonel ? " asked Lord Audrey.   " I'm afraid many of us do that.   Poor Bradbourne !   But here he is at last."

" Hallo, Bradbourne," cried Snider ; " glad to see you out of the ditch.   Here's the Colonel says you throw your bills into the fire without looking at them.   Is it true ? "

" Well, of course," answered the victim, smiling sadly. " What else can a fellow do ?   I can't pay them, and if I read them they would spoil my appetite and take away my sleep ; so I burn them."

" Quite right, too," said Lord Audrey.   " I always do. The only thing that is sacred is a writ.   When *that* comes I am bound to speak to the governor, for fear my horses might go."

" Still, I consider it a most reprehensible and disgraceful practice," whispered the Colonel, stooping over to Mrs. Rainer.   " Don't you ? "

" Oh, dreadful ! " answered she, gaily ; " very shocking indeed ! "

"Yes," continued he, "you see to what you expose yourself with these young men."

"*I?*" asked the widow, innocently. "*I* am not exposed to anything that I know of. They don't send their bills to me; they only burn them."

"But you know they all want you to marry them."

"Colonel, what nonsense!"

"They do, though. Now if you would only trust a man of some experience——"

Mrs. Rainer turned away her horse. "It is no use waiting here all day," she remarked in an audible tone, "the horses will get quite stiff. Let us move on round to the other side of the wood. Perhaps we shall find out what they are doing."

All obeyed the hint, and the Colonel's *tête-à-tête* with her was again interrupted. Nor did he get another chance that day. Whenever he rode up to Mrs. Rainer's side she began talking to some one else, or drew back, or hurried on; and once, when there appeared no other way of getting rid of him, she actually turned her mare short on the road and jumped across a stiff wattle fence into the next field, a leap which the Colonel's charger refused to take.

But not many days elapsed before the gallant officer got another chance. It was at a dinner given by the Crampleton banker, at which Mrs. Rainer and her father were present. He would have dearly loved to take her in to dinner, but the fates and the banker's wife decreed otherwise, and the Colonel found himself in less congenial company, fondly believing the same of her. When, after a "sit" over some old port which was much too long for the amorous ex-plunger, the drawing-room door at last admitted the men, our friend lost no time in approaching the lovely widow, who was sitting on a sofa exchanging mild chaff with Lord Audrey Fantail and Captain Bradbourne.

"Come and sit here, Colonel," was her greeting, as she made room for him on the couch, "and tell me all about yesterday. I could not go out, because we had some people from town staying with us."

"The day had no charm for me," replied the veteran gallantly, "as Mrs. Rainer did not vouchsafe to appear."

"Oh, yes! I know your politeness very well, Colonel. Tell me something I *don't* know! Where did you find? Had you a run? Did you kill? And did your knowledge of the country help you?"

"Captain Bradbourne, here," answered he, rather jealously, "ought to be able to satisfy you. I saw him at the meet."

"I only came to look at them, Colonel," said the Captain. "I have only two horses, and one is lame. I can't afford more, so I rode home after they had drawn all the woods near Barston. It was hard lines, tumbling into that ditch the other day. The mare was as lame as a tree next morning, and I have not paid for her yet."

The Colonel raised his eyebrows. "Indeed! Not paid for her?" A significant glance towards Mrs. Rainer, and the whispered remark, "A most unmethodical, irregular young man, as I told you."

"No!" continued Bradbourne; "I couldn't afford to pay for my horse, and Oakley won't give tick for more than one at a time. So you see I can't manage to hunt four times a week, can I?"

This proposition seemed self-evident, as indeed it might be called wonderful that under the circumstances he could afford to hunt at all. The Colonel, however, at last narrated the very uninteresting events of the previous day, and wound up with the remark, "If you studied the country as I do, Captain Bradbourne, you would be able to make your two horses do a deal more than they do. What is the use of your reckless, harum-scarum riding? Do it methodically, that's what I say. Study your fox's point, and then ride for it. Never jump if you can help it. Trot up the furrows, remember your gates, and carry your ordnance map in your pocket. Then your horse will be fit to go again the next day if you want him."

"Yes, to go along roads and up lanes as you do," murmured Bradbourne to Lord Audrey, as he moved off. "What a terrible old bore! Why does not Mrs. Rainer shunt him for good and all?"

"Why, indeed?" drawled his lordship. "I never can make her out."

The Colonel took advantage of this aside to whisper one on his own account.

"Dear Mrs. Rainer," said he, "when can I have a chance of seeing you alone? I really must. I have a most important question to ask you."

"Ask it now," answered the lady.

The Colonel looked round. He was brave enough, but too methodical to ask a question into which he wanted to infuse the greatest possible tenderness before a host of people in a crowded drawing-room.

"No; I can't indeed. It requires a *tête-à-tête*, even if only a short one. Do grant me this, dear Madam. May I call at your house?"

"You had better not," replied Mrs. Rainer, looking affectionate. "You see, dear Colonel, people have been talking."

"Talking?" asked the delighted lover. "About whom?"

"Well, about you and me," said she, archly. "They have noticed that you are always riding with me when we are out hunting, and often see me home. And papa has heard of it."

"But you are quite independent of Mr. Easton? You are quite your own mistress?"

"Yes; but I would never do anything to displease papa. No; you must not call in a public way, nor at the usual time. Tell me, do you really want to see me so much?"

"Can you doubt it?" answered the gallant Colonel, attempting to seize her hand.

"How can you be so impertinent ?—before all these people too ! Well, if you *must* come, do so. Come to the little back garden gate of our house at ten o'clock next Monday night. Knock gently. I will be there. And mind you don't drive up to the gate. Papa might hear," With these words she rose and crossed the room to the banker's wife.

The Colonel could hardly trust his ears or his luck. Mrs. Rainer had not only made room for him on the sofa, had not only greeted him with twice her usual kindness, but had actually glanced affectionately at him several times and had wound up by giving him a rendezvous in her garden at an advanced hour of the evening.

When an extraordinary piece of good fortune befalls people they begin by being astonished, and then in a very short time discover that they fully deserved it, and that it is a wonder, if not an injustice, that it did not happen sooner. Before the Colonel had taken his leave he had quite got over his surprise, and had arrived at the conviction that nothing was more natural than for Mrs. Rainer to fall in love with him. " She is bound to like me better than that sucking lord or that extravagant fool, Bradbourne," said he to himself, as he jerked his pony's reins on his homeward way. " Of course a woman of her sense would soon see the difference between a man of experience and method like myself and these jackanapes. She knows I should make her a good husband, and she is ready to take me if I ask her. Why should she not, too ?" And the Colonel gave an extra curl to his moustache with the hand which was at liberty. "I have served Her Majesty with honour and credit. I am not middle-aged yet, and as good-looking as any youngster. Know the country, too, better than any of them. Ah !" he concluded, giving the pony a flick, "the Colonel will get the brush yet, notwithstanding all your nonsense, you young asses."

The next few days were spent in delicious dreams of a fair and rich wife, and Monday opened auspiciously; but before noon clouds began to gather, and at four o'clock rain set in with a steadiness and a gloom which promised continuance. It was a long six miles from the Colonel's place to Squire Easton's house, and being anxious to observe the rules of the strictest discretion, our hero did not order a covered fly, but started at about nine o'clock in his little pony trap—"For fear," said he to himself, "of compromising the lady." It rained hard, and ever harder; the road was heavy, and pools formed themselves all over the Colonel's water-proofing, which eventually found their way slowly into his nether garments. He had, as a matter of course, thought of donning dress clothes, but the weather had, at the last moment, deterred him, and he added a heavy high pair of boots to his morning costume.

But even then he would have been miserable in the extreme had not the thoughts of the lovely Mrs. Rainer and her large fortune kept him in good spirits. Instead of following the high road to Mr. Easton's gates, he turned up a lane overhung with the bare boughs of dripping trees. Here he descended and secured the pony's reins round a gate-post. "Polly will be safe enough there," he thought, "while I go and conquer the heiress. You will have a rich man to take home, Polly," added he, aloud, as he stroked the pony's neck. "Stand quiet, and wait for him." Then he trudged up the lane till he reached a garden wall and a little green gate in it. He felt wet and dirty, and was fain to admit to himself that he was scarcely fit to appear in the presence of his graceful lady-love. "But she won't mind," he thought; "she can't expect a man to come six miles on a night like this and turn out as if he had come in a bandbox." And he knocked at the door, first faintly, and then, as nobody came, a little louder. Soon he heard soft steps on the gravel. It was she! Even his old heart began to beat faster. The door was gently opened, and all he could distinguish in the gloom was an umbrella. "Dear Mrs. Rainer!" he whispered. "It is not Mrs. Rainer," a low voice announced from under the umbrella. "I am her maid. Turn this way, and shut the door very gently. Master mustn't hear you—he would kill you if he knew." The umbrella moved up the gravel path, and he followed. "Stop!" the voice suddenly said: "your boots make a horrid noise; take them off."

"Take my boots off?" asked the Colonel, amazed. "Why, I shall get wet through."

"I won't have my missus get into a row," replied the umbrella; "and your boots make such a noise on the gravel they are sure to hear us as we get near the house. Take them off at once, or go back."

"Never!" cried the Colonel, and he sat down on the wet path and pulled off his boots, which he held in one hand, while entrusting the other to his guide, for it was perfectly dark, and though he knew the place well from the outside, he had never been in this part of the premises before.

It seemed a long way to the house. At last the maid again stopped, and pushed open a small door. "Take care," she whispered, "there is a step. Keep firm hold of my hand, and whatever you do don't make a noise. We are going up the back stairs."

The Colonel murmured assent, and followed through a passage, then to the left up a steep flight of stairs. At the first landing she stopped. "There," said she, "lucky man. Now only just go on." With these words she opened a door, and pushed the Colonel forward. There was a blaze of light, and for several seconds he could not make out where he was.

*   *   *   *

At last a roar of laughter brought him to his senses. He was in a brilliantly illuminated drawing-room, surrounded by a semicircle of ladies and gentlemen in evening dress. Among them he instantly recognised Mr. Pottinger, Captain Bradbourne, and Lord Audrey. On his left was a piano, before which sat Mrs. Rainer, who looked at him steadily, and only said—

"Oh, Colonel! How wet you are! And what are you doing with your boots?"

Wet, indeed; and what was he doing with his boots? There stood our hero, in a dripping waterproof, from which little rivulets were trickling down on the carpet. In his left hand he held a pair of muddy Wellingtons; his right was feeling about in an uncertain manner as if for support. With a shriek of dismay he at last realised the situation. It was a practical joke. He dropped the boots and turned to fly. But the door was closed, and Mr. Easton came forward.

"Very glad to see you, Colonel," said the old gentleman; "but you have come rather late. Bradbourne here shall take you up to his room and make you comfortable. He is at home, you know—they are to be married next month."

HE was a grand-looking chestnut, certainly. Sixteen hands if he was an inch; long, short-legged, with fine sloping shoulders. As I stood up against him and placed my left hand on his withers, I felt I had never seen a more likely animal. "Jump?" "Of course he could jump," said his owner, a small farmer in the neighbourhood of the town of Howden, in the eastern portion of Yorkshire. And I did not feel inclined to doubt it, for how could a horse built like Umballah (that was his name) not jump? Besides, the would-be seller was willing that he should be tried over a fence. Giving his boy a "leg up," the lad took the chestnut out of the "moock yard" where the inspection had taken place, and we followed into an adjoining paddock. Here a hurdle with long wings and a small ditch in front of it had been erected for the purpose of trying hunters. Umballah took the place well enough, though laying his ears back a little, and was pulled up on the far side at once, quiet as a lamb.

I looked at him again: I passed my hand down his broad flat legs. He seemed as sound as a bell. His thorough-bred feet were small, but well-shaped, and firm; his hoofs showed no sign of any of those insidious complaints by which the best horse is so often rendered useless for anything but soft ground. His head was a little large, perhaps, for a son of Wild Dayrell, and his eyes were sleepy. Yet the closest inspection failed to show that anything was wrong with them. His wide chest implied good wind, and his teeth were those of a six year old. Why, then, did I not buy him at once, as I was looking for a hunter? I will tell you. The reason was an unusual one; the reader will probably exclaim that it is the most unlikely reason to deter a purchaser. *The horse was too cheap.* Thirty guineas was all that was asked for him. He seemed not only dirt cheap, but actually given away, for the money. Even in these remote parts the canny farmers who habitually bred horses for the market were well aware of the value of a strong, sound, thorough-bred horse up to at least 14st, and the price demanded seemed utterly uncommensurate with the appearance and breeding of Umballah. Fast, too, the man said, nor had I any reason to doubt it, for was not his name in the *Stud Book*, and had he not come out of Lord Stamford's celebrated stable? Not fast enough, however, to win Derbys or Legers, that I knew from his record. He had run several times as a two year old, he had been second in a small race once, but had not otherwise been successful. As a three year old he only ran once, at Newmarket in a biennial, and was not placed. Then I knew not what his career had been, except that he had been sold out of the great stable when it was broken up. But I did not want a horse fast enough to win the Derby. I only required a good hunter, fit to carry me well across a provincial country, in the first flight if possible, but if not quite in the van, at any rate not in the rear. And I could not afford a large sum. So Umballah was tempting. But I was a stranger in the country, and the price was suspiciously small; in fact, as I have said, the horse was too cheap. He would have fetched more at the " Corner " (it was the " Corner " then) on his appearance alone, without pedigree or anything . else. So I doubted still. "May I send a veterinary to look at him ? " I inquired, almost certain that the question would be answered evasively. " Certainly," replied the owner, to my surprise ; " only you'd best drive into town at once and send him out to-day, for unless you buy the horse he is going up to Rugby to-morrow to be sold ; these is bad times, and I can't afford to keep him. He is regular given away at the money." "Very well," I said ; " he shall be here before dark," and I drove off at a great pace to Howden, six miles off, to find a vet. I soon discovered one, and after some difficulty as to a conveyance, persuaded him to return with me at once to the farm. He thought he knew Umballah, he said, but was not communicative at all. He promised to examine him closely, and to give me a conscientious opinion, but beyond the admission that "he thought he had seen the horse," he declared himself ignorant as to his history. It was almost dusk when we arrived, but the leech certainly went to work in a business-like manner. He put the horse through all the usual paces, pinched his throat, carefully examined his legs and feet (by the help of a lantern) tried his eyes, and, in fact, performed all the tricks of the trade. I was still suspicious, and did not leave him alone with the farmer for an instant. Yet nothing appeared to justify my suspicions, except that both veterinary and owner seemed strangely silent. The latter silently opened the stable door, ordered the horse out, and when he had been examined, just called for a lantern, and no more; then, equally silent, again shut the stable door, and walked into the house with us. I drew the vet. aside. "Is he sound?" I asked. "Perfectly," he answered; "the horse is sound in wind and limb." "Very well," I said, "will you give me a certificate?" "Certainly," he assented. Now his character was at stake I felt more comfortable, and determined to close the bargain. "Mr. Broadley," I said to the farmer, "I will take Umballah. Give me pen and ink; I will write a cheque." "On what bank, sir?" asked Mr. Broadley. "On my London bank, the Union." "You will excuse me, sir, I am sure," answered he, "but you're a stranger here, and a London cheque wants four days to cash, and I have known gentlemen from down south change their minds after they had bought a horse, and stop the cheque. Perhaps they had seen something they liked better. I'd sooner have cash." Though somewhat annoyed, I was so much in love with Umballah, and felt that he was such an extraordinary bargain, that I was ready even to meet the demands of the cautious Yorkshireman. "You must come into Howden with me, then," I remarked; "they will cash a cheque for me there, and I will give you the money."

So it was arranged. Mr. Broadley put an old saddle on the horse, and sent his son into town with him, the vet. and I driving back together. We reached my hotel just in time for dinner. I got the cheque changed without difficulty, and handed thirty guineas to young Broadley, who thereupon led Umballah to the stables, where I had secured a stall and decent attendance for him. On the way I had noticed that he seemed an excellent hack, for although the night was dark, and of course the trap passed and re-passed him, I remarked that he was easy to ride, did not stumble, and jogged along quietly enough on the side of the road. The vet. pocketed his guinea, refused my invitation to stop and dine, and went off. Mr. Broadley, jun., having accepted a glass of hot whisky and water, calmly set out to walk his six miles home, with the saddle on his back. The next morning Umballah was after some difficulty, transferred to a horse-box, and we proceeded together by train to the small town of Beverley, about thirty miles off, where I had fixed my hunting head-quarters.

The first time I had my new purchase out with the hounds was on that day week. Meanwhile I had walked him over to a friend's house, some miles off, and had found him pleasant enough, though decidedly sleepy. Nor had my groom any fault to find with him in the stable. He fed well, behaved himself, and gave no trouble. He was led out to exercise with my other hunter (a faithful old mare), and went well enough with a leading-rein. In short, the horse seemed in every respect satisfactory. As I jogged him over to the meet, which was near at hand, several local sportsmen admired him, and, in fact, a grander looking horse never stepped. As we joined the hounds, and I walked him up and down (for it was a cold, raw morning), I heard several of those remarks which make a man feel as proud as a dog with two tails. " Who's that on the splendid chestnut ? " asked one. " Don't know ; but the horse looks a rare good 'un," answered another. " If the man goes as well as the horse," observed a third, " the stranger 'll make Bill Spencer gallop," Bill Spencer being a notoriously hard-riding gentleman farmer of the district. We trotted off to the cover-side, but drew blank. Then to another cover, where a fox was chopped, and so on for some time. To get warm I galloped across from a spinney, which seemed to hold nothing, to a little wood which I knew would come next, and jumped a couple of small things *en route*. Umballah seemed lazy, but took them all right; he appeared to me to be a bit of a sleepy horse, who wanted rousing, but with plenty of latent power. He was, at any rate, wonderfully quiet. Neither hounds, horses, nor men seemed to agitate him. He would walk quietly through a gate, whisking his tail, while dozens of eager sportsmen, on all sorts of animals, were hustling and jostling him. He lifted up his feet when some hound came whimpering round his heels, and put them down again carefully. In short, his manners were perfection. At this last wood, as the hounds were a long time in cover, sandwiches and flasks began to appear. We were standing or moving about on a fine expanse of turf near the bottom of a hill, which the recent heavy rains had made rather sloppy. I was calmly munching a sandwich, and held the reins negligently in my left hand, while the box and flask were in my right, when Umballah suddenly began to sway from side to side. I had hardly time to make out what was the matter when he fell or threw himself down on one side. My sandwich-box and flask flew away, but I fortunately had the presence of mind to jump off while the horse was in the act of falling. I held on to the reins, and the

thought flashed across me that he had the staggers. Not
a bit of it. He simply rolled over and over, kicked up his
heels in the air a few times, then slowly rising shook himself and began calmly nibbling the turf. The condition
of the saddle and the appearance of the horse may be
easier imagined than described. A second horseman,
belonging to a friend of mine, rushed up to help me
to clean the saddle, while the others gathered round
wondering what was the matter. I picked up my
belongings, and we were still trying to remove the dirt,
with which everything was covered, when the cheery
cry of "Gone away!" and the music of the hounds
resounded from the far side of the covert. To jump
on, regardless of breeches, was the work of a moment,
and away we rushed up the grassy hill on the left. As
we topped the easy slope we saw the hounds all together
about a field in front, running almost silently and very
fast, the hunstman and first whip just behind. We
crossed stubble fields, turf and ploughs alternating, but
comparatively few of the latter. It was for the first
fifteen minutes a fairly fast thing over an easy country,
no big fences, but a succession of small hedges and
ditches. Then there was a slight check, and the hounds,
striking off the scent, swerved away to the left. This gave
every one a chance of coming up, and as we cantered
across a wide grass field, cutting off a corner of the
course taken by the fox, a decent farmer-looking fellow

on a very good roan horse ranged up alongside of me.
"Beg your pardon, sir," he said, touching his hat,
"you're a stranger here." "Yes," said I; "I only
know Squire A—— and Colonel C——, and it is but
the second time I am out with your hounds." "I
thought so," said he; "is not that *Umballah* you're
riding?" "Yes," said I; "do you know him?" "I
thought I knew him, sir, but I was not quite sure.
You'd better look out." "What do you mean?" I
said; "what's the matter with him?" "Oh, nothing's
the matter," answered the man; "he's good enough.
But he's a rum 'un. Look out, sir, that's all I say."
And spurring up the roan he jumped a stile into the
next field, evidently unwilling to continue the conversation. We still went on, and Umballah still seemed
to go well enough. In another few minutes, however,
I observed some hesitation in the field, though the
hounds were running straight as a dart. A lot of men
turned off to the left, while a few, including the huntsman, the whips, the celebrated Bill Spencer, and some
more of what appeared to be very hard riders, followed
the hounds. Just then I happened to be close to my
friend Colonel C——. "What is it?" I asked him.
"Why, the Durnford Drain," he answered. "The
Durnford Drain?" "Yes," he exclaimed; "it's the
biggest jump in the country. It's what you'd call a
river in the south, only its got a rotten bottom, and if

you once get into it you can't get out of it. Many a good horse's back has been broken at that place. Better come away to the bridge with us; we're sure to nick in again." But I declined, for I thought it was of no use having a splendid thorough-bred hunter, up to nearly twice my weight, if I turned away funking a "Durnford Drain." Those who followed the hounds were now few and far between, for some more turned off to a ford on the right. We then jumped through a high hedge (easy enough) which had hidden the view, and then at the bottom of a gentle grassy slope, about two hundred yards off, I saw winding along a crooked band of black, sluggish-looking water, with very steep but evidently rotten banks on both sides. A few stunted willows and pollards projected into it at certain places, the banks between them having given way. The leading hounds were tearing up the opposite hill side, the tail ones scrambling through the water and emerging black and slimy. In front of me were the huntsman and Bill Spencer; close alongside, one of the whips; behind me were three or four hard-riding men. The others had turned. "Now, sir," exclaimed the whip as he rushed past me, "go at it as hard as you can. Stick it into him, sir, stick it into him, or it's all over with you." Stick it into him I did. I saw the huntsman tear down the slope like lightning, and flash across. Bill Spencer, on his left, just saved the jump, which kept growing bigger and bigger as I approached it. The whip on my right, whom I was following, had both spurs in his horse's flanks, while his hands were down, and he held the reins in an iron grasp. I did my best. Old Umballah laid his ears back and raced for the "Durnford Drain" like the wind. I kept his head straight for it. At the brink, when he ought to have risen, he suddenly stopped, very nearly pitched me over his head, and then, without any hesitation, and before I could turn him round to have another try, calmly and deliberately jumped straight into the middle, making no more exertion than if he had had to cross a three-foot ditch. Souse! I went in up to my neck in black water, and was for a moment blinded by showers of mud and slime. I soon scrambled out on the opposite bank, and stood there dripping, my boots full of water, the ooze streaming down my face, my cap, and my whole body, loosely holding the reins. Umballah was lying at the bottom of the "Durnford Drain," with his nose just above the water. Nothing was visible of him except nose, eyes, and ears; he seemed perfectly comfortable, did not snort, and did not even attempt to move. In fact, he almost looked as if he were going to sleep. A more hopeless predicament could not be imagined. There was no possibility of hauling him out by the bridle, and he was evidently determined not to try to get out himself; nor could I reach him with my hunting-crop. My friend the second whip came to my assistance. He holloaed a labourer, who had a huge cart-whip.

" Umtsallah was lying at the bottom of the ' Durnford Drain ' "

"Give it the brute," he called out, and when I suggested that the horse might get hurt, he said, "Umballah ? No fear. He has had enough of the run, and he thought he'd jump into the Durnford Drain to get a rest ; that's all. We know all about him in these pairts." After a few vigorous applications of the cart-thong, Umballah roused himself, struggled once or twice, and the whip being again applied, he at last scrambled out. Then, as before, he shook himself, rolled over and over on the ground, and began nibbling the grass. I was thinking of going home, but my friend would not let me. "Git on, mon," he said ; "no stranger's any worse for having been in Durnford Drain. T' horse is a rare bad 'un ; he'd have got over well enough if he'd a tried." And I did get on. I galloped both Umballah and myself dry. We came up with the hounds again, and I fancy that the chestnut, if still living, remembers to this day the absolutely unmerciful way in which I rode him for the rest of the afternoon.

Towards the end of it, he at last began to look warm (all the morning he had not turned a hair) and was quite unsuccessful in capsizing me or shirking a jump. But I soon found out all about him. He was perfectly sound, but a resolute *cur*. Every race he had run he might have won, but laid his ears back when collared, and refused to try. He lost his various owners hundreds of pounds when backed for steeple-chases which, with his power and speed,

he might have won in a canter. He had been put into
harness, but broke the shafts repeatedly by lying down
and having a roll while waiting at some door. At the
covert side he had earned a similar unenviable notoriety.
When hacked, unremitting attention kept him on his
legs; and when he was a new purchase, I suppose I had
kept him going by chance on the one occasion when I had
used him for the purpose. But you had to be always
" at him," and the moment you became careless he used
to lie down. For hunting he had no heart. I tried him
once more, but found it hopeless. He simply would not
trouble himself to leap; he hated the whole business.
If forced at a big fence, he would jump into it rather than
over, in order to get rid of the job. I was glad enough to
sell him to a local fly-proprietor for half the money I
gave for him. How many shafts he has broken since
I do not know.

"Yes," said Roland Glenavon to his friends when the servants left the room after the dessert had been handed round, "I know you all want to hear how it was I married at last. Nay," he added, seeing some deprecating gestures "my wife is fully aware of my previous character, and won't mind my telling you the story. Will you ?" inquired he, turning to the hostess, pretty Mrs. Glenavon, who was assisting her husband to entertain a party of men.

"Certainly not," replied she, laughing. "But I may as well leave you to your wine and cigars. The story will be better told in my absence."

And, rising with a smile for her husband and a gracious bow for young Denton, who held the door open, she left Roland to amuse his friends with the tale of his courtship, which I now give my readers as I heard it.

The previous history of Roland Glenavon must, however, first be briefly told. Heir to a fine estate in the Midlands he was left an orphan while still an urchin in petticoats,

D 2

and the result of a long minority was, that when he took a first-class at Oxford he came into a very handsome sum in Consols, as well as a good rent-roll. Roland, though something of a rowing and riding man before he went up, was studiously inclined, and had been infected by that Balliol enthusiasm which turns out prigs and fine fellows in almost equal proportions. His love of sport saved him from being a prig, and his love of books prevented him becoming a mere athlete. A deep friendship formed at a private tutor's, and cemented at Oxford, induced the graduate to forego the temptations of London and the attractions which were the more powerful that they were still untried, in order to accompany an eclectic young theologian on a prolonged foreign tour, which ended only when the influence of the Church of Rome had induced Roland's travelling companion to modify his views and change his future plans. So at four-and-twenty young Glenavon began his first London season with all the freshness of inexperience, and yet with the University angles rounded off by foreign travel. Well-grown and good looking, a pleasant companion, an excellent dancer, a fair tennis player, and a cultivated man, he was sure to become popular; and his income of over fourteen thousand pounds made him decidedly *the* catch of the season among the commoners. When July drew towards its close, however, Roland Glenavon was still uncaptured, and after a round of country visits he retired to Glenavon Castle—a fine old feudal residence in the Midlands—to shoot and hunt with a party of friends. Several years rolled on, and at last even the most enterprising of dowagers put Roland down as "decidedly not a marrying man." He still danced from April to July, and flirted occasionally, but he remained to all appearances heart-whole, and he was so careful that no big brother nor over-anxious mother had yet dared to ask him his intentions. Sometimes an elderly aunt—a widow —took the part of hostess at Glenavon, and then the old house was filled with young married couples, with bevies of laughing girls, and with men who were not always selected from the most fashionable clubs, but who were always good company at home and in the field. During the hunting season the stables, which Roland had rebuilt, were filled with horses for his friends, and there was no more enthusiastic votary of the Chase than the host himself, who offered stable room to men possessing their own studs, and mounts to those who did not keep horses. He entertained royally, and no one was more popular. But he was rapidly approaching his fortieth year, and yet he did not marry.

It is now time to let Roland resume his own story. "You may remember last winter," he said, "that we began cub-hunting very early, and that there was no frost to stop us till February. Most of you fellows were here then, and there were a lot of women, too, about Christmas time. The ladies rode harder than you did, and what with big runs, and long days, and the chapter of accidents, I had scarcely a horse fit to go when New Year came. I must have turned some of you out, or left you at home to play billiards, if I had not thought of running up to Tattersall's one Saturday to pick up a few. I would not say what I was going for, or I know many of you would have left Glenavon rather than put me to trouble and expense; so I said I had business with my lawyers, left dear old Aunt Veronica and Vickers there (nodding at a man at the foot of the table) to look after you, and bolted. Of course there were all sorts and sizes up for Monday's sale, and with the assistance of my vet. I soon spotted a few that might suit us. In looking down the Fourteen Stall Stable I was much struck by a dappled grey, whose coat was of a remarkably beautiful colour and brilliancy. He did not look much like a hunter, and he had no character in the catalogue; but the horse was so handsome, and had such a singularly intelligent head, that, when I had marked the hunters I proposed bidding for, I returned to have another look at him. 'That is not your style at all,' remarked the vet. 'Don't look like jumping a bit. Not big enough either; has some Arab blood in him, I should think.' This thought had struck me also, for the horse had that very small black muzzle, wide forehead, and deep jowl of the desert-born, while his silvery coat was of a finer texture than I had ever seen before. 'He might do for a hack,' I said, and ordered him to be brought out. His action was showy, and in the daylight he looked still handsomer than in the stable. The surgeon could not pronounce him unsound. Still I was fain to confess that he was not at all the sort of horse I had come to buy. At most fifteen hands, with somewhat straight shoulders, he looked fit neither for the field nor for a covert hack. So I went back to my club, and there again referred to the catalogue, which simply said, 'No. 94. Rajah, a grey gelding.' Nothing could well be less satisfactory, and on that day I thought no more about him. But Monday was a fine bright day, and when Rajah was brought out, and his beautiful coat glistened in the sunshine, while his intelligent head was stretched out, his large eyes gazing wonderingly at the crowd, and his inflated nostrils showing the fine pink shell-like skin, I could not resist making a bid of five-and-twenty for him. To my surprise he was knocked down to me, and when I had bought four hunters, I took the afternoon express down. The horses came on next day, and you may remember that most of you laughed at my anxiety about Rajah, and laughed still more when you saw him.

" I was quite fascinated by that horse. I fancied that he gave me a look of recognition when I had him brought into the stable yard, and certainly when I went up to him in his box he rubbed his nose against my face in the most affectionate way. But I had not the cheek to ride him to the meet, and to face all your chaff, for I was sure that he had some terrible defect which I should discover in half-an-hour's hacking. I was determined to try him myself, and alone. Nor was an early opportunity wanting. There was to be one last day's shooting in the Hedgebury Spinnies, to finish the season, and we fixed the Wednesday for it, as there were no hounds within reach. I left you fellows over the lunch, and sneaked home to get Rajah saddled. I rode him down the avenue at a walk, and he went as quietly as possible—rather sleepily, perhaps, but still at a fair pace. I then trotted and cantered across the park, and his action was unexceptionable, while his mouth was light as a feather. Well, thought I, he is at any rate a charming lady's hack. From the park I turned into the Dipston-road, and then through the farmyard, round the end of the outlying spinnies. I did not want you to see me, but was rather anxious as to how you had got on, so turned into Hedgebury-lane, which, as you know, takes to those cross-roads in the woods where my property joins my late neighbour's, Mrs. Wycherley's. I was cantering along the grassy lane, when one of you fired. Rajah stopped as if he had been shot himself, and thinking it was only natural nervousness, I allowed him a moment to recover, then patted his beautiful neck, and gave him the slightest possible touch with my whip. He did not move an inch, so I patted him again, talked to him, and let him have a very tiny hint from the spurs. Still he would not budge, but looked round at me with a very curious expression in his large eyes. I began to get impatient, and gave him a good cut,—

He planted his fore-feet firmly in the ground, and would not move a step forward, but again looked round at me, as I thought, almost wonderingly. At last I made up my mind to give him a severe dressing, and I shoved the spurs into him, while administering some very sharp cuts of my whip. He turned his head again, and I almost fancied that his eyes were moist with tears ; but he seemed still determined not to move, so that I am sorry to say I quite lost my temper, and thrashed him most unmercifully. The chastisement finally produced some result, for he dashed off at full gallop, and tore down the lane as hard as he could go. I was not unwilling to test his paces, and therefore let him have his head. He was in full swing, and we had just reached the cross-roads, when there was another shot from your party. He stopped still more suddenly than before, and, taken unawares as I was, I was sent clean over his head, and came down against the root of a tree, with one leg under me. I felt a violent wrench, and tried to get up, but unsuccessfully. I sank down again in agony, with the conviction that my leg was broken. But I was fully possessed of my senses, and watched the manœuvres of the horse with ever-increasing surprise. · When he saw me attempt to rise, he stretched out his neck and looked at me with the same wondering expression I had noticed before ; but when I sank back again on the ground he seemed more satisfied, and neighed loudly. He then knelt down by my side and sniffed me all over. Apparently content, Rajah rose to his feet again, and proceeded to push a quantity of dead leaves towards me, working with his nose and his fore-feet. There were plenty of leaves about, and in a very few minutes he had pushed up quite a respectable heap, which he tried to cover me with. I could not move my injured leg in the least, and was in mortal fear lest he should touch it with his hoofs. But he seemed very careful, and, having made a large heap, gently pushed the leaves over me with his nose till some were scattered pretty fairly all over my prostrate body. Then, as I wondered more and more, he galloped away down the lane towards Crampton, neighing loudly.

" I had heard no more shooting, and it was evident that you fellows were working towards home, which was more than three miles off. It was not of much use to shout, and I felt faint and weary, and therefore thought it better to wait for a chance passer-by. Nor had I very long to suffer in solitude, for very soon I heard the tramp of a horse down the lane, and the next minute Rajah reappeared, still neighing. He galloped up to me, and seemed satisfied at finding me in the same spot. He looked towards the lane ; so did I, and from it emerged a pony carriage, driven by a lady, whom I soon recognised as my amiable and charming neighbour, Mrs. Wycherley, who had lost her venerable but (excuse my saying so) very tiresome and silly old husband the year before.

" ' Why, there is somebody under those leaves,' she exclaimed to the lady who accompanied her, and pulled up the ponies. ' It is Mr. Glenavon, I declare ! ' she continued. ' What on earth are you doing there, Mr. Glenavon ? '

" ' I am afraid I have broken my leg,' I answered, meekly. ' At any rate I can't move.'

" In a moment she was out of her carriage. ' Charlotte,' she said to her companion, a lady of more mature age, ' you are something of a doctor. Can you find out what is the matter with him ? ' And she turned away to look at Rajah, who was standing by the phaeton in the most composed manner, with a self-satisfied air which would at any other time have made me roar with laughter. As it was, I could hardly help shrieking with pain, even under the light touch of the lady doctor.

" ' I think Mr. Glenavon's leg is broken,' said this lady ; ' we must either take him home or send for help.'

" ' Oh, take him home,' answered Mrs. Wycherley, quickly ; ' your husband can attend to him at once. Dr. Clarke and his wife are stopping with me,' she explained, ' and he can set your poor leg at once, if you don't mind. The groom will walk back, and Mrs. Clarke and I will drive you. It is not half a mile to the house, and it's ever so far to Glenavon.'

" In a few minutes the ladies had piled up all the cushions in such a manner as to make almost a horizontal couch of the front of the phaeton, and while I endured tortures the three helped me into it. Mrs. Wycherley sat down beside me on the bare boards, while 'Charlotte' perched herself on the seat behind, and the little groom led Rajah back to Glenavon. It was a very short drive to Mrs. Wycherley's pretty home, and the rugs and cushions made it fairly easy. There was, however, time for me to admire my fair companion's eyes, which were large and liquid, and seemed full of pity and anxiety; her dainty gloved fingers, which so deftly handled the reins and whip; her——But why describe her, gentlemen? You have seen her and know her. Excuse the enthusiasm of a husband who is still a lover.

"To resume, Dr. Clarke had me carried to a spare room and set my leg at once. He absolutely prohibited my being removed for a week at least. He, his good wife, and Mrs. Wycherley took turns at nursing me, and when after a few days his professional avocations called him to town, Mrs. Wycherley was my constant companion. An invalid couch was brought, which enabled me to be wheeled into the adjoining room, and my fair hostess was so kind, and made my convalescence so pleasant that I was quite sorry when I was able to hobble about on crutches, and had no longer an excuse for trespassing on her hospitality. The party here broke up when you heard of the accident, of which you could not guess the details, and you were all good enough to come and pity me, while

I felt that I was the happiest man alive. You know the rest. As soon as I recovered the use of my leg I knelt at Mrs. Wycherley's feet, and she is now Mrs. Glenavon."

"But what about Rajah?" we all asked.

"Oh! Rajah's history is this: I discovered it afterwards. He came out of a travelling circus, and had been taught to perform as a Life Guardsman's horse in Egypt. His master was supposed to be wounded by a shot from an Arab, and to fall off. Rajah had then been trained to bury him in the sand all but his head, and to gallop away to fetch an ambulance. The poor horse expected me to fall off at the first shot, and was very indignant at my not doing so. When at last I did tumble, he was grieved and astonished at my not remaining motionless like the circus rider. He then covered me with leaves, as there was no sand, and galloped off for the ambulance, which he met in the shape of Mrs. Wycherley's pony phaeton.

"Her attention was of course attracted by the riderless horse, and his neighing and other extraordinary antics induced her to follow him, with what result you know."

"What have you done with Rajah?" I inquired.

"He has the best and most comfortable box I could build," replied Roland, "and my wife rides him from May till August. In the shooting season he is led about by a lad for fear of accidents, and when he gets old he will be pensioned, for he has made me the happiest man alive."

IT had not been a very satisfactory day, and I was jogging towards home in no very contented frame of mind. The scent had been catchy and the field unruly, though small; the weather wet and cold until the afternoon, when it cleared up as if for a frost, and the scent grew worse every minute. The ground was tremendously deep, and the fences blinder than they usually are even in the first half of November. My new purchase—a youngster with a pedigree as long as my arm, whom I had bought at the Oxbridge Agricultural Show, where he had won the first prize for jumping—had scarcely acted up to his price nor to his reputation. The former was the longest I had ever paid for a horse, and the recollection that a small bill, the balance of the purchase money, was rapidly maturing, did not become pleasanter since he had dropped his hind legs into a ditch after refusing a flight of sheep-hurdles before the whole field. And among the powerful horses of— never mind which—Vale, I was fain to confess that he looked small and weak, scarcely able to cross the formidable oxers, and unlikely to live through a long run over heavy grass land. Corky he was, pleasant to ride, and pretty to look at, but, like Mr. Sawyer's roan, he seemed to have dwindled wonderfully in size since I bought him. Two or three friends had asked me whether *that* was the new horse I had (imprudently) talked a good deal about, and on receiving an affirmative reply had remarked, " A niceish little horse, but scarcely up to your weight, is he ? " I hoped that no one but the huntsman had seen his blunder at the ditch, for we two were the only ones then in the same field with the hounds, but I knew that all had watched him refuse the hurdles. So altogether I was thoroughly out of temper, and began to doubt, not only the wisdom of my purchase, but even the reality of the pleasure of hunting. Nay, more, my depression went so far that I felt much less certain than usual of my own knowledge of horseflesh. Need it be said that, as a rule, I "fancied" myself very much on this subject ? Doubts now began creeping over me as to my 'cuteness and ability to cope with dealers—doubts which unfortunately came rather late in the day. I recollected how proudly I had begun the previous season with a powerful youngster, who had cost a lot of money (but not so much as the Oxbridge prize-winner), and two screws, whose jumping powers were better than their legs; how when one of them broke down badly in the middle of a run over deep plough and steep hills I rather overdid the other two, and my brave youngster, after carrying me gallantly through several big days, had given way altogether under the strain, so that he had to be put on the shelf for a twelvemonth. So before half the season was over I was reduced to one screw only, and the poor thing did her level best, but also succumbed early in March. Thus the value of my stable had dwindled to a mere fraction; in fact, a "pony" would have bought the lot. And this year, it seemed to me, was likely to be still worse. Determined to have at least one real good one, I had spent more than I could afford; and, lo! on the very first day he was out he had made two mistakes. One of my screws was, indeed, patched up, and had gone well enough the previous week, but she might, as I well knew, "turn it up" at any time. So my reflections were melancholy, and my temper was irritable. "Hold up, you brute," I said in an unkind tone of voice as the thorough-bred (who was of course something of a daisy-cutter) tripped over a loose stone, and I caught hold of his head roughly, in a manner he scarcely understood. Just then I heard galloping behind me, and turning round I saw a young girl on a powerful chestnut, which, if not actually running away, had certainly got the best of his rider. She was sitting well back and pulling "all she knew," but as the horse flashed past me I noticed the curb chain hanging loose, and perceived at once that the chance of the young lady stopping her steed sooner than the latter liked

"She was sitting well back and pulling 'all she knew.'"

Page 48.

was very remote. It is a bad thing to gallop after a runaway horse, and I was still considering how to act, when I heard the same sound again, and this time was nearly upset by a regular bolter, on to whom a groom clung, much more discomposed than his young mistress. He had lost his hat; he dropped his whip as he passed me; his horse's head was straight out, and the bit between his teeth. Of course my own "Herald" did not witness all this without some discomposure; he made a violent plunge, and attempted to join in the frantic race going on before him. For a moment I had enough to do to keep him in hand while setting him going, and this moment sufficed for the arrival of the third member of the party, a little girl on a rough Exmoor pony, which was of course running away after the rest. On the whole, thought I, she is in the least danger, as she won't have far to fall; so I gave Herald his head and tore down the road after the others. There was a sharp turn to the right a few hundred yards on, followed by a steep descent, and I was fearful lest the young lady on the chestnut should come to grief here, as it was just the sort of place to bring a runaway horse down. As I neared it, however, I just saw her hat over the intervening hedge, gliding swiftly, but apparently safely, down the hill. Not so with the groom. The horse slipped up in turning the wet corner, tried to regain his footing, stumbled, and fell heavily, the groom, who by this time had lost, not only his presence of mind, but grip and balance as well, landing on his hatless head. I did not stop to pick him up, as my youngster was also getting excited; besides, I was more anxious for the young lady in front, so as soon as I reached the foot of the steep but short declivity I let Herald have the latchfords, and at last began to appreciate the value of my purchase, as the moment I gave him his head he began to overhaul the chestnut in front stride for stride. I knew there was an old-fashioned, narrow, and steep bridge a little farther on, and felt that the runaway *must* be stopped before getting there, as otherwise a serious accident must happen, for, like many country bridges, this one was not in a straight line with the road, but slightly on one side, the old road having led through the brook by a ford, now impassable on account of the recent heavy rains. We therefore raced in earnest, and it was well we did so, for only about a hundred yards from the black, deep brook was I able to range alongside the chestnut. Fortunately Herald, with all his blood and speed, was the most manageable of horses, so when I laid hold of the chestnut's head and gave him "the office" he helped me by gradually shortening his stride and acting as a drag on the runaway.

"Sit quiet," I called out to the young lady, whose brown hair, flying in the wind, added not a little to the charm of her appearance. "Sit well back, and give another pull. The mare will stop now."

So she did, but only just in time. In fact, the sight of the dark waters in front of her probably stopped the mare as much as our united efforts. I was off, of course, in a moment, and, as I fastened up the curb chain, inquired whether the rider was hurt.

"Not at all," she replied; "and the mare has never run away before. I can't make it out. But where is my sister?"

I then told her what I had seen, and we at once turned back to the scene of the catastrophe, meeting the little Exmoor, as I expected, still galloping away like a race horse. When he saw us returning, the tiny brute suddenly shied on one side, and put his little rider down in the neatest manner. Her skirt somehow got entangled in the saddle, and gave way, and there she stood in the road without it, her pretty baby face hovering doubtfully between laughter and tears. The pony then immediately began cropping the grass on the road-side as if nothing had happened, with the rent garment hanging loosely from the saddle. The elder sister was in dismay.

"What shall we do?" she cried. "This gentleman says Charles has fallen off, and you're an awful figure; and how shall you ever get home? And perhaps The King's knees are broken."

Of course I was bound to help. "You had better get off," I said to the eldest, as I helped her from her now placid steed, "and try and make your little sister more comfortable. I dare say you have got some pins; and here, take my hat-string, that will do to tie up the pieces." At the same time I took the skirt off the pony's saddle, and opened a gate through which the two young ladies could pass into a field, so as to get as tidy as circumstances would permit under a friendly hedge. I secured the pony's bridle to the gate, and told them to wait for me while I looked after Charles. Remounting my Herald, I led the mare till I reached the turn of the road, the scene of the recent disaster. Here I found Mr. Charles standing dazed by his trembling horse; the latter was apparently uninjured, but the groom's coat was torn, his head and right side all over mud, and his forehead grazed. I saw at once there was not much the matter, and proceeded to examine the horse, much to Mr. Charles's disgust, who considered his own injuries much more serious. The horse was lame. He had probably sprained himself, and could scarcely walk. "Are you far from home?" I inquired.

"About nine miles, sir," was the reply. "Oh dear! my poor 'ead. Our 'ouse is Furze 'Ouse, sir—Mr. Weddingfield's."

This was just about nine miles in the opposite direction to my own head-quarters, and therefore eighteen out of my way. But I felt that I could not let the girls go home alone, and it was quite clear that neither Charles nor his horse could go with them. Looking about, therefore, I soon spied a cottage about a quarter of a mile off the road, and telling Charles to wait, I cantered up to look for accommodation. The good woman had a tiny farmstead with a small cow-house, but she boasted neither horse nor trap, and though willing to take the sick man in and to give the horse shelter, could not help either of them home. I summoned the young ladies to the council, and they were of opinion that they would wait in the cottage until I sent them a fly from Mudford, whither I was bound, which would take them home. I argued that this would be a bad plan, as their horses would have to remain in a shed, without food or clothing, an indefinite time; and my arguments were none the less forcibly put that I had by this time discovered that Miss Weddingfield was an extremely good-looking, graceful, and pleasant young lady.

"If you are not afraid to ride again," I said, "the best plan will be for me to take charge of you as far as Furze House while this good woman takes care of Charles and The King; then Mr. Weddingfield will no doubt send for both in the evening." As we were some distance from the nearest village, and the short afternoon was drawing to a close, my advice was at last taken, and abandoning Charles, who was evidently not only a bad rider but a sulky brute, we turned our horses towards Furze House. My ill-humour had strangely vanished, though, logically speaking, it ought to have been largely increased by the prospect of a nine miles ride on a tired horse, and eighteen back in the dark on a cold November evening. Miss Weddingfield was full of pity for me and my horse, and attempted, after we had ridden a mile or two safely and quietly, to persuade me to return and let them go home by themselves. She assured me that their horses always went quietly enough, but that her mare had been suddenly startled by some pigs, which rushed out of a farm-yard, and The King, not having done much work lately, bolted as soon as he saw the mare gallop. Of course, I resolutely declined to abandon my trust, and Miss Weddingfield then became somewhat silent, as indeed was not surprising, for she knew nothing of me except that I had stopped her horse and otherwise helped, and having thanked me for my assistance had, strictly speaking, nothing more to say. Her little sister, Effie, however, was more communicative, and told me all about her two brothers at school, a certain demoniacal Miss Brayger, the plague of Effie's life (who, it afterwards turned out, was a harmless governess), her garden, her games, her pony, and her dog. She told me that Mr. Weddingfield had gone to London on business, and that it was partly with a view of meeting him on his return that they had ridden so far towards Mudford. They had, however, been disappointed. He would probably come by a later train. *I* was not at all disappointed, and should not have minded if he had not come at all, though my efforts at a sustained conversation with the elder sister were almost fruitless; she seemed determined to keep to common ground—that is, to the adventure of the day and my assistance. At last we approached Furze House, just as darkness had completely fallen in. As we turned into the grounds past a brightly-lighted lodge we heard a voice out of the night, "Your papa has just come home, young ladies;" and indeed the carriage was still at the front door, Mr. Weddingfield's traps being in the course of unloading. In the hurried embraces, questions, and answers which followed on our joining the group on the steps, consisting of Mr. and Mrs. Weddingfield and some friends, my presence was for a minute overlooked; but I was soon brought into the light, and took the opportunity of introducing myself by name, which formality seemed greatly to relieve Miss Weddingfield, who at once dropped the reserve she had assumed, and became the frank, pleasant maiden she was by nature.

Furze house became for the rest of the season a favourite "fixture" for me. Need I tell the sequel? A month later Charles was discharged, and a year later I became the happy partner of Miss Weddingfield. We have seven children now, and I cannot afford to hunt. Herald is pensioned, and trots about the paddock, eating apples which my little ones give him.

A REAL OLD SPORTSMAN.

THERE is a man whom I used to meet in the hunting-field for two successive years, and who was my *bête noire.* My heart is not, I believe, worse than other people's, and my bosom does not generally cherish sanguinary feelings against a fellow-man. But all my milk of human kindness turned into (is it whey ?) when I saw this modern imitation of Squire Western, without the old squire's hearty good-nature. His name is Blister, and very proud he was of it. He thought it was a name to conjure with. Years ago, it appears, Blister was a very fine rider across country; years ago (a very great many, I am sure) Blister "sported silk" and won steeple-chases, at a period when the expression "gentleman rider" was rather less vaguely interpreted than it now is. Blister traded on this past reputation of his as a staunch old sportsman, as a careful preserver of foxes, a first-class huntsman (for he also wielded the horn in Blankshire for several successive seasons), as a rough rider, and for aught I know, even

as a cock-fighter. On the strength of his prowess
in old times he made himself a nuisance to all his
juniors, who were very many, and a bore to his con-
temporaries, who were few. Seniors he had none. He
bullied us, he ordered us about, he growled at us, cursed
us, and even threatened more than once to fight any of
us. For two successive seasons I vainly endeavoured to
satisfy the old ruffian. I assented to all he said, I obeyed
his orders without a murmur, accepted his curses with
a deprecating smile, and even agreed with him when he
asserted that he could pound me into a jelly if he
liked. For the odour—not perhaps of sanctity, but of
what smells better in the nose of most of us—that of a
true blue, a sportsman of the old school, clung to him,
and inspired respect. I was desirous of pleasing the
sportsman of the old school; I wished metaphorically to
sit at his feet and learn the words of wisdom. Though
he now rode over fifteen stone, he had once weighed
less than ten, and had led fields of the best amateur
jockeys perhaps in England, mounted on the best horses.
He it was, I was informed, who saved the fox from utter
destruction in the districts surrounding his house; he
exerted himself to get the country in order, and having
begged or purchased drafts from various packs, hunted
it himself, and handed it over to his successors with a
reputation due to his own skill and perseverance alone.
With the stud, the kennel, and the ways of wild creatures

he was perfectly familiar; and he was also well known in connection with more than one useful and charitable institution. So in truth Mr. Blister possessed all the qualities necessary to make him an idol to the younger generation of hunting men. But he was a most objectionable idol. He had a tongue, and he spoke roughly; and his ears were sharp, notwithstanding his age. If his manners were those of a sportsman of the old school I am very glad that the old school is, as we are so often told, fast dying out. I do not see why strong language and overbearing behaviour should be necessary to a genuine hunting man. I imagine that courtesy and toleration denote the gentleman, whether it be at home, in general society, or in the field. At least so I was taught at Oxford, and I have hitherto had no reason to modify my opinion. Mr. Blister certainly fell far below my standard of an ideal English sportsman even in the days when I was sanguine enough to suppose that I could by soft answers and gentle behaviour turn away his wrath, and bask in the sunshine of his smiles, which, though they came but seldom, were cheery enough when they did come.

On one occasion, towards the end of my second season with Mr. Blister, he at last succeeded in breaking down my humility and causing me to lose my patience. I had been consistently trampled on for something like twenty successive hunting days, and the worm turned at last. A good old dog fox had broken from Rise Spinney, and old Mr. Blister was as usual abreast of the body of the pack before they had crossed the first field. He knew the country as well as any man out, and the ways of Reynard better. He had studied hounds to some purpose, and though both his age and weight prevented his riding very forward, and the "thrusters" were to him what a red rag is to a bull, he was always there or thereabouts. So I generally stuck to him till the fox was fairly away, or at least went the same side of the covert as he did. This Wednesday in March, I had, as usual, kept my eye on his movements, and when I saw him suddenly thrust the spurs into his horse and hurry for a gate, I knew that hounds had gone away, though I neither saw nor heard anything. He dashed through, and let the gate swing violently back without the slightest effort to hold it. But this was only Mr. Blister's usual way. Hounds were creeping through a black-looking hedge into the next field. The huntsman and a couple of "thrusters" took it in succession at the only practicable place, and Blister followed them. There was no reason for me to try to make a gap for myself alone; it would have been selfish, and besides I might have hung myself up in the attempt. I therefore calmly jumped at the same spot, about four lengths behind Blister. As I crossed he angrily turned round, and ex-claimed, "Don't jump on my back, sir! Ride a line of your own, if you can ride at all!" As this, again, was quite the old gentleman's style, I took no notice, but resolved not to be behind him next time if I could help it. We were in a large ploughed field, the hounds crowding and bustling under a gate at the far end. In the plough my horse, carrying eleven stone, naturally went away from Blister's weight-carrier, and I reached the gate first, just behind Manners, one of the best and most forward riders of the hunt, a charming fellow, whom our true blue bullied as much as he did every one else. Manners held the gate for me, and I did the same for Blister. "Get on, sir, get on! What do you mean by stopping up the gate?" he shouted, but not until he had his crop fairly against it. And get on I did, beginning to feel that I was scarcely treated with the courtesy one gentleman may fairly expect from another. Again we approached a gate, and this time Manners had not been able to hold it, or some *contretemps* had occurred. At any rate I found it closed, and had to endeavour to raise the latch —no easy task, with a young horse burning to join the hounds, who were racing away on the far side. I fumbled somewhat in my endeavours, and my nervous anxiety to get the gate open made me more awkward than usual. "D—— you, sir!" screamed Blister, riding up; "can't you open a gate?" Just then I succeeded in doing so, and he thrust through, exclaiming, "Now, don't crowd like that, sir; there's plenty of time," as he hustled his horse along over the springy grass. This was the last straw. I had consistently endeavoured to be polite, I had lost a good deal of ground by holding gates for him, and I had received nothing but curses in return. At the other side of the field, a long way off, for it was a large one, I saw the huntsman and Manners riding for what was certainly a very formidable obstacle, though I could not from my position at the moment determine its nature. The huntsman was a little in advance on the right : I observed his horse refuse; Manners then took a tremendous bound into the air and disappeared on the other side, and the huntsman, putting his horse at the same place with great determination, got over. "Now," I thought to myself, "I will give Mr. Blister something to swear at. He has cursed me for being civil; he cannot do more if I am rude. But I wonder what language he will use." With *malice prepense* I waited till my friend was about thirty yards from the obstacle, which I could now see to be a wide ditch, guarded by a post and rail on the near, and a very thick hedge on the far side, the place where Manners had jumped, and to which we were now steering, appearing to be about the only possible one. An outsider would have thought that Blister did not seem to be quite certain whether he would go at it or not ; but *I* knew that he was afraid of nothing, and was merely steadying his horse. Taking advantage of this circumstance, I rushed past him, and went at it at racing pace. I yelled out a wild " Hold up!" as my good horse, with a tremendous leap, landed safely on the far side. But even my shout was not loud enough to drown Blister's angry curses. They rattled through the blackthorn like buck shot, and came hustling about my ears like a shower of hail. A rapid glance backward through the twigs just enabled me to descry Blister's horse refusing the jump, nor could I wonder at this, for he had been thrown out of his stride, and his rider had lost the little temper he had ever possessed.

That fox ran very straight, and for three fields I had peace from Blister. Manners and the huntsman were still in front, and I rode about six lengths behind; no one else near the hounds. But I could scarcely believe my eyes when, in the fourth field after the big jump, I saw Blister ranging up on my right. How he got there I could not guess. Either he must have managed to negotiate that big place, or his knowledge of the country had served him to find a handy line of gates. At any rate, there he was, cursing and swearing worse than ever. This time I took matters into my own hands. " Do you think you are the only one who can curse?" I called out; " I could if I tried." His reply, divested of the expletives with which it was studded as plentifully as tipsy-cake with almonds, was to the effect that I was incapable of doing anything but riding over other people, and through gaps they had made for me, and that I was a perfect nuisance to the country. I did not stop to answer, but rode at the next fence, shouting, "Don't jump on me, sir; give a man time." But it was a very poor revenge. Blister had got the better of me. I did *not* succeed in pounding him. He stuck to the hounds like a leech, and when at last we ran the fox to earth, I was fain to confess that he had ridden as fast and as straight as the best of us, and had had the monopoly of profane language into the bargain. In this respect I felt myself his inferior. I did not try to compete with him, for I could not.

But my day was to come. A man of Blister's weight could not ride hard three days a week without producing some slight fatigue in his horses, and when the season was done so were they. The next winter was a very cold one, and men with large studs were often inclined to use language scarcely weaker than the old sportsman's. This gentleman came out early in November on a fresh horse, a beautiful animal well up to his weight. But before we drew the first covert his portly back was visible on the road home. "What is the matter?" we all inquired. "How is it that old Blister,. the keenest sportsman in Blankshire, turns back early in the morning?" "The poor fellow has got sciatica," a local hunting doctor explained. "He has had several touches of it since September, and this morning it has come on so badly that he can scarcely sit on his horse. Poor old man ! such a fine sportsman, too ! That's a *real* hunting man ! None of your fellows with aprons and cream tops and nosegays." Will my readers be disgusted when I confess that I did not sympathise with the doctor ? nay, that I even rejoiced over Blister's sciatica ? Then let them be disgusted, for I *was* glad. He had bullied me worse than ever on our way to the meet, though we had tried to avoid him as much as possible. He called the perfume of our best Havanas a stink, and asked us satirically whether we came out to smoke or to ride. He objected to our riding behind him, as he hated having fellows always jog, jogging behind him ; and when we went on in front he called out to us to stop as we made his horse pull. In short, he had been a greater nuisance than ever. So we rejoiced in our hearts, though we bore hypocritical sympathy on our lips. Another hunting day came, but no Blister. Blister was using strong language at the Three Tuns—the favourite old-fashioned inn, which was a handy *rendezvous* for the Blankshire meets. He had come from town in the hope that his sciatica would be better; but it wasn't. It was worse. He could not even move from the sofa in the hunt-room, which he made too hot to hold the younger members of the party. In order, however, not to miss a chance, he ordered his servant and baggage down from London, and stuck to the Three Tuns. For several weeks there was open weather, and his sciatica did not improve. We

had continual bulletins of his condition either from himself—and then they were sufficiently forcible—or from
the landlord, and then they were combined with bitter
complaints of the guest's temper. At last, one evening,
when the hotel was full of hunting men in anticipation
of a favourite meet on the morrow, Blister announced
himself quite well. The, well, let me say "blanked" sciatica
had left him. He cursed less heavily than usual. He
was silent, which was a distinct step in advance. Of
course he was grumpy and rude, for 'twas his nature to,
but he was not actively offensive unless spoken to. We
went to bed under the impression that sciatica had done
Blister good, but with serious apprehensions as to his
behaviour in the field the next day.

We need have had no fears. In the morning we woke
to a cloudless sky and severe frost. Hunting was out of
the question. It froze hard for ten days afterwards, and
all this time Blister was, to use his own language, "Fresh
as a ——— two year old." At last the barometer fell
and the south wind rose. A day's rain followed a snow-
storm, and we all looked to our horses and tops. Again
Blister returned to good temper—for him. There was
not much cursing in the hunt-room that night. He had
a few misgivings about the weather, but he was so urbane
as even to tell a funny story—funny, though rather strong.
But there was no Blister at breakfast. No oaths ex-
ploded between thick slices of buttered toast; no growls

accompanied demands for more ham and eggs. Our incubus was once more down with sciatica, and we rode to see the hounds without him.

And so it went on all the winter. Whenever the weather was mild Blister was unable to ride; as soon as he got better a frost was sure to set in. Though he stuck to his quarters and never lost a chance, he was not able to ride a single time until the young wheat and budding fences stopped hunting for the season. The regularity with which he got well the night a frost set in, and was laid up again the day a thaw came on, improved neither his temper nor his language. Mine host of the Three Tuns was a victim to both. His habitual joviality disappeared; he became moody and thin. It was very wearing, he said, and " Mr. Blister's langwidge was horful!" But there was no help for it, short of turning the genuine old sportsman out by main force. We youngsters enjoyed ourselves in the short intervals of open weather, rode over each other, and opened and shut gates without let or hindrance. At last, when all hope was gone, Blister's horses were sent to Albert Gate, and he gave up the struggle.

But only for that year. He hoped for better things in the season to come, and bought a fresh lot. It was, however, the same story over again. Frost alternated with thaw, and good health with sciatica. When we hunted, Blister was laid up; when he got better, we had to stop hunting. Again his stud went to Tattersall's, and his only consolation was that he had not tried them, and therefore did not know how good they were.

When this second season of misery came to an end, Blister resolved to effect a radical. cure. Consulting a distinguished physician, he went to Harrogate, and really got rid of his complaint for good. All the doctors assured him that it would not return again unless he was particularly imprudent. So Blister, who had hitherto bought rather cheap horses, relying on his extraordinary ability to get them over anything and make the best of them, resolved to have a fling and buy. a couple of real good ones. Price, he determined, should be no object. He spent a month during the early autumn in travelling about to look at various animals which had been recommended to him, and at last selected two of a stud about to be sold at Tattersall's. There was a large crowd assembled at Albert Gate on that Monday, partly because the stud in question was really considered a good one, and partly, I fear, because some of Mr. Blister's young friends determined to make him pay for any horse he wanted to buy. Old hand as he was, Blister was too mistrustful of other people to buy through a commissioner. He was always in the habit of bidding himself. So some of us who may have had more money than wit, posted ourselves near the rostrum to watch his proceedings. After a few lots had been sold, a fine black horse was brought out, a weight-carrier, well bred, winner of prizes, and with a high character. At a hundred Blister began to bid; at a hundred and fifty he began to swear, but continued bidding; at two hundred he swore louder, but still bid; and finally the horse was knocked down to him at three hundred and seventy. He walked off, with curses audible all over the yard, declaring he would wait another day to buy a couple more, and that that one was good enough to cut all those youngsters down with. Eventually, as we were informed, he bought something just to go on with till he found an opportunity for a cheap purchase, the three hundred and seventy having, to use his own expression, "about dried him up."

Once more at Rise, on a fine, mild November morning; everybody in high spirits except Blister, and he was on his recent purchase, grumpy, ill-tempered, but proud. Undoubtedly his mount looked the best in the field. Genuine compliments were showered on him in such numbers that they might almost have consoled him for the loss of two seasons and the expenditure of nearly £400 on one horse. They did not quite effect this wonder, but they visibly pleased the old man, who was delighted at heart to be once more with hounds, and on the best horse he ever rode, as he repeatedly said. Again, as on that memorable occasion, he was away with the pack, but not quite in the same direction. The fox pointed for Scarsbury, and there was a fair hunting jump out of the first field. A few of the leaders went over easily; then

"Where he was trying to get his horse over the first fence."

came Blister well clear of the ruck. He rode his magnificent horse steadily, as usual; but what was his horror, and the surprise of the field, when the beast refused, and being put at it a second time, refused again!

The fox ran straight, right through Scarsbury Covert, where there was a check. Everybody asked what had become of Blister, and then somebody replied that they had not seen him since Rise, where he was trying to get his horse over the first fence. And no one *did* see him again that day, for the fox ran on for another half hour, nearly straight; and when at last Blister got his horse over, horses and hounds were ten miles away!

HE was gloomily looking at a heap of letters lying on the breakfast-table. He knew the contents of them without opening the envelopes. They were all bills, or duns, or threats of proceedings. Was it any use reading them?

The December sun shone cheerily into the windows of the chambers, perched high up among the rooks in Gray's Inn. Its rays gilded the cottage loaf on the table with a finer tinge than the baker could have given it; they were reflected in the teapot, and lighted up as if with scorn a copy of Frith's *Derby Day* on the wall. Ay, Derby Day, and Ascot, and the Cesarewitch, and the Cambridgeshire—between them they had pretty well done for poor Jack Ponsford. He had paid his debts of honour, he had found the money to settle with the Ring, he could walk into Tattersall's with his head erect, and he could attend Newmarket races without being warned off the Heath; but these

wero almost the only privileges left him. His tailor
his hosier, his bootmaker, the man who had supplied
his horses with corn, he who had shod them, he who
had sold them on credit, and many more—all combined
to make poor Jack's life a burden to him. Would to
heaven that he had never backed a horse, never trodden
a race-course in his life! Vulgar and noisy, too, wore
these race-courses, not scenes in which Jack Ponsford
took any pleasure. He felt that the disagreeable journeys
to and fro, the pushing, swearing crowds, the horrible
talk, the deep mud or stifling dust, the disgust at seeing the favourite done by a head, were evils not
compensated for by a pleasant half hour under the
trees, or a jolly lunch on a drag, or the rare spotting
of a winner.

No, he would not go racing again. But what was
he to do now? There was Smiles regretting that he
would have to place matters in the hands of his solicitor ;
Larks & Co. had served him with a writ; Gokes Brothers
had a judgment against him; Merrifield was even now
waiting in the tiny ante-room to see Mr. Ponsford on
"private business," the nature of which might be guessed.
He did not know which way to turn. No more money
was to be raised on his small property ; it had been
mortgaged up to the hilt to meet a series of black
Mondays, and the last hundreds had gone in settling
over the Cambridgeshire. After deducting the sums

due for interest, he had exactly a hundred a year left to meet all expenses, which hundred was inalienable, being strictly tied up in the hands of trustees. Eight pounds six shillings and eightpence per month, and four or five hundred pounds to pay away out of it. No briefs yet and not much prospect of any. Horses gone, dog-cart sold, nothing to dispose of except what are termed personal effects. Jack tore open the envelopes one after the other. "After all," thought he, "I know what's in them, but I may as well see which of these devils is the most savage and the least patient." The contents were such as he had anticipated—threats, duns, *et hoc genus omne.*

"May as well file them, and be tidy for once in my life," said he to himself, smiling bitterly, as he passed the letters over the point of one of those wires specially constructed for the immediate reception of correspondence. "Hullo, what's this?

It was a country letter, and read as follows:—

"My dear Ponsford,—Sorry to hear through Whelks that you had a bad time of it at the Houghton. Come down here for a week, and have a few days with hounds. I can give you a bed, and we'll find you a mount. Pretty Mrs. Grieves, whom you admired so at Goodwood, is stopping with us. Telegraph when you are coming, and I will send to meet you. Kind regards from wife.

"Yours ever,

"Arthur Poppleton.

"Poppleton Hall, *Dec.* 2."

The writer had been Jack Ponsford's most intimate friend at Cambridge, and they had come to London to read for the Bar together. They were "called" on the same day, and at first shared the same rooms. But very few months after they had donned the barrister's wig, Mr. Poppleton, senior, had died, leaving his son Arthur the possessor of a fine estate in Northampton-shire and of a handsome sum in railway securities. Arthur was of course obliged to leave town to look after his property; he promised to return to their snug chambers in a month or two, but fate overtook him in the attractive shape of a pretty and well-dowered neighbour's daughter. In a year after his father's death Arthur Poppleton married, and settled down at Poppleton Hall, definitely retiring from the practice which he had not had time to acquire. It was now eighteen months since Jack Ponsford had acted as his best man, and in these eighteen months the friends had only met occasionally. Jack knew that Arthur's purse would have been opened to him, but he had been hitherto too proud to appeal to it, particularly as he saw no prospect of being able to repay what he might borrow. Now, however, things were becoming so serious that he resolved at once to go to Poppleton Hall, not, indeed, with a view to a loan, but with the intention of consulting his friend on his future course. Should he sell up and emigrate? Should he try for a land agent's situation?

or should he make an effort to pull through and stick to the Bar? What to do, and how to do it, puzzled Jack, and he felt that a long talk with his kind and sensible friend would strengthen him for the struggle, or nerve him for the final plunge, if plunge there must be. Besides, though he scarcely confessed it to himself, a week's respite from duns, a week spent in the healthful atmosphere of a pleasant Northamptonshire house, a week, too, in the attractive company of such a charming woman as Mrs. Grieves, would rest him from old troubles and brace him for new ones. It was a famous hunting country, and they were sure to have some good gallops. Yes, certainly, he would go as soon as he could get away. But how about funds? He had two pounds seventeen shillings in his pocket, his banker had given him notice that he could not honour any more cheques, and he felt that he could not very well write to Arthur for a fiver to be able to go down like a gentleman. This was a puzzle.

There was still another letter on the table—a thin one, with a French postage stamp and the postmark Nice. Jack knew no one at Nice, and opened it with some curiosity. It came from a man who had lost fifty pounds to him on the Derby. Jack had never been paid, his debtor having come to grief and gone abroad; but Captain Rashleigh now sent him a ten pound bank note on account, having, as he said, had a turn of luck at the Monte Carlo tables, and being anxious to settle with every one as far as he could. This was, indeed, an unexpected piece of luck, and Jack went out to talk to Merrifield, and console him for not getting his money, with more courage and better spirits than he had displayed for a long time. Mr. Merrifield was not an easy man to deal with; but Jack was no novice at pacifying creditors, and finally got rid of him without any disturbance. He then sent for a Bradshaw, and finding a convenient train at four o'clock telegraphed to Poppleton that he would arrive in time for dinner that very evening.

The guests at Poppleton Hall were Mrs. Grieves, whom our hero had not met since Goodwood, a gentleman who was introduced to Jack as Colonel Whelks, and an insignificant young man of no particular account. At dinner our hero sat next to Mrs. Poppleton, the Colonel being on the other side of her, and before the meal was over he took a decided and unmistakable dislike to the gallant officer. Whenever Jack told a good story, the Colonel capped it with a better one; whenever Jack attempted to become confidential with Mrs. Grieves (his neighbour on the left), the Colonel talked across the table to her; and when Jack casually mentioned the names of friends, the Colonel looked satirical, and talked of earls and marquises, leaving out the mention of their titles altogether.

When the ladies had left the room, Poppleton said, pushing the claret towards Jack—

" Hounds meet at Horsley Green to-morrow. You can still ride, can't you, old man ? "

" I hope so," replied Jack ; " though I am not sure."

" Well," continued the host, " I have old Safeguard in the stable; he won the Oxshire Hunt Steeple-chase last year, you know, and he's a wonderful jumper, just about up to your weight, too. Will you ride him ? "

" Why not ? " asked Jack.

" There is no reason that I know of," Poppleton said ; "except that he pulls a little. I have promised Colonel Whelks the Irish mare, or you might have had her ; but the fact is, Safeguard is not up to *his* weight, so I don't quite see how otherwise to arrange matters."

"I'm sure you'll like your mount," the Colonel remarked, with what Jack interpreted as a sneer ; " no doubt *you* can ride Safeguard."

" Oh ! " their host threw in, " Jack will be all right on him. All he will have to do is to sit well down. I'll warrant Safeguard will carry him to the front."

Jack would have had no misgivings if he had not noticed a peculiar smile playing round Whelks's lips. But he was not the man to refuse a mount because the horse might pull a little, and did not feel in the least afraid. When they joined the ladies the Colonel at once went over to Mrs. Grieves, who was sitting in one of those comfortable

little Pompadour chairs which the progress of high art is
gradually expelling from our drawing-rooms, and leant over
her in what Jack chose to consider an offensive manner.
The fair widow and the Colonel were evidently on good
terms, and impartial spectators might have suggested that
they would form a very handsome couple. She, slight as
a girl, but with gracefully sloping shoulders, rounded
figure, frank blue eyes, and fair hair of a tinge between
golden and brown, of which the luxuriance was scarcely
concealed by her simple mode of wearing it ; he, tall and
stalwart, with cheeks browned by an Indian or African sun
and worn either by campaigning or dissipation, a drooping
black moustache, black eyes deeply set under bushy
eyebrows, and a certain languid air which betrayed the
cavalry man and scarcely quite harmonised with those eyes
and that broad forehead. The chin only was the unpleasant
exception to an otherwise handsome face—weak and re-
ceding, it seemed to denote indecision. Whatever doubts
there may have been of the Colonel's beauty being strictly
classical, there was none as to his voice, which he soon
practised in a duet with Mrs. Grieves. It was soft, full of
melody, and yet powerful—one of those rich baritones
which, next to tenors, are most likely to affect an im-
pressionable woman. Jack could scarcely get a word with
Mrs. Grieves during the evening, and at last fell back on
Mrs. Poppleton, a charming woman, who possessed the rare
virtue of being kind and polite to the friends of her

husband's bachelor life. Jack, however, was determined not to waste any time, and when "flat" candlesticks were brought in, asked his host whether he could have a quiet chat with him.

"Certainly," said Poppleton, leading the way into the deserted dining-room, while Whelks went up to don a smoking-coat. "Fire away here. There will be no one to interrupt."

Jack told his tale, with which our readers are already acquainted, and wound up by asking his friend's advice. As he had expected, Poppleton at once volunteered a loan of a couple of hundred.

"No," Jack replied; "many thanks, old fellow, but that will not really help me. I would not take your money merely just to stave off the evil day, and without a chance of repaying it. Nay," seeing Poppleton raising his hand deprecatingly and about to speak, "don't interrupt me, and don't think me ungrateful, dear old man. But the fact is, I must get square altogether, or turn it up and emigrate, or get a land agent's place, or something of that sort. It is not a bit of use my taking your money. I could keep the duns quiet for a month or two, perhaps, but after that things would be as bad as they are now, perhaps worse. And I can't live on a hundred a-year, nor can I wait till briefs come."

"Marry Mrs. Grieves," suddenly suggested Poppleton.

"Ah!" sighed Jack, "I wish I had ten thousand a-year,

I'd ask her directly," and his eyes suffused with tears. "*That* woman, Arthur, has prevented my funking it altogether, and bolting out of the world to get rid of my troubles, and since I met her at Goodwood, somehow, the thoughts of her have stopped me from many things worse than backing horses. But these very thoughts make my worries harder to bear. For what chance have I of winning that angel? No money, and not much to look at, am I?"

With these words Jack stood up, and held his dress-coat open with a comical gesture, in order that his friend might have a good look at him. Poor Jack Ponsford was certainly not good-looking. Too slight for his height, though with fairly broad shoulders, he appeared a good deal younger than his age. His nose was rather a snub; his candid grey eyes, though bright and steady, were small; his long upper lip was not much improved by a moustache of doubtful brown, his check-bones projected, and his jaw was square and heavy. Certainly he was not handsome, but he knew it, and did not pretend to be otherwise than nature had made him. But Poppleton was obliged to admit reluctantly that in Jack Ponsford, who had only a good old name to offer, the rich and beautiful Mrs. Grieves would scarcely find her ideal. The conference ended by his repeating his generous offer, and assuring our hero that he had better accept it while the friendly lender thought over more permanent means for setting him up.

The next morning broke gloomily, with a touch of frost in the air, but matters improved a little during breakfast. Mrs. Grieves appeared in her riding-habit, which made her look still more attractive, if possible, than on the previous evening; the Colonel was in pink, got up in a manner so entirely perfect that not even the most fastidious critic could have found a button or a fold to object to. Poppleton also sported scarlet, though with less pretension to elegance than the soldier; and Jack was in sober black, and had devoted a little more attention to the whiteness of his breeches than he would have done if Mrs. Grieves had not been of the party. Hursley Green being only four miles off, they rode their hunters on, and by dint of manœuvring Jack succeeded in keeping Safeguard abreast of Mrs. Grieves's mount, a fidgety but well-bred mare. When a man is much in love he is supposed to be tongue-tied, and, indeed, for a mile or so Jack was no exception to the rule. But the brisk easterly wind, the recollection of Poppleton's promise to help both in word and deed, and the vicinity of his fair charmer in the most becoming of costumes, her face glowing with the wintry air, a stray lock fluttering from under her hat, her small hands steadying her fidgety mare, all combined to raise his spirits and to make him rattle away merrily, though not without an occasional tinge of sentiment. He spoke of his pleasure in seeing her again, of the anxiety with which he had sought for opportunities of meeting her, of the pleasant afternoons they had spent at Goodwood, and of many other topics—all in his usual frank and straightforward way, which could not offend the most sensitive. To his own troubles he merely alluded quite superficially, knowing that to tell a woman a long story of one's own money matters is not the way to please her. All this time Safeguard was as good as gold, his only fault being that he slouched along lazily, like so many thoroughbreds, and never raised his feet more than he could help. The Colonel attempted to interrupt the *tête-à-tête* more than once, but unsuccessfully, for Poppleton gallantly helped Jack as much as he could by keeping his supposed rival deeply engaged in conversation. At Hursley Green, of course, the small party was scattered among the larger one there assembled; but when a move was made for the covert side Jack again managed to get next to Mrs. Grieves, who was, it appeared to him, not so very desirous of the Colonel's company as to cause him any immediate anxiety. Safeguard, however, now began to be troublesome, putting his head down and laying it into his bit in his struggles to get on, and dancing along sideways in his inability to do so. That he bounded to the left into a puddle and splashed Mrs. Grieves's habit all over was the sort of contingency which might have been expected, and although the lady assured Jack very kindly that it did not matter, she did not look altogether pleased, and our hero was much put out.

Her mare, too, was becoming more tiresome by seeing the other horse dancing about, and Jack was much relieved when they turned into a ploughed field, and he was able to take Safeguard away to a respectful distance. The spinney they first tried was blank, and on the way to the next several gates had to be opened. Of course Jack was anxious to do the polite, and tried to hold the gate back for Mrs. Grieves. Safeguard, however, was not used to gates, and did not like them. He jammed himself against the latch, very nearly squeezed Jack's leg flat against the rails, and finally, as his rider could not get his hunting crop out of the latch in time, backed out and left Jack prostrate on the poached ground, a spectacle for the whole field. It was a disagreeable and stupid fall, for of course the horse got away, and Jack's coat was plastered with mud. He had to remount and ride after the fast advancing crowd in a condition far from enviable, and when Safeguard was put into a canter Jack found it difficult to prevent his bursting into a racing gallop. There was no chance of being able to rejoin Mrs. Grieves at once, and if there had been Jack would not have taken advantage of it in his present state. He thought he would allow the incident to be forgotten, if not erased altogether, by the brilliant figure he expected to cut in the run he hoped for. For his horse was a fine fencer. Rather than try to open any more gates, Jack sent him boldly at the next one, which the last of the field had allowed to slam behind him, and Safeguard took it handsomely—a little too fast indeed, and shaking his head more than Jack liked, but still with so much to spare that there could be no doubt of his powers.

Scarcely were hounds in the next covert when their music resounded, and before Jack had reached the crowd of horsemen gathered at the far corner there was the cry of "Tally-ho! Away! Gone away!" Everybody knows the rush that follows on this welcome cry, and Safeguard was not inclined to wait. Probably he thought that the flag had fallen for the start; at any rate, when the first lad on a rough pony galloped past him, he was not to be denied, and bolting away at full gallop bore straight for the next fence in the wake of the field. Jack was too old a sportsman not to know that it was hopeless to try to stop his horse. All he might do was to guide him; and this he tried, with some little success. Safeguard was heading for the blackest and highest part of the hedge, but all Jack thought of was, if possible, to keep him clear of the other horses; and, holding his arm over his eyes he faced the jump. Nothing worse happened than a severe "whip" across one ear from a thorny bramble, but he had not a hand to spare to wipe his face and staunch the blood he felt trickling down, for on the far side of the field, which Safeguard was approaching at racing speed, was a formidable-looking fence, with but one practicable gap, over which the others were now successively hopping.

Jack had passed a great many, but several, including some ladies, were waiting their turn at the gap in front, and, notwithstanding all his exertions, Safeguard raced straight for it, seeing the horses there. At his approach the group scattered like chaff, the men using bad language, the women half scared and quite angry. With one almost superhuman effort Jack pulled Safeguard over to the right and avoided banging right into the thick of them, but the horse flew the fence scarcely a yard from the gap, and landed almost on the top of Mrs. Grieves, who had just jumped it. Over went Safeguard, with Jack under him. Mrs. Grieves's mare, who received the impact on her haunches, slipped, struggled, and finally slid down sideways, her fair rider quickly disengaging herself, with the exclamation, "Oh, Mr. Ponsford!" She was not in the least hurt, and, with the assistance of the handsome Colonel, was quickly in the saddle again, not, however, before Jack had also remounted, his left leg feeling sore and bruised, but not otherwise injured. Safeguard, by no means done with, would not give him time to apologise, but was off again at Derby speed, as there were still some on in front. These fortunately were passed without accident in the long fallow which followed, and Jack sincerely hoped that the deep ground would settle the horse. This was, however, not the case, for, as often occurs, Safeguard pulled harder and in a more determined manner now he was getting a little blown than he had even done at first, and to steady him appeared hopeless. Jack was out of condition, he had not ridden since his horses had been sold, and his leg hurt him; he was getting very weary when they jumped the next fence, and narrowly escaped being thrown over his horse's head. Here the stubble had been soiled by sheep, and hounds were at a loss. The huntsman cried, "Hold hard!" Jack held as hard as he could, but it was of no use, for Safeguard dashed among the pack, treading on the feet of one, knocking over another, and causing yelps of pain and fright all round. Louder yet were the imprecations of huntsman, the Master, and those of the field who witnessed the performance. "Stop that cockney!" halloaed one. "Who the devil is that fellow?" cried another. "Send the beast home!" was the suggestion of a third; and Jack, hearing all these howls, ceased trying to stop his horse, but would have been glad to get anywhere out of hearing.

Safeguard, no longer seeing any horses in front, was now not unwilling to pull up; but Jack would not let him. He jumped the next fence at the risk of over-riding the fox, and finding himself in a lane, at once turned the now manageable horse towards home. Of course he reached the Hall long before the rest of the party. By this time his leg had become very painful, and he could scarcely hobble to his room. To remove his hunting garments was no easy matter, even with the assistance of Poppleton's valet, and when his toilet was at last completed, Jack felt as thoroughly miserable as any man could. To be put down as a galloping cockney snob, to knock over the lady he most wished to please, to make a fool of himself before a hundred people—all this was so galling that his anger found vent in expletives against Poppleton, who had given him the mount. He had almost made up his mind to start for London at once without meeting any of them, when a silvery voice on the staircase which could only be Mrs. Grieves's, and a heavy tread which he recognised as the Colonel's, told him that the party had returned, and that it was too late to disappear undiscovered. Mrs. Grieves went at once to her room, which was under our hero's on the first floor, his own being on the second. Jack could hear the door close, and the subdued sound of talk between mistress and maid. What should he do? Should he calmly go down stairs and talk with Mrs. Poppleton, who would be sure to sympathise and soothe? But probably the Colonel would be there, and he would be terrible to face. Yet the Colonel and all of them must be faced some time or other. In his vexation he approached the window and looked out into the garden, dull as gardens are in December, but neatly swept and trim. Under his window was a balcony—Mrs. Grieves's—and under that again the gun-room, now deserted. From his position he could see a little bit of the drive, and up it came Poppleton, slowly riding home. Then the Colonel and Mrs. Grieves had come back together! No, he would not go down now; he should meet his host in the hall. He would sulk up stairs in solitary grandeur. In a few minutes there were steps on the stairs, then a knock at his door. He threw himself into the armchair, and pretended to sleep. Another knock, then the cheery voice of Poppleton, "Are you asleep, old man?" and his host, with the *sans gêne* of old friendship, walked in. "Are you hurt?" he inquired, seeing Jack prostrate.

"Not much," replied he; "a little bruised. But, I say, Poppleton, how *could* you put me on such a brute?"

"I'm awfully sorry, my dear fellow," Poppleton asseverated. "I had no idea that the horse pulled so. He has not been hunted since he was chased, and it appears to have spoilt him for the field. I am really dreadfully sorry. I've been telling every one that it was not your fault. But I thought you could hold anything."

"So I could at one time," answered Jack; "but I am not in training. I can't now. At any rate, I could not hold Safeguard. I've made an awful fool of myself, I can't show my face down stairs. What does Mrs. Grieves say?"

"Well," admitted the truthful Poppleton, "I'm afraid you have not improved your chances with her; but never mind, old man, cheer up. Come and have some tea. I'll stand by you."

Jack at last allowed himself to be persuaded, and limped down stairs. Mrs. Poppleton was full of compassion and sympathy, nor did Mrs. Grieves, when she at last appeared, show any signs of displeasure. She was, however, sensibly cooler than in the morning, and when Colonel Whelks began a narrative of Jack's escapade, told in a gentlemanly way enough, but not calculated exactly to soothe our hero's ruffled feelings, she laughed outright more than once.

Several neighbours came to dinner, and the party was a merry one. Mrs. Grieves was in high spirits. Her face had acquired additional colour from the healthful exercise of the day, and the handsome diamond necklace she wore scarcely sparkled more brightly than her eyes. Poor Jack, whom fate and Mrs. Poppleton had placed opposite to her, had ample opportunity of contemplating the large brilliants of her necklace, the graceful curve of the fair neck on which it rested, and the sweetness of the smiles with which she responded now to one, now to the other, of her neighbours. Never had the object of his affections appeared so attractive, and never so entirely beyond his reach. It is true that the frame in which the object was set was, on this occasion, of the richest and most imposing nature—diamonds, velvet, and antique lace; but had not the picture itself been lovely the accessories would have been unable to lend it charm. Jack felt morally and physically depressed—out of it, as he said to himself. His limbs were stiff with bruises, and every movement was painful; his mind seemed dazed, and he sank into a dull and hopeless torpor which neither the sparkle of Mrs. Grieves's jewels, nor of her eyes, nor of Poppleton's champagne was able to dispel. He retired early, slipping away when the inevitable duet between the fair widow and Colonel Whelks was being listened to in polite silence. His bruises, his disappointment, and his debts combined to make a heavier load than he could bear, and he resolved to "turn it up" and go back the next day. Back to what? To town and his duns? Or to make such preparations as he could for a new life beyond the ocean? He was too tired and too much knocked about to come to any resolution. While he was endeavouring to decide on some course of action, while strains of music, hushed by doors and distance, still occasionally found their way up to his bachelor's room, he fell into a heavy sleep.

But not for many hours. He awoke, as men often do when quite wearied out, feeling particularly wakeful and almost lively. His leg, too, ached violently, and that alone would now have sufficed to drive slumber away. The house was quiet; the guests must have departed. For some time no sound was heard except the soughing of the night wind through the trees. Jack turned from one side to the other, punched his pillows and altered the curtains, but was unable to find any position comfortable enough to induce sleep. He tossed about restlessly, tried to think out future plans, and then gave it up because no plan seemed possible without money. Then, somehow, his thoughts wandered to Mrs. Grieves's diamonds. Every single stone of that necklet must be worth a hundred at least, and some much more ! How pleasant to have such ample funds that one could afford to lock up a few thousand or so in those unproductive gems ! What bliss it would be if he, Jack Ponsford, were able to present Julia Grieves with a pair of earrings to match that necklace ! Men always gave jewellery to the ladies they were going to marry. Why not he ? Yes, but he was not engaged yet, nor had he much chance of becoming engaged to her. Besides, if he were, he could not afford diamond earrings——

Hark ! What was that ? It sounded like a step on the gravel walk. No, it must have been fancy. Yet again ? Surely there was some one in the garden ? Who could be amusing himself by taking a stroll at two or three o'clock on a winter's night ? Jack listened intently; his nervous condition lent his ears exceptional sharpness. The noise, though very slight, certainly appeared to proceed from footsteps — from some one taking excessive care, and stepping with extreme caution. Jack jumped from his bed, and slipping on a dressing-gown drew the blind aside. He looked out into the garden. It was a dark night, but still it was lighter outside than in his room, and he could just make out the black outline of the shrubs and the lighter stripes of the walks. But he saw no one. Then, dropping his eyes, he closely scrutinised the flower-beds under his window. From them they naturally fell to the balcony of Mrs. Grieves's room under his own. What was that dim outline at the balcony? Surely a man climbing over. Jack was so near that he could not make a mistake. Pressing his face against the window-pane, he peered eagerly down. There was undoubtedly a man outside the balcony, standing on what seemed to be a ladder. The figure raised one leg and then the other, and stepped out of sight over the parapet, right under Jack's window. In this brief glance Jack fancied he recognised the tall stature and broad shoulders of Colonel Whelks !

He looked again, and then gently raised the sash, which enabled him to stretch his neck out and look down on the balcony. There was no one there; the man had disappeared, but Jack was certain that he had not gone down again, or he must have seen at least a grey shadow. The man had therefore entered Mrs. Grieves's room by the window. Jack seized a big stick he generally used for country walks, and rushed to the bell, intending to ring it loudly. But a horrible thought stopped him. That man looked like the Colonel ; perhaps it *was* the Colonel, and possibly Mrs. Grieves was acting Juliet to the Colonel's Romeo. His blood almost froze at the thought! He listened intently. Undoubtedly there was the sound of voices from the lower room. They were hushed and subdued as lovers' voices might be. What should he do ? If he raised an alarm and it turned out that Mrs. Grieves was secretly conversing with the Colonel at her window, he would be betraying the woman he loved best in the world, and calling the world's attention to her indiscretion. But if the intruder was a malefactor that very woman might be being murdered at this moment, and he (Jack Ponsford) was standing close by without stretching out his hand. Further hesitation might be fatal—he would rouse the house. No! he would first try and find out what was going on. He opened his door as gently as possible, and stepped swiftly down the stairs. In a few seconds he stood at Mrs. Grieves's door. He must, for the first time in his life, listen at a keyhole. If what he heard was a conversation between Colonel Whelks and the fair widow, the words might kill him, but they should be buried with him. He bowed his head and listened. For a few moments he heard nothing but a subdued sigh or groan, and some rustling which might be footsteps, but sounded more as if some one were carefully moving furniture about. Jack's ear was pressed against the door. Suddenly a louder groan reached him, muffled, like the last, but almost resembling a shriek. This was followed by a low, gruff, but perfectly audible whisper, "If you don't hold your row, I'll shoot yer!"

Jack now had no further hesitation. Mrs. Grieves's room had evidently been entered forcibly. No doubt the door was locked on the inside. It would never do to try it, and thus give the alarm too soon. Stepping from the door as far back as he could, Jack suddenly hurled his whole weight against it; the hasp gave way, and he burst into the room. A glance round was sufficient to tell the tale. In the full rays of a bull's-eye lantern was a figure clad in white kneeling before a chair, the face concealed and the head muffled in a cloth, the hands raised as if in supplication, a stray lock of fair hair the only bit of colour. Jack saw a hand dart forward and seize the lantern, which was instantly extinguished. From the far corner of the room came an imprecation, then there was a flash and a report. Short as was the former, it lighted up the whole room, and showed two ruffians with blackened faces, one still busy breaking open a wardrobe, the other holding a pistol. Quick as thought, Jack stepped aside, and his heavy stick came down with a thud on some part of the burglar, who at the same moment fired a second barrel. There was a yell of pain, a shriek from the fair victim, and then another report. Jack felt a sudden sting in the upper part of his arm, as if a sharp lancet had gone through it; but he had strength to hit out with his stick right and left, and there was a dim glimmer of light from the open window which enabled him to make out the outlines of the robbers. " Ring the bell, Mrs. Grieves ! " he shouted, " or run away and scream ! " There was no occasion to repeat the order : the fair widow rushed down the passage yelling loudly, and the burglars tried to make good their retreat through the window. But Jack's next thought had been to rush to the balcony and knock the ladder down. Scarcely had he done so when he was seized round the neck by a powerful grasp, and the blow he aimed at his assailant fell harmlessly in the air. He felt that he was choking· Throwing his arms round his opponent, he attempted to force him down; but the burglar was the heavier man, and had gained a great advantage by almost suffocating Jack before the latter could do anything. Poor Jack was now being squeezed against the balcony railing, his strength fast ebbing away, and his efforts to disengage himself vain against the weight of his antagonist. He made one final effort when he saw that the burglar would in another instant jump over and escape. He struggled to his knees, and using his heels and body as a purchase tried to force the man back; but the weight was too much for the frail railings, and with a crash they gave way, Jack and his foe both falling fifteen feet into the garden below.

Our hero was prostrate on his back, and a shout from above told him that the house was now aroused; but Jack determined, if possible, to catch his man, and jumped up as well as he could. There was no one there. The burglar had got away. But where? How? Jack looked round dazed. Then he made a bound into the laurels on the other side of the path; a crouching figure had disappeared into them, and he seized it. There was a howl of agony, and a volley of oaths. " Leave me alone," cried the man, with sundry frightful ejaculations. " I've broke my legs, and I sha'n't try to bolt now. May as well get my five years without any more row about it." But Jack gripped the man's arms with all the strength he could still command, which was not much. He shouted for help, and it soon arrived, for Poppleton and a servant came up and relieved him of his charge. The other burglar had, it appeared, escaped.

When order was restored and the pieces picked up, it turned out that the captured man was Colonel Whelks's groom, whom the gallant officer had but recently engaged and brought down to the Hall. This man was, of course, on excellent terms with the female servants in the establishment, and had heard of the great value and beauty of Mrs. Grieves's diamonds. On this point he was enabled to convince himself by helping to wait at table. He made a full statement of his mode of operations, and explained that he had had to wait for the arrival of a confederate from London before effecting his purpose. The men had easily cut a pane out of Mrs. Grieves's window in the way much practised by burglars, had then moved the hasp and raised the sash, and finally carefully lifted the bar of the shutters by working the blade of a blunt table-knife through the joints. The rest was easy. One of them half suffocated Mrs. Grieves by twisting a towel round her head, and effectually muffled her cries, while the other tried for the jewels. They had actually opened the drawer in which they were contained when Jack unexpectedly burst in the door. A revolver was kept levelled a yard from Mrs. Grieves's head, ready to fire if she tried to give an alarm. The groom assured every one that they had no intention of killing or even of hurting her, "for," said he, "we know'd the governor was sweet upon her, and we 'adn't no call to interfere with 'er so long as she didn't interfere with us."

The confederate — a tall man, who of course only resembled Colonel Whelks in outline—was taken a few days later, on the information supplied by the groom.

Mrs. Grieves was much upset by the occurrence, and took a great dislike to the Colonel, whom she could not help associating with the unpleasant attack of his servant. The one who suffered most—at any rate physically—was Jack Ponsford, whose arm had been pierced by the bullet of the burglar's revolver, while his head and neck had been severely bruised in the struggle on the balcony, and his back hurt in the fall from it. A few hours later he was in a high fever and the doctor prescribed absolute rest of body and mind. The latter, however, was beyond the medical man's power to bestow, as poor Jack scarcely ceased raving of his debts, of sparkling eyes, and bright diamonds. Poppleton was unremitting in his attention, and when Jack had

a lucid interval informed him that his creditors were
settled with. The good fellow had gone up to town and
arranged with his solicitor to settle Jack's affairs, giving
him an open credit for the purpose. The moment our
hero had this worry removed from his mind his condition
improved, and it became still more promising when a
mine in which he had placed an odd hundred or so
two years back, knowing that it was a gamble, proved
to be worth a very large sum, and yielded so good a
return that its shares rose to a huge premium. He
resolved to sell the shares, and left Poppleton Hall to
receive the considerable amount of ready cash due to
him on the transaction. When he had paid Poppleton's
solicitor there was still a fair amount left. " How would
it do," thought he, " to try his luck in diamonds ? " And
he purchased a pair of earrings which would about match
the necklace, and with these in his pocket he drove to
South Kensington. Mrs. Grieves gave him a warm
welcome, a cup of tea, and — something more. For
he left her house the happiest man alive, and she wore
the earrings on her next visit to Poppleton Hall.

THERE probably never was a man keener on sport of all kinds than Harry Marston. He preferred hunting for choice, but, when he could not hunt, he was just as anxious not to miss a day's shooting as the most enthusiastic votary of the gun; and when neither foxes nor birds were fair game, he would go in for ratting, or any other "chivy" which was to be discovered or invented. Harry was the son of a neighbour of ours, but was supposed to be in town "reading" for the Bar. I believe he did read a little, but, after he was called, his chambers were, as he himself confessed, almost the least likely covert to hold him. Supplied with a good deal of money by a somewhat too liberal father, and possessing some social talents of his own, he was popular wherever he went, and got asked to too many country houses in the autumn and town houses in the spring for him to sit in his chambers waiting for clients who never came. He stuck to our own hunt like a man, though sorely tempted by wide Leicestershire pastures. It was seldom that, in a good run, Harry Marston was not there or thereabouts, while his fond parent imagined he was poring over dull law books in the Temple, or hearing a masterly exposition of a subtle legal technicality from the Judges of Appeal. There seemed to be a general agreement among his friends not to tell, and it was only very occasionally that the squire heard of his son's escapades.

One winter we missed him from several successive meets, and it was whispered on the whole country side that Harry was really working hard at last. Men who knew his ways in London, and frequented the localities which he had patronised during his idle days, confirmed the report, and assured us that he now never did more than to turn out half-a-dozen rats in his rooms to teach his terriers " manners." " That is handy," remarked Harry, " for I have my sport on the premises; and, if a client should come, why the rats would bolt as soon as the door was opened, and no one would be any the wiser." All this was confirmed by the son of a well known solicitor, whose father had been anxious to put something in Harry Marston's way. The old attorney rang at the rising junior's bell, and when the door was opened, after some delay, he found three young gentlemen of a somewhat sporting appearance, and a very disreputable looking individual with a box under his arm, a short pipe in his mouth, and a very disagreeable bull-terrier at his heels. Harry merely remarked, " Clients of mine, Mr. Costs; clients of mine," and tried to get rid of them unostentatiously; but the

terrier growled, and declined to move from the door, inside
which something had taken refuge, while his owner pulled
his forelock in so sheepish a manner that Mr. Costs soon
understood the state of the case.   When young Costs told
the story, as we jogged over to meet the hounds one fine
February morning, we all felt that Harry was not very
much to be pitied for his sedulous application to his work.
On that day I determined on trying a special cut of my
own through Standish Park and across the London-road,
and turned off to the right by myself.   The fact was that
I was on the back of a new purchase, and thought that it
would be as well to see, privately, what sort of an animal
I had bought before I exhibited him to the very considerable field which would no doubt be assembled.   It was a
fine-looking horse enough, and had passed sound, but the
price asked was so low in proportion to his size, looks, and
breeding, that I had very serious doubts as to his being
able to jump, and thought that the little fences on the line
I selected would enable me to form an opinion without ex-
posing myself to the chaff of my friends.   It was well I did
so, for at a flight of sheep hurdles my new horse resolutely
refused, and I had to take him into the middle of a field
and give him a bit of my mind, which I did through the
medium of a piece of whalebone I happened to carry with
me.   I succeeded, it appears, in making myself intelligible,
for not only were the hurdles crossed without further hesitation, but the rather more serious fence between the copse

and the London-road was taken with a bouud that meant business. As we landed on the grass by the side of the road, I had just time to pull my horse back to avoid colliding with a carriage moving slowly along. It was one of old Field's "mourning flies," a vehicle constructed like a large "growler," but painted black and elaborately lined in the same hue. Field was our local builder, livery-stable keeper, carpenter and joiner, undertaker, and general contractor, who would provide marquees and refreshments for a cricket match, or build a complete manorial residence. He would supply lunches and ices for a ball, or turn out a first-class funeral. It was his pride that he had buried everybody's father, and many people's grandfathers, while he was not unwilling to relate how he had cleaned out somebody else's drains, and cured another man's smoky chimneys. On the box of this sad equipage was seated Jack, the most popular and civil fly driver within a twenty miles radius; the Jehu universally sought after to drive nervous elderly ladies or timid young ones to distant balls or dinner parties, one who could be relied on to drink any amount without its affecting either his care, his eyesight, or his civility. He was sure to bring his charges safely back; no one had ever heard of his running into anything, or meeting with any sort of accident; and his attention to the fair sex on wet or cold nights was positively touching, for it was quite fatherly without ever being familiar. To-day Jack was, of course, carefully dressed in a suit of seedy black, with a long crape round his hat, and black worsted gloves on his large hands. He raised one to the salute as I landed, and "hitched" his head towards the inside of the conveyance. Somebody looked out. I could scarcely believe my eyes! it was, it positively was, Harry Marston! Harry, dressed up in full mourning, which his overcoat scarcely concealed, and looking as melancholy as the occasion demanded.

"Where do they meet?" was his first question, without any previous greetings.

"Halford Gorse."

"Oh, Halford Gorse, of course! Just like my infernal luck! The *only* place in the whole country where you're sure of a run! And probably won't come here again this season."

"Not if we kill," I answered; "but tell me, Harry, whose funeral are you going to?"

"The old woman at the Grange is dead," he replied, looking very grave. "She was my aunt, you know, though no one would have thought it. Only got the telegram last night, for I was down at Brighton, and had to get some black clothes and come here sharp. Halford Gorse, is it? What beastly luck to be sure! Why the deuce didn't she live till next Sunday?"

"Well, you don't seem very much cut up about her."

"How should I be?" he answered. "I don't think I've seen her half-a-dozen times since I was a baby. I say, old man," he continued, "have you a second horse out?"

"No," I replied. "Why?"

"Because, you know, you might have lent him to me just to see them throw off. I should get there quite soon enough; the funeral is not till twelve o'clock."

"Nonsense, Harry," I retorted. "You could not ride in those clothes! Besides, what would people say?"

"Oh, nobody knew her," he continued; "but it's of no use if you have not got a horse, there's an end to it. Confound this beastly funeral!"

"Well, good-bye, old chap," I said, waving my hand. Jack shook up the old black horse, who must have been pulling this identical fly for the last twenty years, respectfully touched his hat, and jogged on. I put my new purchase at the opposite fence and lost sight of the mournful vehicle and its sad occupant.

Harry was right. Halford Gorse was a famous place. It always held one fox, sometimes two; and you were sure of a run from it, because there was a deep ditch defended by a black fence all along one side, and there was no bridge over this place. It was, therefore, always clear on that side at least, and our men were too fond of sport to jump the place before the fox had gone away. This February morning was no exception to the rule. Hounds plunged eagerly into the thick furze and underwood, and in less than five minutes old Lively proclaimed that

Reynard was at home. Then two took up the cry, and in less time than it takes to write this the whole pack echoed the welcome notes. Once round through the close vegetation, and then he broke as usual on the side towards the big ditch. That turn round the gorse was a wise move on the part of Master Reynard, or he would have been chopped in covert. But hounds were not so quick through the furze as he was, so he got a fair start, and had crested the hill before the hounds were fairly out of the covert, exactly a field behind. Then there was rushing for the two best places for jumping the ditch; there was a scurrying of knowing farmers away to the right; three or four hard riders turned their horses round and took the jump at a fresh place to avoid the crowd; one man was in, another came down on the right side of it and scrambled up again; and in five minutes more about twenty of us had breasted the hill and were taking the small fence into the turnip field on the top, the hounds running mute.

There was a little hesitation in the next field, which let up some road-riders, then they hit it off and away again, to the left, down a small grassy valley, running at a good hunting pace, and crossing small "grips," which were of little account. There was a stream in the bottom of the valley, and here hounds again checked, the foremost riders holding up their hands. The delay was, however, not long enough to enable the horses to get their wind, for they

"Harry was on a black horse of somewhat uncouth appearance." *Page* 105.

were away again directly, through the gravelly bed of the stream and up the hill beyond. It was a long, nasty, treacherous hill. At first I fancied my horse would almost get up to the top in a bound or two ; but the ground was heavy and the hill kept rising and rising the further we went, till the fleetest and freshest horses dropped into a trot, or at best a slow canter. I was wistfully watching the sterns of the tail hounds, fast diminishing in the distance, wondering how I should ever get up to them, when I heard a voice at my elbow saying—

"Go on ! Go on ! For goodness' sake, go on !" And looking round there was Harry Marston, hard at work on his horse, whom he was thrashing unmercifully with a cane.

"Please go on ! For heaven's sake go on !" he kept saying to the panting brute, as he was labouring up the ascent. "Go on, or they will get away from us altogether ! Confound you, you brute, go on !" and gave him another cut with his stick.

Harry was on a black horse of somewhat uncouth appearance which I had never seen him ride before. He had an old snaffle bridle on him, and the saddle looked very much the worse for wear. One of the stirrup leathers was tied up with a bit of string. Master Harry himself was still in his full mourning costume, with his legs naked up to his knees.

"Halloa, Marston ! Glad to see you out !" exclaimed one man.

" Taking one of the governor's nags out for an airing, I suppose ? " asked another.

" Came across the hounds by chance, did you ? " inquired a third, gazing at Harry's legs, which were certainly curious objects.

A shrewd suspicion crossed my mind, but I could not stop to inquire. We had at last topped the beastly hill, and hounds ran streaming down the other side, a gentle slope of fine grass. We put on steam and soon reached the valley, where the fox began to run short. A slight check ; then away across a couple of fields to the right, a turn which was favourable to many. There was a forbidding-looking ragged place in front of me, and I sent the persuaders into my horse to rouse him up. As I came to it I saw some one forcing an unwilling horse—a black one—a little on my left. There was a yell of " Hold up, you brute ! " then a scramble, and what looked very much like a bad fall. But by this time I was busy with myself. Landing safely after a somewhat near shave, I saw the hounds tumbling over each other in the middle of the field in a manner which betrayed that the good fox's end had come. I galloped up, and then recognised in the man who had so nearly fallen our friend Harry Marston. The buttons of his beautiful go-to-meeting frock-coat had burst, and one sleeve was nearly torn off. His hat was crushed in, and the mourning band all ruffled up and scratched with thorns. What was left of his trousers scarcely reached below his knees, and great splashes of mud disfigured the whole of his sable suit. But there was no opportunity of getting near him to ask questions. The rest of the field galloped up, the fox was thrown to the eager hounds, everybody jumped off his horse and turned the poor animal's head to the wind—in short, there was, for a few minutes, the usual scene of excitement and confusion which concludes a successful run. When it was over, when sandwiches were produced and flasks pulled out, Harry was nowhere to be seen, nor had any one noticed which way he went. I had a sort of notion, and beckoned young Costs.

" Are you going on ? " I asked.

" No," said he; " I have no second horse, and this one has had more than enough. I shall go home."

" So shall I," I chimed in, "but as it is early we can afford to go a couple of miles out of our way. Let's canter across to the Blue Lion in the London-road. I think we shall have some fun."

Costs agreed without asking questions. When we reached the Blue Lion, a small roadside public-house, we perceived a dusky vehicle in the yard. It was the identical mourning fly I had passed in the morning. We walked into the bar and asked for gruel for our horses.

" I'll get you some in a moment, gentlemen," said a voice, and a man came out from behind the partition, whom we at once recognised as Jack.

" Where's Mr. Marston, Jack, and what have you.done with your horse ? " I asked.

" Well, sir, you see, Mr. Marston he was so *very* anxious to see the 'ounds, sir, that he took my old 'orse out of the fly, sir. And the landlord 'ere, sir, lent him his saddle and bridle, and I don't know where he's got to. Can't have gone very far, though, with that old black."

"Didn't he, Jack ? " said I. " Well, he was in at the death, and got the old horse along at a pace that must have astonished him. But how about the funeral ? "

" Doan't know, sir, I'm sure," remarked Jack, scratching his head. " I'm afeerd we be a'most too late now."

There was the sound of a horse's steps outside. Here came Harry, leading his woe-begone steed, who was so done that he could scarcely put one foot before the other.

In a quarter of an hour I galloped off to the railway station, with the following telegram :—

" From HARRY MARSTON to JAMES MARSTON, Esq.

" Sorry I missed the train and too late for funeral. Will come on in the evening."

Harry, however, was truly repentant next day, for on reaching home he heard that the old lady had left him the Grange and a thousand a year to keep it up. He never forgave himself for having missed that train.

The following are extracts from the diaries kept by a young man and a young lady. The young man is a captain in the 30th Hussars, and the young lady is the daughter of a wealthy railway contractor. The captain follows his regiment, and therefore lives nowhere in particular. The young lady lives at Duncombe Priory, a few miles from the garrison town.

His.

Sept. 19.—Want a horse badly for hounds and to do as second charger. Found an attractive one in Sir Thomas Lennard's catalogue; " Scaramouch, brown, six years old, by Arthur, bold fencer, fast, good manners, has carried a lady, up to thirteen stone." Decided to go and see him.

Sept. 20.—Went down to Belhus. Scaramouch would suit me exactly, as far as I can tell. Seems willing to face any jump, has a light mouth, capital legs, and a clever head. Feel inclined to go up to a century for him, or even a hundred and twenty. On my way back, finding the only first-class smoking carriage full of ruffians, got into one where there were two ladies—an elderly mother, who looked rather cross, and a filly, rising seventeen or thereabouts. Chestnut—I mean fair; healthy and bright looking, and *such* eyes. I could not take mine off her till they asked for tickets. A splendid mane, too, and well bred, I bet a monkey.

HERS.

Sept. 20.—I have always kept a diary since I left Mrs. Appleby. She said it would keep up my English, which otherwise might become slipshod when she would no longer be able to correct it. Keeping a diary is more amusing than translating *Télémaque* into English prose; but things refuse to happen. So it is not always easy to fill up a page. To-day we went to Aunt Sophy's place in Essex. I played with my little cousins and roamed all over the fields with Tom. Tom is not a bad boy for fifteen, but he's dreadfully shy. On our way back a gentleman got in at Rainham, who looked awfully cross because he could not smoke. He had a cigar in his hand. I saw it and smelt it till it went out, and a little time after the gentleman looked at me very hard; in fact, he almost stared. I did not look back at him, of course; but I think he was rather nice-looking, and seemed very good-natured when he left off being cross about the smoke. He had a black moustache, and was certainly good style. Mamma smelt the cigar too, and said he was horrid. A fast man, she was sure. Why does mamma object to fast men?

His.

Sept. 24.—At the Belhus Sale. Bought Scaramouch for £75—very cheap. Looked out for the chestnut girl but could not find her anywhere. Suppose it was a mere chance journey. Wonder where she lives and who she is when she's at home.

Sept. 26.—Back at Cranborough. Shall be glad when hunting begins, for it's not a lively place. Stables, and guard, and parade, and an occasional escort are not always entertaining. Scaramouch arrived last night, and looks as fit as a fiddle to-day.

Hers.

Sept. 24.—Papa says Nellie must not carry me to hounds next season. I am afraid he is right about her legs, for she has stumbled more than once lately, though of course I would not tell. But papa is so good, he says he will look out for another horse for me.

Sept. 26.—Papa came back from town in great spirits. It seems he met an old friend of his in the train, a colonel whom he had known years ago in India before I was born, and he says the colonel's regiment is "quartered" at Cranborough.

His.

Sept. 29.—Jogging along the London road on Scaramouch to-day, whom should I meet but the chestnut filly? She was with a comfortable-looking squire, whom I believe to be old Heavytoft, a magistrate and local swell, and a small boy on a short-legged pony, and there was a respectable-looking groom behind them. I did not much like the looks of the mare she was riding, though as they cantered past us I had not a chance of seeing much of her. She seemed groggy about her fore legs—no action. I should say she was about done, the mare I mean, not the girl. At mess I tried to find out who she is. Nobody was able to tell me; they say there are a lot of fair-haired girls about, and I'm sure she is not one of those they mentioned. *She* is not a baker's daughter, nor the vet.'s young wife, nor a young lady connected with the stage! The idea! And yet that is what the fellows suggested. "Must be one of that lot," they said. "All fair, all rather good-looking, and all ride old screws. In fact, they all ride the same old screw hired from Fetlock." No, they're wrong.

Hers.

Sept. 29.—Frank and I went out riding with Mr. Heavytoft. Nellie *is* getting very bad: even poor old stupid Heavytoft said she was hardly safe. We met the young man that got into our carriage when mamma and I were coming back from Aunt Sophy's. He looked very well on horseback—not at all cross. He had, oh! such a pretty horse; and pulled up sharp to look at us. Perhaps it was rude; but he did not stare in a rude way. I wonder who he is!

Sept. 30.—Papa has asked his friend the colonel to dinner for next Wednesday. We are not to have a party, as they are such old friends. My birthday is October 4, and papa says he will find me a new horse by that time. He won't let me go cub-hunting on Nellie.

His.

Oct. 1.—Scaramouch is improving every day. I never rode a horse I liked better. He jumps like a cat, too, and is handy as a glove. Went out cubbing to-day, and jumped him over a couple of nasty blind places, just to see what he was like.

Oct. 2.—Met the chestnut filly again. She was coming out of Jones's, the draper's in the High-street, as I passed by with Donovan. Donovan's a good fellow, but he need not have shouted out loud, "What a d———d pretty girl!" She looked up and blushed scarlet, thinking us no doubt a couple of infernal cads. I'm sure I blushed as red as she. The old lady came out behind her, and looked as if she would eat us. They got into a very neat turn out—a sort of landau. She is certainly a most lovely girl, and I *must* find her out. Donovan says we're sure to see her somewhere in the course of the winter, as if I could wait all the winter on the chance. I'll put Jenkins on the scent; he'll run her to earth if any one can.

Hers.

Oct. 2.—We were shopping at Cranborough to-day and went into Jones's ! I came out first and almost knocked up against the same gentleman again—the one that got into the carriage at Rainham. He was walking with another man, who said quite loud, " What a (naughty word) pretty girl !" I could not help looking up. My old friend was scarlet, evidently ashamed of his companion's remark. He looked so much the more gentlemanly of the two. I wonder if I *am* pretty ! Mamma said : "There are two of those horrid officers. Whatever you do, child, don't marry an army man." As if I were likely to marry any one, and leave dear papa ! But why does mamma dislike officers ? "

Oct. 3.—The Colonel dined with us to-day. He is rather an old twaddler; at least, I don't suppose he is very old, but he twaddles all the same. At dessert papa told him that he was looking out for a horse for me. " Perhaps you know of one, Colonel," suggested my darling papa ; " there must always be one or other going among your officers. I have not been able to find a horse quite to suit

Kate (that's me). I want a made hunter, quiet, clever, with good action, and fairly young."

"I know the very horse for Miss Lee," replied the old Colonel, "but I doubt whether he is for sale. He belongs to one of my captains. I will ask him." After all I am not sure that the Colonel is an old bore, as I at first thought. At any rate he is very good to look out for a horse for me. It would be dreadful not to have one before the regular season begins; it's bad enough to lose the cubbing.

HIS.

Oct. 3.—This morning I summoned Jenkins after stables. "Jenkins," I said, "I've seen a young lady about, and I want you to find out where she lives and what her name is." Jenkins winked. "You need not wink, Jenkins, it *is* a lady this time." "Very well, sir,' answered Jenkins, as grave as a judge. I must admit that he has sometimes had to find out the names and addresses of ladies whom he would simply term "young persons." I went on to describe the carriage my chestnut charmer drives in—a dark blue landau picked out with red, two powerful roans drawing it, a spotted dog behind, a fat coachman and a thin footman in neat liveries on the box. Then I told him of the mare she rode and of the small boy on a short-legged bay pony who rode with her. Jenkins asked leave for the day, and I found him in my room after mess to report progress. The beggar had found out all about her! After all, these fellows do more in a day than we could in a month. However, he did not boast of his success. It seems that he had waited all the morning and had discovered nothing; but this afternoon, loafing along the parade, what should he see but the landau, the roans, and the spotted dog. There was no young lady in it; only an old one and a small boy. Jenkins can run like a lamplighter, and he followed the trap at a respectful distance till it stopped at a shop. As soon as it had gone on again he asked the shopman who his customers were. According to his own account, he did not ask plump out, but first bought two yards of red ribbon for his sweetheart. He could not think of anything else to buy in a ladies' shop. Of course I paid for the ribbon. And then he was told that the lady was the rich Mrs. Lee, of Duncombe Priory, and that little boy was her only son, and that she had a girl besides, a " sweet pretty girl," the shopman said, and "very civil and nice-spoken." They thought Mr. Lee had something to do with railways, but they did not know precisely. Jenkins seems to have had a good gossip. At any rate he has found out all about it, and now it is my business to get asked to Duncombe Priory. That is certainly a most charming girl; I never saw a better seat on horseback in my life. I knew it could not be the baker's daughter, nor the vet.'s wife, nor any other "young person." She must be thoroughbred. What tiny hands she has, to be sure!

Oct. 4.—This morning after stables the Colonel asked me whether I wanted to part with Scaramouch. Of course I said I did not. "Well," said the Colonel, "would you not even sell him to a very pretty girl?" "No," I calmly replied, "not even to a pretty girl." "That is a pity," the Colonel went on, "for I had hoped to oblige my old friend Lee. He wants a really first-class hunter for his daughter, and I think Scaramouch would just suit her. Money is no object. However, do not let us say any more about it." I pricked up my ears when he mentioned "his old friend Lee." "Is that Mr. Lee of Duncombe Priory, Colonel?" I asked. "Yes," he replied; "do you know him? He's a real good fellow; he helped us all through the cholera when I was with the 36th Lancers at Scrungabad." "I do not know Mr. Lee; but to oblige you, Colonel, I do not mind his having Scaramouch, if the horse is likely to suit his daughter." "Thank you, Belvoir," said the Colonel, apparently quite touched at what after all was a piece of hypocrisy on my part. "You're very good. I will tell him about the horse : if Miss Lee likes him, you may depend upon getting any price you ask." What a delightful opportunity to approach that lovely girl! But how can I sell her the horse? I could not take money from *her*. And yet I can't make her a present of him; she would not accept him. It is awkward.

HERS.

Oct. 4.—This afternoon (my birthday) the Colonel called. Mamma and I were at home, papa had gone to town. He said he had called so soon in order to tell me that the officer he had spoken of would part with the horse, and would send it up for me to try. How nice of him! I told papa about it in the evening. The old dear said that he knew the Colonel would not recommend anything but a first-rate horse, and I might buy this one if I liked him; he would leave it all to me when the veterinary surgeon had certified him as sound. And before I went up stairs he gave me a cheque for a hundred and twenty, and told me to see whether I could get the horse for the money. I wanted papa to stop here and see him; but he has to go to France on business, and won't be back for a week, so I have to look out for myself. Mamma says she does not know anything about horses.

HIS.

Oct. 5.—Scaramouch was advertised as " carrying a lady." But I don't always believe in horses' characters when they are printed in catalogues; so, after parade to-day, I got Jenkins to ride him in the school with a rug round his waist. Scaramouch went quite quietly. But still I had a misgiving. He might fidget, or shy, and throw that lovely girl. So I had a side-saddle put on him, and fastened a rug round my waist, and got on him myself. It was very uncomfortable, and I never cease wondering how women manage to ride at all in such an unnatural position. In the middle of my exercise Donovan came in and burst out laughing. I certainly must have looked awfully ridiculous. However, in the afternoon I started Jenkins off to lead Scaramouch over to Duncombe Priory (it's only three miles), and then got on old Peony myself to meet him there. It's a fine old place, in the middle of a large park, beautifully kept. I sent my card in, and was at once shown into a room all panelled in oak, and looking very snug and comfortable. Before I had had time to look about much the old lady walked in, with my card in her hand. She looked as stiff as a poker, and bowed ceremoniously. " May I ask what has procured me the honour ? " she inquired, as if she did not care about visitors. I felt rather a fool. " I have come about a horse for Miss Lee," I stammered. " Oh ! I am sure we are much obliged to you. Pray sit down ; my daughter will be in directly." And the next moment the girl came in, looking as majestic as a princess, and as graceful as a nymph.

" This is Lord Belvoir," said the mother, " of whom Colonel Bruce spoke. He has been good enough to come about the horse for you." I never felt such a fool in my life. As far as my experience goes, mothers generally run after a fellow, particularly if he has a handle to his name, and girls are ready to be made love to. But Mrs. Lee almost snubbed me, and her daughter only bowed and blushed most becomingly. I said the most stupid thing I possibly could have said. "I think that I have had the pleasure of meeting Miss Lee before." The mother pricked up her ears like an old hunter when he hears the hounds. "Where?" she asked quite sharply, while Miss Lee blushed more than ever. "You never told me, Kate." I murmured that I had only met Miss Lee on the London road, when out riding, but the old woman looked suspicious, and evidently thought we had had a flirtation somewhere. I only wish I had had the chance! I don't know how I got on, because somehow every word seemed to stick in my throat, though I am not generally shy with girls. But I could not take my eyes off Kate. Her voice was soft and musical, and I hate a woman with a loud or gruff voice. Her every movement was graceful, and the little struggle she had to conceal her impatience under company manners was pretty to behold. At last I made her understand that I had brought Scaramouch for her to look at. "How good of you!" she said. "Mamma, I'll go and see him at once." Off we went, and I am thankful to say left the old lady behind. She was afraid of the damp autumn air. Miss Lee sent for the old coachman, and petted Scaramouch and gave him sugar, and called him a dear pet, till I wished that I could change places with him. Jenkins clumsily put in a good word for me. "He will carry a lady beautiful,

Miss," said my batman. "His lordship rode him in the school for an hour to-day with a rug round his waist to try." Stupid ass! Of course she said: "Oh! how kind of you, Lord Belvoir;" but I know she thought what a fool I must have looked in a lady's saddle with a great rug hanging down. I asked her to keep Scaramouch for two or three days on trial, and if she liked him, to keep him altogether. It was all arranged, and we seemed to be getting on capitally, when Mrs. Lee appeared with her head wrapped up in a shawl. Her daughter told her how delighted she was with Scaramouch, and what we had arranged. "Well," said Mrs. Lee, "I don't know anything about horses, and you had better settle it as you please with Lord Belvoir. But what is the horse to cost?" I had forgotten all about the money, and so, it appears, had she. Kate turned to me and said, in a hesitating sort of voice, "I am dreadfully stupid. Of course, I ought to have asked first. Scaramouch must be a very expensive horse, I am sure." "Oh!" I replied. "I can settle that with Mr. Lee." "No," she said, "papa has given me a cheque for £120, and I am to do everything. I hope that is enough." "A great deal too much," I answered; "the horse cost £75, and I shall be delighted if you will take him at that price." "But I am sure he is worth more," said Mrs. Lee, gazing at him through her glasses, "though I am not a judge." "I think that is his full value," I repeated; "and he is not up to my weight (an awful story); he will be much happier here than with me." At last I went away, not having been able to find anything to talk about except snaffles and martingales, and how much hay and oats he ought to have. I never was half so stupid before.

HERS.

Oct. 5.—I have seen him. It is the same man, the very one we met in the train, and on the road, and at Jones's. And he is nicer to talk to than to look at, much nicer. He brought over the horse for me to see, and I saw his card. His name is Belvoir, Lord Belvoir. Mamma does not like lords, and can't bear officers, and I don't think I should like a nasty man, simply because he was a lord. But if it is a nice man, I don't see why his being a lord should make me dislike him. And I always rather like officers. Anyhow this one was very kind and charming, and I think, I really think, that he is selling his horse only to please poor little me. It is a most delightful horse: I shall ride him to-morrow. Lord Belvoir was so thoughtful, and did not say anything that mamma would not have liked. But mamma has been puzzling all the evening as to where we met him before. She does not remember seeing him when we went to Aunt Sophy's.

Oct. 6.—I rode Scaramouch this morning: he is such a

darling. A baby could manage him, and he seems to understand exactly what I want. So safe and pleasant too. I am to keep him for a few days.

Oct. 9.—Papa arrived this morning, and looked at Scaramouch. He thinks him too cheap. The Colonel called in the afternoon, and they talked it over. The Colonel said that Lord Belvoir is very well off, and certainly will not take more than the price he mentioned. The Colonel says we had better return the politeness by asking the young man to dinner. A very poor return, I think; but I hope he will come. Mamma did not seem to care much about inviting him; she says she can't bear soldiers, and a man who is a soldier and a lord as well is sure to give himself airs. We will see.

Oct. 11.—He has accepted. I am afraid they are going to have a big party to meet him. What a pity!

His.

Oct. 11.—They have asked me to dinner, and I am going. But I fear it will simply be a big spread. Never mind, it will be a chance of knowing her better, and of making arrangements for seeing her oftener in future.

Hers.

Oct. 18.—He came last night. Mamma would insist on having fifteen people to dinner. She had arranged that he was to take in Lady Clanronald, because she is pretty and lively, and recently married, and a swell; but he had the cheek to say that he would rather take *me* in to dinner, and he *did*. Mamma was awfully angry, but she could not say anything to him; and papa was so pleased with him that it was of no use talking against him. I was very glad. He is nicer and nicer. He can play and sing as well as ride. We are to go out cubbing together; but of course Frank will come too, and the coachman.

Oct. 19.—Mamma says she won't let me go, and considers my hunting altogether improper. She never objected to cubbing or anything before. I said I would write and tell him I could not come, but mamma declared she would do it herself. And then after all she gave in, though she grumbled a good deal, and told me to be very careful. As if I should fall on Scaramouch! Is it likely?

His.

Oct. 18.—She is the prettiest girl, with the best manners, I have ever met. Not a bit of nonsense about her. Open as the day, straight as a die, simple, and unspoiled. What next? It was a very good dinner, I believe; but I paid more attention to her than to the grub. The old woman wanted to shunt me with that flirt Gerty Clanronald. No! it was not good enough. Going cubbing with her and her little brother on Wednesday. She is very kind to the little devil.

Oct. 20.—Called to-day, as a *visite de digestion.* Could not decently go sooner, though I would have liked to turn up the very next morning. The old lady does not like me at all. She asked me what church I went to, and whether I took a class at the Sunday school. It is not in my line; never was. I respect the people who do, but cannot do it myself, and would rather not learn. Felt more stupid than ever. Mrs. Lee would talk of a lot of things I don't understand, and never gave me a chance of a word with Kate. She is going to keep the horse, of course; I found that much out at any rate. Settled to go cubbing on Wednesday, though the old woman tried to make out that her daughter had a cold, and that it was not safe, and that they were engaged elsewhere, and all sorts of rubbish.

HERS.

Oct. 20.—He called to-day, and I almost think he looks as nice in morning dress ("mufti" he calls it) as in uniform. Mamma worried him about church matters, and I think he was wonderfully patient; answered all her questions, and looked quite good. When he was gone mamma said, "I don't trust that young man. He has the eyes of an unbeliever." I do not know whether unbelievers have bright brown eyes that look right through one, but if so I would almost learn to like them. Why should he be an unbeliever?

His.

Oct. 21.—I can't make up my mind about it. It's a big fence, but it's a beautiful country the other side. Yet the filly might refuse! She is so awfully straightforward and nice, and not a bit of a flirt. She might not really like me a bit. And the old woman does not, I am sure. Shall I face the fence and go at it?

Hers.

Oct. 22.—We went cubbing this morning. Somehow we lost George and the coachman in Beechwood, and he actually asked me to be his wife. It was very sudden, after so short an acquaintance. I said I must think it over. I wanted to ask papa.

His.

Oct. 22.—I went at it, but I rode as clumsily as possible. Heavy hands, no doubt, and went too fast. Nothing is worse than rushing. She asked for time. What does she mean? Is there another fellow in the hunt, or does the *mater* object?

Hers.

Oct. 23.—I never said a word to mamma, but went straight to papa. He kissed me, and said I was a good girl, and he would find out whether Lord Belvoir was worthy of such a prize. Worthy indeed, of poor little me!

He is a great deal too good for me.   I said so, and I think
I cried a little.   But papa told me to dry my tears, and
to keep my own council, and then he went off to Cranborough.   And he did not come back till tea, and he and
mamma have been having a long private talk.   Oh dear,
oh dear!   I am afraid she won't let me.

THEIRS.

Oct. **21.**—We are engaged, and quite happy.   We have
been reading each other's diaries.   Even mamma approves,
and there is nothing more to be said.

YACHTING YARNS.

K

YACHTING YARNS.

THE LAST CRUISE.

(1879.)

WET and cold as the summer has been, and destructive to the farmers' hopes, it has not passed entirely away without a few days of sunshine and a few bright, moonlit nights. Pleasure-seekers have, like the farmers, suffered much, even though less seriously; many have been forced to spend less on their holiday, and many have not taken one at all; but still the majority have managed to throw off the cares of work for a few weeks at least, and of those who have done so none have, this terrible year, been so favoured as the yachtsman. Not he of the Thames and the Solent, who rejoiceth only in smooth waters and light breezes, but the man who requires no captain with a gold band round his cap to steer the yacht—the one who gathers new life from the spray which splashes his face, and, fearless of a swell, quits the ports "Saunterer" described as the head-quarters of the yachting fleet of England, and wings his way to more distant

K 2

shores across rougher seas. For him, this summer, rainy and stormy as it was, has not been entirely joyless. Seldom, indeed, has the sun shone down hotly on a glassy sea, and still more rarely has a light north-easterly blown steadily for days, bringing cloudless skies and wholesome freshness. Heavy rains have followed strong gales, and these, again, have been succeeded by squalls, with occasional sunshine. Yet there has been generally wind enough and to spare, and the want of wind is the greatest misfortune which can befall the yachtsman who has not as yet taken refuge in steam. Those who have shared and those who have witnessed the regattas of the year have therefore rejoiced, and few of the races degenerated into drifting matches. But now the glory of the season is over, and with the shortening days the graceful craft are gradually seeking shelter in the creeks and harbours, laying aside their "white wings" for the winter's sleep.

This year there was no counter-attraction to make the yachtsman send his vessel to "lay up" on the 31st of August. Generally the first half of September brings us, in the south of England, the finest weather of the year; and even 1879 has been no exception. But these brilliant days are of course devoted to the slaying of partridges; and many good sailors, being equally enthusiastic sportsmen, hasten from the decks to the turnips. This year, however, as there are no birds to slay, the yachting season, which began late, has been prolonged for a little;

and those who had the patience to battle with the heavy showers of July and the fierce storms of August, were rewarded by the gentle breezes and the warm air of early September. As we glide gently over a rippled sea, the full moon shining down from a pure sky, a bright, ever-moving path stretches from the yacht to the horizon. The little wavelets in her wake are caught by the moon's rays, and a thousand tiny pale sapphires fall in quick succession from her bows. There is just enough motion to betray that we are not on shore, but on the ever-changing sea; no more. The brass stanchions and white man-ropes stand out against the blackness of the ship's shadow; a tender light falls on the deck and on the sails, softening the colours and toning down the glare of the white canvas. The water flows past with a gurgling murmur, which tells of swiftness, but not of violence; of quick silence, but not of danger. The lamps from the cabin, tempered by the skylight, mark a ruddy spot in the blue surroundings. We can look out to sea and dream of Naples and the blue grotto of Capri and Masaniello, and lo!—the dream is continued as the sweet southern fisher-song—

> "In una notte
> Così soave
> Ah ! com' é dolce
> Star sulla nave "—

sounds across the waters, to mingle with the flickering

moonbeams, and to amaze the solitary hand on yonder pilot cutter. As the last note dies away, the sailors, who had crept a little way aft from the fore hatch to listen, return to their pipes, and the stillness is undisturbed, save by the murmur of the waters and the soft whispers of that couple near the companion-way, which is perhaps exchanging vows to be confirmed under another vault, more confined than that of the starry heavens above. No wonder, for the air is soft and full of love, and there are no indiscreet eyes to peer under the shadow of the mainsail, nor eager ears watchful for every word that falls. Those two are far from the prying gaze of worldly gossips, and the careful scrutiny of dower-hunting mothers. If warm lips are kissed, what then? We are listening only to gentle rushing waters. If an arm steals round a slender waist, what then? We are looking away to windward at the moonbeams on the sea. The gurgling ripples hide, perchance, the beating of two hearts which in the rush and clatter of the land would never have heard each other. Perhaps the mainsail conceals what the glare of a ball-room would have betrayed. But what matter? Can any harm come of a temporary escape from the trammels of an overwrought life, from the weary treadmill of work, and amusements more wearisome than work? Another moment, and the stillness is disturbed, for the cry sounds, "Light on the port bow," and the skipper having made out his destination, cruelly calls out, "Ready about." Over goes the boom with a crash, and the lovers are rudely disturbed, their snug nest behind the mainsail exposed to the full moonlight. Then the steward from below summons all hands to a prosaic, but necessary, repast. The dream is broken, but let us hope that the reality remains. The vows scaled under the shadow of the sheltering canvas, under the twinkling stars, are surely strong enough to bear the lamplight of the cabin and the tossing of the curling waves: they will hold against the ruder billows of the world's contempt, and will brave the storms of the shore, which are more severe, more pitiless, than those of the ocean.

And as the sun rises, a globe of fire, from the sea, and the mystic light gives way to the red glare of morning; as the vessel bends to the freshening breeze and the sails fill—the landsman wonders how he could wakefully watch through the night without the excitement of dancing, and music, and thronged staircases, and lively epigrams, and hot, crowded supper-rooms. He is neither exhausted nor weary; a calm contentment steals o'er him, and the waves rock him to sleep in the tiny cabin, to awake in port, at the end of "The Last Cruise."

OCTOBER.

IT is now high time to lay our vessel up, and to make everything snug for the winter. The days are getting short and the nights cold. There is not much fun in sailing when you have to shiver on deck in a drizzling mist, and when it becomes necessary to light the cabin fire. Yet some enthusiastic yachtsmen whom I know never desert their vessel even in the winter. They bring her up the Thames to Erith or Greenhithe, and live on board as if they were ashore. They put on dress clothes and go to the play, just catching the last train down at Charing Cross. They often attend evening parties and balls, and seldom ask their friends for a bed, as a cabman can be generally found willing to drive any distance at any hour for a sufficient remuneration. However, when it is possible, they disappear about midnight, to turn up again the next afternoon, making calls like other people, who dwell on *terra firma*. They sometimes ask friends to dinner, and send their boat to meet them at the pier, when the snug cabin will be found well-warmed and well-lighted, and the yacht almost as " wet " inside as out. I knew a man of this sort who was the happy owner of a fat old thirty-tonner, which was to him house and home. She was, like most of the old boats, ballasted with iron, but on the occasion of a great wine sale, at which many good brands of Burgundy and champagne were sold at very low prices, my friend purchased a great many dozen, and vowed to get rid of the iron, which, as he said, was lumbering up his vessel and occupying a quantity of room which might have been better employed. He took up the floors and substituted for the pigs a hundred and thirty dozen of champagne, sparkling Moselle, and Burgundy. It was asserted that the vessel was afterwards not in such good trim ; but whatever truth there may be in this assertion, it cannot be gainsaid that my friend was in very good trim indeed until all the hundred and thirty dozen had been con- sumed. When any one came on board, the carpet on the main cabin floor was instantly turned back, and some planks, kept loose on purpose, lifted. There were the vintages of France and Germany beautifully laid in rows in a bed of sawdust, filling the vessel from side to side, and extending downwards as far as her keelson. On the port side was sparkling Moselle, on the starboard, cham- pagne, Burgundy amidships. There was therefore no difficulty in putting his hand on the wine required. But a certain difficulty soon arose in connection with this novel and distinctly expensive ballast. The vessel's trim, of course, rapidly altered with the consumption of the fluid, and a few " wet " nights might have made so important a difference that the first breeze would have capsized her, crank as she was already. However, my friend's ingenuity was fully equal to the occasion. Every "dead man" was instantly handed to the steward, whose duty it was after he had ascertained by personal and close inspection that no wine was left in the bottle, to re-fill it with water, cork it carefully, and replace it in the hold. The steward, who was not as clever as his master, used at first to push his precautions so far as to seal each bottle up. But this led to unpleasant consequences. For having asked a jovial party on board, my friend, having ascertained their wishes with regard to wine, lifted up the cabin floor as usual, and placing two black bottles on the table, ex-claimed, "There! I am sure you will call that splendid Burgundy." Just then, something or another in the river fouled the yacht, and the host went on deck to exchange polite courtesies with the owner of the guilty craft. While he was absent, his friends, of course, filled their glasses, and when he reappeared they were sitting before some tawny liquid which they did not appear to be enjoying to any extraordinary extent. "Well," exclaimed he, "how do you like the wine? A1, isn't it?" His friends hesitated, but one of them, gaining courage, at last said, "I wish you would try it. I rather fancy there must be something wrong with this bottle." "Try it, of course I will," exclaimed the owner, filling his glass; "it *does* look lighter than usual." He had hardly set it to his lips when he exclaimed, "Why, d——n it, it's sea water. Here,. you infernal fool, Jim, what the h—ll have you been doing?" and it then appeared that James, in his anxiety to replace the ballast which had been drunk, had at once filled up the bottles of Burgundy without rinsing them. It need hardly be added that a more genuine wine was soon produced, and that in future the bottles containing water were no longer sealed.

There was a piano on board this vessel, and dulcet strains, continued to the small hours, not unfrequently attracted the attention of the watch in surrounding craft, and roused sleepers from their slumbers. On one occasion, the owner of a yacht moored close by became very irate and sent on board to inquire "when that row would be stopped." My friend replied by a very polite message, requesting Mr. S. to come and stop it himself. Very soon we again heard the splashes of oars, and Mr. S. ascended the gangway, swearing audibly, "Where's the owner? It's disgusting that a fellow can't spend a night on board his vessel without being disturbed by a lot of heathens singing all night. I shall speak to the Thames Conservancy." Mr. S. was politely asked below, and on arriving there my friend rose with great solemnity, and welcomed him on board. "D——n you, sir," exclaimed the irate S.; "what the devil—" "I beg your pardon, Mr. S.," answered the host, "will you favour me with sitting down? I shall be very happy to explain, but before attending to business I must really beg you to take a glass of wine." "But, sir—" "Excuse me, Mr. S.; pardon my interrupting you, but permit me to introduce my friends to you. Mr. S., Lord A.; Mr. S., the Marquis of B." Now A. and B. were no more lords than they were legislators; the titles were purely invented on the spot. But Mr. S. was a little taken aback, and had only just time to mutter, "But, really—" when my friend again broke in, "What wine do you prefer, Mr. S.? Champagne, Ruinart, père et fils, or Burgundy (real Romanée, I assure you), or Nonpareil Moselle? All are on the table. Or would you like a drop of the craythur better? Now, no refusal! We can talk business afterwards. A., old fellow, just hand the Moselle this way. B., dear boy, do fetch Mr. S. a glass." B. rushed to the pantry, bringing back a huge tumbler, and a large thin champagne-glass, while S. could hardly believe his eyes, and felt utterly confounded by being waited on by a real marquis. "Really, my lord," he began, "I don't know what to say; allow me—" "Nonsense, sir," chimed in the host; "we are all equal here. You are a friend of mine, and so I am sure their lordships will treat you as one of themselves." "Certainly," said B., who was gradually recovering his *sang froid*. "Have a glass of something. *I* always prefer Burgundy, but Lord A. sticks to fizz. Then we'll have a song." So poor S. was obliged to swallow his anger with a glass brimful of Ruinart; and it may well be imagined that he did not return to the subject which had brought him on board. Very soon the host exclaimed, " Now, Marquis, give us that song you promised us," and S. listened with some amusement and great patience to a noisy music-hall ballad, and himself joined in the chorus, for it made all the difference of course, whether it was roared out by a couple of plebeians or by two real live lords. Glass followed glass, and song followed song. Cigars were pressed on the unwilling S., whose boat had been meanwhile sent back to his family craft with the message that Mr. —— was going to stay on board and make a night of it. She soon returned, the men saying that Mrs. S. had sent them for their master. But by this time the poor man was far advanced in his cups. He was shaking hands violently with his hospitable entertainer, saying, " Thank you, old feller—very kind of you—glad to see you on board ; letsh enjoy ourselves—good fellow, the Marquish, so is Lord A., but not such a good feller as the Marquish." So the boat went away without him ; and as the dawn began to steal over the March sky the keen wind became sensible even in the snug cabin. S. was gently lifted by three pair of stalwart arms over the side, still murmuring, " Good feller, the Marquish, very good feller." How he was hauled on board his own yacht, and what reception he met with there, we never ascertained ;

but he no longer attempted to interfere with our legitimate (?) amusements.

Another seafaring character I knew had a mania for shooting, which he combined with yachting in all sorts of ingenious ways. A bottle on the bowsprit end was the favourite sport when no birds were to be had. It is not so easy to break one attached to the end of this spar by a line two feet long as might at first be supposed. The yacht pitches or rolls, and the bowsprit does not seem to bob with the yacht, so although the distance is absurdly short, there are more misses than hits. Each competitor used to pay a shilling into a pool, and the best of ten shots took the lot. It was all very well at first, but after a time the deck hands used to get a little tired of climbing out to attach fresh bottles to the end of the bowsprit, and when a little liquor was going, the competitors frequently volunteered to do it themselves. The result was, on more than one occasion, a cold bath, and, though life-buoys were handy, and the boat towing astern, the amusement was hardly to be recommended as absolutely safe. When off the Devonshire coast my friend was, of course, in his element. Popping right and left between the islands he used to bring on board huge bags of gulls, curlews, and every imaginable bird. Hardly one was ever fit to eat, but the vessel was made to resemble a shamble by the process of curing and cleaning the feathers, which he pursued with uninterrupted industry.

THE ORDEAL.

THE ORDEAL.

CHAPTER I.

THE "APHRODITE."

" HERE are the men! Let them take your things. Be careful of the step, Mrs. Kingsworth, the platform is not high enough. Dubois will look after your maid."

With these words Mr. Ansdell helped two ladies from the train on the narrow platform of the Southampton Docks Station. The speaker was a middle-aged man, of moderate height, slightly inclined to stoutness. His face was round, jovial, and lighted up by a pair of bright black eyes, which darted quick glances in every direction—eyes watchful and merry, but frank and open. His cheeks and chin were clean shaven, while his grey moustache and the stray locks of hair visible under his yachting cap gave his otherwise youthful appearance the lie. He was dressed in blue serge with the studied carelessness which betrays care.

The lady he handed out first was Miss Kingsworth, the American beauty who had taken the inclosure at Ascot by storm but a few weeks since. Alma Kingsworth was tall,

L

well-grown, and faultlessly dressed in a suit of dark seaside blue, with narrow red braid laid on to relieve the sombreness of the costume. A sailor's hat covered with shiny black stuff was set forward on her pretty head, which she carried erect with an air of self-possession and courage which not even her female enemies—for she had no male ones—could call pertness or assurance. She did *not* wear the huge pile of hair and cushions on the top of her head which is so much affected by some of our Transatlantic cousins; her fair hair was simply twisted into a plain knot. A certain quickness of movement and slenderness without angularity were, possibly, points in which she might differ from a genuine English girl. Most of our young ladies are either well-formed strapping damsels, who promise some day to develop into portly matrons, or they have a tendency to spareness which art has not taught them to convert into supple grace. Alma was certainly slight, and her complexion was paler than might have been thought consistent with perfect health. But she dressed and moved about like a Parisian who has gone through a dozen seasons, although she had only seen one in New York and one in London. She had a nose slightly—very slightly—aquiline, bright hazel eyes with long lashes under well-marked arched eyebrows, a mouth admirably cut, but by no means small, displaying two rows of the whitest teeth, and a chin which was anything but weak. No description, however, can portray the indefinable charm which fascinated the most *blasé* of London men and elicited expressions of admiration even from the beauties whom she eclipsed. There was something new and strange about her frankness and *naïveté*, combined with culture and power of conversation, which attracted almost everybody, and many women said that " they could not make her out." In Washington she might have created little sensation, as she was only a very good example of the best type of American beauties; but in England we are not yet accustomed to these young ladies, who appear to unite the shrewdness and knowledge of a woman of fifty to the grace and freshness of early girlhood.

Mrs. Kingsworth, her mother, was nothing but Alma's mother. She would talk nicely and sensibly, nay, sometimes volubly; she was gentle and pleasant and good-natured, but she let her daughter do exactly as she pleased, submitted entirely to her judgment, and never presumed to have an opinion of her own. She was the widow of an enterprising American financier whose affairs were found in some confusion when he died. There was enough money for the two women to live in comfort, but not enough to keep a large house at Washington, or to entertain in the style Alma would have desired. The young lady was no heiress; the moderate fortune Mrs. Kingsworth possessed was entirely her own, and what the father had left belonged to her only brother, who had settled at " 'Frisco " and was supposed to be getting on well.

Mr. Ansdell was also an American ; but a sojourn of many years in Europe had almost entirely destroyed every trace of his origin. He might have been, and often was, taken for a distinguished Englishman who had spent much time on the Continent. He called himself a cosmopolitan, and was as much at home at the Orleans as in the French Jockey Club : as comfortable in the Prater at Vienna as in Hyde Park. The only country he did not wish to live in was his own ; yet he was kind and hospitable to any Americans sent to him by friends across the water. Mr. Ansdell occupied handsome chambers near St. James's : he was a member of some of the best clubs, and his very large fortune enabled him to run racehorses, and to give his friends the best of shooting in Norfolk without exceeding his income. For some years he had been much sought after by enterprising mothers of portionless girls, but it had now been long accepted that Mr. Ansdell was a confirmed old bachelor. It was perfectly understood that ladies would be asked to mount his drag and to make use of his box at Ascot, to join his dinner parties at Greenwich, and to tea and strawberries in his pretty rooms, but that he was not a marrying man. It was only a very silly or very inexperienced person who would, in recent times, have dreamt of setting traps for Mr. Ansdell ; and he was quite sharp enough to avoid them. Years were advancing on him, and young ladies had come to consider him as quite old, while their mothers had to admit that he was certainly elderly. So he could now enjoy himself among his friends, and invite people of both sexes and every age, without *arrière pensée.*

This summer Mr. Ansdell had determined to take a longer trip than usual in his schooner, the *Aphrodite.* He was a little tired of the Solent, and the " Cowes week,' and thought that a cruise further to sea would be a pleasant change. The one difficulty was to form an agreeable party, for it is no easy task to bring together half a dozen people who are not likely to fall out when confined for weeks to the limited space of even a large yacht. Mr. Ansdell had no notion of filling his boat with a crowd; on a pleasure cruise, he thought, every one ought to be as comfortable as possible, for discomfort breeds ill-humour and quarrels. Finally, therefore, he invited Charles Clitheroe, a bright young fellow who was supposed to have been in the Foreign Office, but, in fact, had abandoned diplomacy for journalism and literature generally, and had created some sensation by a recent work called " Our Future Faith," in which he had successfully combined a little philosophy, and a little theology, with a great deal of worldly wit, so that those of the fashionable people who called themselves " thinkers," began to believe that a new Apostle had appeared amongst them. Clitheroe had a small fixed income, and was believed to be making money by his works. The other guest was the Hon. Reginald Audley, the eldest son of

Lord Edgware.   Audley was well off, and would be very rich some day: he was a capital companion, a thorough sportsman, and able to make himself generally pleasant and useful; his good looks, too, were undeniable.

These five, all warranted to be good sailors, composed the *Aphrodite* party.

CHAPTER II.

EARLY DAYS.

" How nice the men look," remarked Mrs. Kingsworth, taking Mr. Ansdell's proffered arm; "I hope they will take care of our boxes."

"Dubois will look after them," replied Mr. Ansdell. "He is very careful, and knows how to deal with ladies' things. Don't be anxious. Is your maid a good sailor?"

"We hope so," answered the lady. "Alma engaged her before we went to Paris in the winter, and she was not ill when we crossed."

"Where is she?"

"Brayger is looking to the luggage with Mr. Ansdell's servant," Alma interposed. "We can leave them to take care of themselves and it."

The still surface of Southampton Water was glowing in the evening sun when they reached the pier. The taper masts of the yachts stood out black against the golden sky, and the burgees were hanging down almost motionless. A six-oared gig was waiting at the steps, her hull brightly varnished, the Squadron burgee gaily enamelled on her bow, her stern sheets comfortably filled with cushions, and her crew, all in white, with "*Aphrodite*" marked on the front of their jerseys, and appearing in gold on the ribbons of their straw hats. They saluted respectfully as the party approached. "Shove off," said Mr. Ansdell, when he had taken up the steering lines and the ladies were settled comfortably on either side of him with their bags, shawls, and sunshades. "Give way!"

And at the word the five oars, hitherto held up in one vertical line, dropped into the water simultaneously, and the gig shot out from under the shade of the pier into the bright surface beyond.

"Which is the *Aphrodite?*" asked Alma.

"That schooner to your left, just behind the steamer with a yellow funnel," answered Mr. Ansdell.

"Oh! I see her. Look, mamma," exclaimed the girl, "how pretty the yacht is!"

The *Aphrodite* was indeed a vessel of which any one might be proud. She was a fore and aft schooner of about a hundred and seventy tons, a powerful craft holding a medium place between the old-fashioned heavy cruiser and the modern racing machine. She had a large free-board, but a gold line and the graceful curves of her bow and stern took off from her height out of water. A little golden goddess, her figure-head, seemed to float over the ripple of the tide caused by her cutwater. The ladder was out, and the captain, with a gold band round his cap, stood at the gangway ready to hand the ladies the white man-ropes. As they pulled up alongside, and Mr. Ansdell said, "Way enough," Alma recognised in two figures standing behind the captain, Clitheroe and Audley, both of whom she had met before. The former pushed forward eagerly to shake hands as soon as she stepped on the deck, while Audley was busy handing up all the small requisites, which had been stowed in the stern sheets. Not till everything had been taken below, and the gig was hauled up on the davits, did he approach the group on the quarter-deck, where the four were all talking in an animated manner. Alma and her mother greeted him warmly, and Mr. Ansdell then offered to show the ladies their cabins, which were comfortable and private. In the steerage was a small retreat for Mrs. Brayger, the indispensable maid, who shortly afterwards came alongside in the steam cutter with the heavy luggage. Until dinner time the sunny decks of the *Aphrodite* were dotted with black trunks of all sizes and shapes; and it was late ere even a semblance of order was brought about, though the mate and a "fatigue party" did their best to meet Brayger's wishes. That lady was scandalised at the limited space at her disposal, and retired to her supper in no very amiable mood. Meanwhile a very merry dinner was going on in the bright main cabin, brilliantly lighted and decorated with flowers. Dubois waited on them; he was a brisk, good-natured Frenchman, who had been all over the world, and, unlike most of his fellow-countrymen, did his work as well in a rough sea-way as in harbour. A cook and a cabin-boy made up the staff. The principal subject of discussion at dinner was their next destination; and after some doubts and suggestions, it was resolved to begin with a cruise to the westward, the wind being in a favourable quarter.

"High water is at eleven to-morrow," said Mr. Ansdell, when dinner was over; "we ought to get under way about nine. Look over your things, ladies, and see if there is anything you want from shore before we start. We must send for provisions, and leave directions at the post-office for forwarding letters."

Of course, next morning, there turned out to be a long list of wants, and it was suggested that Alma should go on shore with Brayger and the mate. But Mr. Ansdell was too old a hand to permit this. He knew that if Miss Kingsworth began shopping, they would certainly miss the tide or have to leave her behind. So, after some *badinage*, she gave way, and agreed that she could, if she were obliged, entrust her commissions to Brayger. But that was worse still. Brayger, uncontrolled, was sure to run amuck in the High-street, and spend all day Above Bar. Some one in authority must go with her; but who? Audley volunteered at once; and with many expressions of doubt as to his intelligence being sufficient for the task, he at last stepped into the boat with the ungracious Abigail. Mr. Ansdell went below to write some last letters; Mrs. Kingsworth attempted to put things straight in the ladies' cabin with the assistance of the boy; and Mr. Clitheroe sat on deck and smoked, and talked philosophy and theology to Alma, who listened and talked also, while the men loosened the covers from the sails, and hove the anchor short, and hauled the tackle out of the sailroom, and got number two jib ready, for it was very fine and sunny; and after Mr. Ansdell had poked his head out of the companion and gazed anxiously to the pier more than once, and after the captain had looked at his watch a dozen times and had glanced towards shore, shading his face with his hand, a boat at last appeared, laden almost to the gunwale, and Audley climbed on deck, wiping his forehead and saying " Well; I've got back at last; but I never thought we should. Your maid wanted to buy a wardrobe with plate-glass doors, to hang your dresses in. She said it would stand on deck all right."

CHAPTER III.

BOTH.

A WEEK had passed, and the *Aphrodite* had called in at Weymouth, had been laid to off Lulworth Cove, while they explored it in the steam-cutter, had brought up in Torbay, and had remained in Dartmouth a couple of days for them to steam up the lovely Dart and drive to the borders of the wild moor. So far, scarcely a cloud had disturbed the serenity of the sky or of their party. Of course it was evident that both the young men admired Alma, but then every one admired Alma, and there was no reason to suppose that either of them had been seriously smitten. It was a splendid evening when, with a light air off shore, the *Aphrodite* was heading for the Start under all sail. Her boom was well over the quarter, and her deck sloped but slightly to leeward as the towering white canvas drove her through the calm sea. Tiny waves rustled past her curved sides, and only the gentle flowing of the water told that they were moving through it. It was the pleasant hour after dinner when, as usual, Audley or Mr. Ansdell took the helm so that they might have the quarter deck to themselves. Far away forward, separated by a long length of deck glowing red in the evening light, were a couple of hands looking out; the rest were all "keeping their watch below"—the servants at supper, and the captain entertaining the party with forecastle yarns. Soon Audley took the helm out of the owner's hand, saying, "Now smoke your cigar quietly, Mr. Ansdell; I'll keep her going."

The ladies were reclining in comfortable deck chairs, Mr. Ansdell and Clitheroe lighted their cigars, and all became silent, feeling the soothing influence of the scene. As the darkness increased a bright flash suddenly appeared out on the beam. "What is that?" asked Alma, half alarmed.

"Only the Start lighthouse," answered Audley. "If you look to the left, just ahead of the fore rigging, you will see the Eddystone directly."

Just then Dubois put his head up. "Tea is ready, if you please, madam," he said, addressing Mrs. Kingsworth; "will you have it on deck or below?"

"I am getting a little chilly," said the lady, "and will go below." She rose and moved to the companion, Mr. Ansdell following. The other two also got up, leaving Audley at the helm. The companion was nearly amidships, and before Alma reached it, Clitheroe said, "Don't go below yet, Miss Kingsworth! You are not cold, are you?"

"Oh no," replied the girl.

"Then come and look at the lighthouse for a minute."

They moved over to the weather side and leant against the bulwarks.

"It is very beautiful," murmured Alma, gazing on the dark waters, over which, in the distance, flashed the brilliant light, while the stars were appearing one by one, and the high Devonshire cliffs loomed black against the sky.

"That light guides our way, though we are not steering towards it," said Clitheroe. "If we were to make straight for it, the *Aphrodite* would go to pieces on the rocks. It is like man's ideal."

"How?" inquired Alma.

"Why, thus," replied the young man. "We strive and strive for our ideal, but the best of us fortunately don't reach it. If we did, we should go to pieces on the rocks of overweening pride and gratified conceit. Some do; and see what pompous, overbearing beasts they are. Morally they are shipwrecked."

"A funny notion," said Alma. "And it depends upon the direction of the ideal. I do not think the comparison quite successful."

"Perhaps not. Perhaps," continued Clitheroe, "I should say that the light rather resembles a beautiful and clever woman, who lights up the path of an aspiring man. She shows him which way he should go, though the way need not necessarily lead to her."

"That is better," remarked Alma. "He continues in the right track as long as the light remains in view, and then he drifts off again. At least most men seem to do that, and_many pilots, too, I believe."

"Yes, but not all. The light may be obscured for a moment, but it reappears again; and even if it did not, the mariner would know its bearing."

"Mariners may, but how about the men?"

"The men?" said Clitheroe. "Oh! no doubt they are mostly quite as foolish as you fancy them. But not all, Miss Kingsworth, not all. I, for instance—forgive my being egotistical—have been groping about for years seeking my beacon, my guiding star."

"Have you?" asked Alma, quite seriously. "By your last book, I should have thought you had long since discovered it; at any rate I hope you will soon find it."

"I *have* found it, Miss Kingsworth! At last I have found that brilliant light which, if I can only keep it in view, will illumine my path in the world. Miss Kingsworth," he continued, seizing her hand, "can you not guess whom I mean? The ideal I have so long sought for is now by my side! Alma! will you remain by it?"

"What do you mean, Mr. Clitheroe?" gasped the astonished girl.

"In the language of the world, I mean, will you be

my wife ? " said Clitheroe.   " In my own language, will you guide my path in literature, may I look to you to inspire me, may I regard you as my ideal and my goddess ?   I am not at all insane," he continued, volubly, "and know what I am asking.   I feel that I have done something in the world, but I could do more, much more, with such a one to help me as you."

" I'm afraid I could not help much," answered Alma, withdrawing her hand, half amused at his egotism.

" Ah, but wait ! listen.   The fate I ask you to share is not that of a mere Bohemian !   You would be rich in many pleasures, if not in money.   I have achieved but the first rung of the ladder; but if you help me to ascend it, you will ascend it with me.   Your life would be spent in its proper sphere; all that is clever and interesting and beautiful would surround you."

" Let us go down stairs," said Alma, who never could remember the proper nautical expression.

" What ! without your giving me an answer ? " exclaimed Clitheroe.   " Miss ·Kingsworth—Alma ! I adore you; tell me that you do not reject me."

" I want my tea ! " the girl remarked.

" Tea ! "   And he could not help throwing a certain contempt into the word.   " While I am struggling for my light, my star, my very life ! Miss Kingsworth, please give me a word—and do not let it be No ! "

" Well," replied Alma, as she placed her little foot

on the first step of the companion; "I won't say No, then. I will think it over. You have taken me by surprise, and I am not prepared to answer to-night. I will tell you another evening."

"When?" cried Clitheroe, seizing her hand almost roughly.

"Well, this day week, then," answered the girl, disappearing.

Five minutes later, both the young men appeared in the main cabin, the mate having relieved Audley, who, from his position at the helm, had not been able to tell what had been going on. But Alma was very silent, and watched Clitheroe closely. He talked just as usual, in the tone of somewhat cynical fun usual to him, and amused the party by an account of the last thought-reading humbug's exposure.

The ladies retired early, and Audley remarked to Mr. Ansdell when they paced the deck for a final constitutional:

"The weather is likely to change before morning. The wind has fallen altogether, and I doubt whether we shall get into Plymouth Sound till next ebb, if then. We are drifting astern fast."

"How is the glass?" inquired Mr. Ansdell.

"Fallen nearly half an inch since lunch. The skipper has noticed it," continued Audley. "See!"

A group of men were silently at work in the main

rigging, and another lot forward.　Shouting and stamping at night were particularly obnoxious to Mr. Ansdell, and they lowered the big topsails, and let down the heavy yards, as quietly as if they had been feather-beds.　Jibs were shifted, and soon the foresail was noiselessly hauled down, tied, and covered.

"May as well make all snug, sir," said the captain, coming aft.　"The sails are doing her no good, as there's no wind at all.　It's no use their flapping and heaving about."

"Quite right, Osborne," remarked Mr. Ansdell; "and it looks like a hard breeze before morning."

"I doubt we might get a little wind," answered the seaman, looking out over the port beam.　"However, we'll be comfortable enough now."

In the night Audley was awakened by the tramp of footsteps over his head, and turned out to see what was going on.　He was met by a violent pelt of rain, and could scarcely see his hand before him.　They were housing topmasts, and putting a reef down in the mainsail. There was not much wind yet, but the captain was mindful of the old adage—

> "When the rain comes before the wind
> Stand by and well your topsails mind."

Out of the showers the Start light still shone at intervals, and it was now over the starboard bow, proving that they had drifted astern several miles.

"Then he sat down on the wet boards at her feet."

Page 163

The morning was rough and gloomy. The *Aphrodite* was plunging violently against a short, angry sea, and the wind being strong from the south-west, the captain was making short tacks on and off. They were, however, gradually working to the westward. Breakfast was served under difficulties ; Brayger was groaning in her cabin, and Clitheroe did not appear at all, though he sent a message to say he was not at all sick—quite an unnecessary piece of information, as no one believed it. Mr. Ansdell and Mrs. Kingsworth declared that they would spend the morning in the cabin ; but Audley donned his sou'-wester, sea-boots, and waterproof, and went to take a turn at the tiller. In a short time he was surprised to see Alma emerge from the companion.

"I am tired of that cabin," she said, staggering aft with the assistance of one of the men who had sprung to help her. " May I stop on deck, Mr. Audley ? "

"Certainly, if you do not mind getting wet. Wait a moment : I will make you comfortable."

He called out for some one to take the ship, and then lashed a chair against the bulwark. " Sit there," he said, helping her across the slippery deck. And then, as a sea struck the weather beam and the spray came flying over, he got an oilskin and covered her up altogether, so that no water could possibly hurt her. Then he sat down on the wet boards at her feet, and though the *Aphrodite* plunged, and the seas came over every two minutes, and though the wind howled and the boom creaked Audley felt happier than he had been for some time.

He could not refrain from a disparaging remark about Clitheroe, who had not yet appeared. Miss Kingsworth rather stood up for him. "We are not all fitted for the same pursuits, Mr. Audley," she remarked.

"No indeed we are not," he assented, cleverly changing the subject; "I have often thought how different must be your own life in New York, for instance, to that of English ladies at home."

"Very different indeed," said Alma. "We are all town mice in New York and Washington, though we may go to the seaside or to the mountains in the hot months."

"Have you considered, Miss Kingsworth," continued Audley, "how you would like to settle down in England in a comfortable country home on an estate of your own?"

"No," answered Alma, simply; "I have never thought about it."

"Why not?" asked Audley.

"Well, I suppose, because it is not likely to happen," replied the girl; "why should I bother my head about such a thing?"

"Because you can realise it at any moment, if you like," said Audley.

Alma opened her eyes wider, notwithstanding the salt sea water which still occasionally came over.

"Dear Miss Kingsworth," Audley went on, hesitating a little, "I had not intended, perhaps, to speak quite so soon, but——"

Alma did not help him by a word.

"But the chance is too good to be lost," he burst out.

"Because I am tied up here like a mummy," exclaimed Alma, now guessing what was coming. "Oh, don't go on, Mr. Audley."

"Yes; now I must," answered he. "I—I love you very dearly, Miss Kingsworth, and if you will only like me a little, you will make me the happiest man alive!"

There! he had taken the plunge, and it was not so awful, after all.

"I am surprised," began Alma—but he interrupted her:

"Oh!" he went on, "I am not half clever enough for you, I know, and not good enough. But I will try and make you happy. My father and mother would be delighted to have such a daughter, and we should do all we could for you and your mother, so that you might like England better than America. Dear Alma, will you say yes?"

"Beg your pardon, sir," interrupted the captain, at a most inopportune moment, "will you kindly move the lady to the starboard side? We're going about; we can weather the head of the breakwater now."

The spell was broken. Audley had to assist Alma to

rise, and to remove the tight oilskin. She became her own mistress again, and at once tried to bolt for the companion.

"Will you not answer me?" he asked imploringly.

"I can't to-day. Wait for a week," she replied, descending the stairs.

CHAPTER IV.

THE ORDEAL.

SOME rough days followed; the *Aphrodite* rode them out quietly in the Tamar, and our party spent their time very pleasantly, though not as privately as the young men might have wished. For there were friends of Audley's on the Channel Fleet, just then anchored in the Sound, and there were friends of Mr. Ansdell in the neighbourhood. So they had to dine ashore; and there was a ball on board the *Lord Warden*, and an afternoon party in a charming house in the valley of the Tavy, and there were other dissipations of a like nature. Alma had to rebuke each of her lovers once, and once only, for not patiently waiting till the week had expired. They were both on the tenterhooks of anxiety, and neither suspected that the other had proposed.

At last the barometer rose, the sky cleared, and sailing orders were given. It was on the morning of the seventh day that the *Aphrodite* was heeling over to a fine northerly wind, making her eight knots an hour as she ran along the Cornish coast, bound for the Scilly Islands. That evening Clitheroe would come for his answer; next morning at latest she would have to give a reply to Audley. Alma was in sore perplexity. After breakfast she whispered to Mr. Ansdell—

"Will you come on deck? I have something to ask you."

Her courteous host, of course, at once assented.

"I want your advice, Mr. Ansdell," she said, taking his arm, and leading him to the comfortable place close to the davits, where the friendly foresail concealed them from view.

"I will give it with pleasure, if I can do any good," replied Ansdell. "What is it, dear Miss Kingsworth?"

Alma blushed. "It's a delicate matter," she began.

Ansdell's quick black eyes looked into hers.

"What?" he asked. "Which of them?"

She was almost glad that he understood so quickly. But it was not easy to reply.

"Well," he inquired, after a pause, "which of my young friends has proposed to you? He is a lucky dog, at all events, for I see by your face that you are almost inclined to say Yes."

"But I can't marry both of them!" Alma suddenly blurted out.

"Both? of course not! Have *both* of them asked you? Well, I can't be surprised, considering how entirely fascinating you are. Why I am nearly fifty, and yet I assure you you are the most charming girl I have ever met, with all my experience."

"Do you *really* think so?" asked Alma; "without compliments, am I *really* so nice?"

"Upon my word of honour, I mean it," answered Mr. Ansdell. "You are the very nicest girl I have ever known. But what about these two young men? Have you accepted either?"

Alma shook her head.

"Have you told your mother?"

"Yes, but mother* says I am to do as I like. She won't exercise her authority one bit."

"And what do *you* say?" continued Mr. Ansdell.

"I can't say anything," replied Alma.

"But surely you like one better than the other?"

"I don't think I do," the girl went on. "I like both very much. But I can't make up my mind which I like better."

"Then refuse both," suggested Mr. Ansdell.

"I am afraid I have not the courage to do that," replied Alma. "It would hurt them so much."

"Oh, never mind their feelings," exclaimed the gentleman. "It is my fault for bringing them here; I might have foreseen the consequences. I am sorry to have

---

* American ladies seldom say "Mamma."

caused you this annoyance. We must put them ashore at Falmouth."

"I would not hear of it," said Alma. "No! I think I like them both, and I believe either could make me happy. How shall I decide?"

"Take Audley," suggested Ansdell. "He has the best position." Alma shook her head.

"No, I cannot decide on such a ground. Oh dear, I wish we had ordeals now, as in olden times! I wish young men had to fight with each other for the girl. That would save all trouble. I should like to marry the one that really loves me best; and I have to answer to-night. It is dreadful."

"Wait a minute!" exclaimed Ansdell. "I have a plan. We will find an ordeal. You shall fall overboard, and the one that jumps in to save you shall be the happy man."

"But we might both be drowned!" observed Alma. "Otherwise it would be delightful."

"There is not the slightest danger, if you will leave it to me," replied Ansdell. "You can swim, of course?"

"Yes," answered Alma, "fairly well."

"Then," continued Ansdell, "if you arrange your dress as I tell you, and conceal a life belt under it, there is not the remotest chance of either you or your preserver coming to grief."

The American then explained his plan, and Alma

clapped her hands when she understood it, exclaiming joyfully: "Oh, that is delightful! And whoever saves me shall know nothing of the trick till we are married."

When Audley and Clitheroe came on deck after lunch the former was rather surprised to see the foresail stowed and three reefs down in the mainsail. The weather was fine and the wind lighter than ever. The mate told him Mr. Ansdell had ordered them to reduce sail during lunch, so that there might be less motion, and of course Audley had no right to interfere. Soon the ladies came on deck, and Mr. Ansdell himself took the helm. Alma did not come aft, but went to the lee davits, where the two young men joined her.

"I should like to look into this boat," said she; "I wonder whether it is the same one we came from the ball in." And with these words she put her little foot on the rail, and, catching hold of the davits, swung herself up.

"Take care, Miss Kingsworth," cried Audley; "you will fall overboard."

The vessel was, of course, heeling over on the lee side. It was not far to the water, and scarcely had Audley cried out when there was a shriek and a splash. All was confusion, or apparent confusion, in a moment. "She is in the water," yelled Clitheroe, frantically. "The lady's overboard," cried the men on the forecastle.

"Steady!" shouted Ansdell, who had put the helm

hard down. "Lower away, boys," cried the captain, as the vessel shot into the wind. And in five seconds the men, standing ready at the weather davits, had the boat in the water.

But the two young gentlemen had not waited so long. There were two successive splashes, and two cries of "Man overboard!"

Clitheroe jumped over the bulwarks, and not being able to swim a yard, sank for a moment and then drifted away to leeward. Audley knew better; he made for the taffrail and almost caught Alma as the schooner came round. But before he could seize her he was himself hauled on board the boat,·while Alma was calmly and gently beating the water with her hands, and waiting for the certain rescue.

"Give me a rope," she said, and was helped over the gunwale without any trouble.

It was more difficult to secure Clitheroe. He was nearly sinking for the third time, and his struggles were getting feeble when they hauled him in at last.

Nobody could quite make out Alma's coolness. When all had been brought safely to the yacht, and Clitheroe had regained consciousness, she returned to the deck, where she found Mr. Ansdell.

"Don't be anxious about me!" she said, in reply to his inquiries. "I have only had a bath, and now I've put on dry clothes I'm quite comfortable. And Dubois says

Mr. Clitheroe will be all right again before dinner. But, Mr. Ansdell, this is worse than ever!"

"So it is," admitted Ansdell; "they both jumped in."

"Yes," answered Alma; "and what is more, the stupid one of the two was the cleverest about it, and the clever one nearly got drowned himself."

"I think Clitheroe showed the most affection for you," remarked Ansdell.

"No," answered Alma; "for Mr. Audley did all he could. It is not a proof of affection to be an idiot. I must think."

She thought for a minute or two, and blushes appeared on her fair face, and disappeared as rapidly.

At last she spoke.

"Mr. Ansdell," she said, looking at the good little man's face, "you said this morning that I was the nicest girl you ever met."

"So I did, and it is true," replied he.

"Then," she answered, "I have made up my mind. I shall refuse both!"

"Will you really?" asked Ansdell, taking her hand. "They are both good fellows, you know, both young and good looking."

"I don't care about their youth and good looks," replied the girl; "I won't marry either."

"And you will leave the *Aphrodite* fancy free?" he asked.

"Nearly," she answered, looking down.

"But not quite?" he said, taking her other hand.

*　　　*　　　*　　　*

"Audley, old man, and Clitheroe," said Mr. Ansdell when they were all three on deck together after dinner. "I am so much obliged to you for what you did to-day. You behaved like real good fellows." He shook hands with them as they murmured deprecatingly. "Of course you must both come to my wedding."

"Your wedding?" they asked with one voice.

"Yes, Alma has asked me to invite you. It will be early in September. Can you give up your shooting for a day or two?"

THE CRUISE OF THE "MOONSHINE."

THE CRUISE OF THE "MOONSHINE."

CHAPTER I.

FIVE OF US.

PEOPLE who take up these pages must not be surprised at the name we gave our vessel. It will be explained in due time. First it behoves to tell how and why we got her at all. We were five. We were extremely fond of boating on the river. To launch our four-oar and have a good pull from Teddington Lock to Sunbury and back we were not afraid of braving even the traffic arrangements (?) of the South Western Railway on a Saturday afternoon. Week by week during several successive London seasons we had to elbow our way through the crowds which encumber the station at Waterloo and fight for room in a stuffy carriage; and only on wet afternoons could we hope to find a seat. When our annual holiday came round we took small but extremely expensive quarters somewhere up the river. We spent our time either in the water or on it, and in our rush for the element so dear to Englishmen we resembled nothing so much as a brood of young ducks when they leave their careful foster-mother screaming in vain on the bank. We were very proud of our four-oar. None but really trained crews could beat us, and we had serious thoughts of entering at Henley. But after a few seasons we got tired of the dust, scramble, and crowd of an almost daily railway journey, we began to grumble at the charges of our waterside landlady, and the scenery of the Thames no longer awakened the same enthusiasm as in our earlier years. One of our crew proved unfaithful. He declined to share our lodgings at Pipnell-on-Thames, and started for the Continent. He actually crossed the Channel and bathed at Ostend. In the water he made the aquaintance of a delightful man, a real sailor, who owned a yacht. Repeated joint immersions cemented a friendship commenced under watery auspices, and the yacht owner gave our chum a run to Dover in his boat. The results, which he admitted made him feel rather queer, were momentous. For in the first place, our summer boating had been a dead failure. It rained all through August, while *he* was writing of cloudless days and rippling seas at Ostend. Then the boat was nothing without our bow oar. The little cox, who only pulled eight stone, could not take his place, and of the volunteers who joined us none understood our stroke nor our jokes. They were alawys out of time and swore that we rowed badly; we swore back, and then they turned sulky. Finally, our misfortunes came to a crisis when we went out one day without a cox at all. We got jammed in between a steam launch and a barge, had to leave our favourite boat in a hurry, and lost, not only our and Messenger's pride, but also our jackets and their contents, which we had taken with us in view of lunch. When the traveller returned triumphant, he found us grumbling over our bills at Pipnell and lamenting over the cedar splinters which an enterprising waterman had rescued out of the Thames mud at a price far exceeding their value.

"What are you fellows growling at?" said he. "Boating is poor fun, after all, you are nothing but a lot of fresh-water sailors. Why, not one of you could splice a halliard or luff the jib-sheet."

We were much impressed by the nautical knowledge displayed in the last sentence. We did not know in the least what "luffing a jib-sheet" meant (nor, it appears, does any one else); but of course we thought it must be very tremendous. We looked at each other, and one of us ventured timidly to remark, "You used to like it yourself."

"Of course," answered the traveller, "before I knew of anything else. But now I have been to sea (he said this in the deep bass adopted by the late T. P. Cooke in nautical transpontine dramas), I feel that I was born to be a real sailor, not a sort of fresh-water horse-marine. Every Englishman is, in fact, born a sailor, if he only knew it. It is not your fault; you fellows have never had a chance. But it is the only real thing. You will never want to pull on a river again when you have once sailed at sea."

"I daresay not," remarked our stroke; "but I cannot give up my place at Doubloon and Dollar's bank to go away as a common sailor." And I chimed in, "No. I certainly don't intend to leave the Cat and Dog Tax office. They don't pay much, but I like it; and I can always have a day when I want one."

"What rot you are talking. The idea of going before the mast!" (we did not quite know what this meant, but expected it was the same thing as "walking the plank.") "No! You should go to sea like gentlemen. We ought to have our yacht instead of that miserable paper thing of Messenger," at the same time kicking the venerated remains of our dear old boat as if they had been dirt. "Then we are independent of landladies and bills. We can come and go when we like. We take our hotel with us. No one can prevent us crossing the blue waters in any direction we please; we become, in fact, free men; untrammelled by considerations of dress, of locks and lock-keepers." And then he took his hat off, lifted up his nose and seemed to sniff the briny as he waved his hand.

"That is what we ought to do next year, instead of simmering at Pipnell, and being crushed by beastly barges or run into by steam launches."

At last our little coxswain spoke. He was a small man, gentle, good-tempered, and rather shy, but sensible withal. "It is all very well, Smythe," said he, "to talk big about yachting, and the flag waving in the breeze. I should like it as well as you, perhaps better, for I was not seasick when I went to Margate with my aunt seven years ago, and I am sure you would have been, if you had been there." (An indignant start and scowl from Smythe. The cox had touched him in a sensitive place.) "But yachting is very expensive indeed. How are we to afford it?" "Yes," said the rest of us in chorus, "we should like it very much, but we can't afford it."

"You are wrong," replied Smythe. "I know all about it from my friend Seasalt. His is a splendid craft—a schooner of seventy tons, and we should not think of such a big one. But he tells me that it is cheaper than staying about at hotels. He positively saves money by yachting. He gets his wine out of bond and catches a lot of fish, so he has not much to buy when he does run in somewhere. All you have to do is to buy a yacht cheap; keeping her is nothing."

And so the discussion went on, to be resumed many times as the autumn evenings waxed longer. We never met without speaking of the topic nearest our hearts

What should we do next season? Should we get Messenger to build us a new boat and return to Pipnell or Styecombe? or should we adopt Smythe's suggestion and go in for the sea, the deep blue sea? One evening we were surprised by Smythe, who had never shown any talent for music, sitting down to the piano and accompanying himself singing—

> "When we lay,
> In the Bay
> Of Biscay, oh!"

There was no resisting this. The song settled the matter. We decided to go yachting next summer. We held a solemn meeting at the Barnacle Club—a very smart, but very young, institution which Smythe had recently joined, and of which the object was to follow, at a respectful distance, the noble example set by the Royal Yacht Squadron. The whole air of the Barnacle Club was distinctly and decidedly nautical, though it was not a hundred yards from Piccadilly. There was a builder's model of a yacht hung in the hall; there was a telescope on the table of the reading-room; the walls were decorated with list of yachts and yacht-owners, codes of signals, and pictures of regattas. The secretary wore a blue pilot coat with gilt buttons; among the ordinary "society" hats on the pegs there peered out two real unmistakable sailor hats.

CHAPTER II.

WE felt awestruck as we ascended the stairs (companion, Smythe said), to the strangers' room, and felt that we were entering on a new and unknown world. This time the discussion was not long, for we were all agreed. We were to buy a yacht and sail in her. We unanimously elected Smythe the captain, or, as our stroke called it in a moment of ill-timed facetiousness which jarred on our highly-strained nerves, "head boss." He graciously took the chair, and, pushing pens and paper towards Sturge, our little cox, begged him to perform the functions of secretary. We became still more impressed, for the thing began to look like a board meeting, and Goggles (No. 3), who was sub-manager for a Joint Stock Company, and had a wholesome horror of board meetings, whispered that he did not like it. However, Smythe explained that we must have a distinct understanding about ways and means and that it was better to put the arrangements down in black and white. We fully agreed to this, and then proceeded to discuss matters. It was at last agreed that Smythe should have full power to choose and purchase a suitable yacht for us, but that he was not to exceed the limit of 200*l.* We then each wrote him a letter promising to pay him 40*l.* when called upon. Our president pointed out that we were now in the best position to find a good and cheap vessel, as in the winter plenty of yachts were to be had at moderate prices. " But," said he, as he closed the meeting and rang the bell for beer, " I intend to be very careful. I shall justify the trust you have reposed in me ; you shall have a beautiful vessel for your money, gentlemen." And then we fell to talking of our summer cruise, of the ports we would touch at, the splendid regattas we would attend, the ladies we would take out, and the importance in their eyes the possession of a yacht would give us. We separated full of nautical dreams, and walked home with something of a sea swagger.

For the next few weeks whenever we saw Smythe he was busy scanning advertisements in the paper or writing letters to yacht agents stating his requirements. To our surprise and disappointment we found that the sum which we had voted with so much liberality, which it would cost us each some sacrifice to raise, and which we thought so splendid, did not dazzle agents or owners at all. In fact Smythe admitted that having inquired the price of sundry well known racing or cruising yachts advertised for sale, the sum demanded for them far exceeded what we could afford; yet our requirements were but simple. We wanted a yacht with five sleeping berths at least, and a spacious saloon; she must be a fast and weatherly vessel, and above all handsome (of course Smythe made these conditions, and told us they were necessary; we could not have mentioned anything in particular). Weeks slipped away; our president was more absorbed than ever in looking for yachts, and seemed even further from success, when one afternoon each of us received an urgent summons to the Barnacle Club, which we all reached, panting, several minutes before the time.

"I have found exactly what we want," said Smythe, "Here it is. Read." We eagerly scanned the following advertisement :

TO BE SOLD, at a great sacrifice (owner going abroad), the beautiful cutter yacht *Ocean Queen*. She is 28 tons O.M., makes up five berths, and is a splendid sea boat. Has won several cups. Inquire, &c.

"Now, gentlemen," continued our president, "I have made the necessary inquiries, and find that the vessel is exactly what we desire. She is on the Clyde. I therefore beg you will authorise me to go and look at her, and vote me ten pounds for expenses at once."

CHAPTER III.

HOW WE BOUGHT THE " OCEAN QUEEN."

WE were startled, but soon each produced two pounds towards Smythe's expenses, and we accompanied him to Euston, wishing him God-speed. The next evening we received a telegram : " The *Ocean Queen* suits us. I have purchased her. Return to-morrow." And on the third morning at six o'clock we were all waiting on the platform in the chill February twilight to hear of our new acquisition. Our ambassador turned out of the train rather sleepy and cross; we could not get much information from him, and he merely requested us to come to his rooms in the evening after dinner, when he would be thoroughly rested and tell us all about it. We felt ourselves rather ill-treated, as we had all got up in the middle of the night for nothing at all, and did not know what to do with the time until ten o'clock. However, we could extract nothing from Smythe in answer to our urgent inquiries of, " How about the *Ocean Queen* ?" " Has she plenty of cabins ?" " Is she pretty ? " " Is she fast ? "

and so on, except: "Oh yes, she is all right. Can't you leave a fellow alone when he has spent two nights out of bed for you chaps?" Finally we all went home to bed. We could not sleep, thinking of the *Ocean Queen*, and of the pleasures of cruising in her. What a lovely name to be sure! We pictured to ourselves a majestic craft proudly riding the waves and excelling all her surroundings in size, beauty and speed. We did not quite know what a "cutter" was, and we did not like to ask. Had a cutter two masts, three, or four? We never supposed an *Ocean Queen* could only have one. Had such a possibility been suggested we should have laughed it to scorn. We had read and heard much of the luxury with which yachts are fitted up—of the silk settees, beautiful panels, and gorgeous hangings of these floating palaces. We dozed and dreamed of amber curtains, satin couches, and gilt mirrors; of six stalwart men in open blue jackets and hats with brims turned up rowing us in a beautiful blue boat with cushioned seats. Of Miss H—— and Lady Alice F—— calling our attention on the pier to that lovely yacht just sailing in and of our proud reply, "Yes, she is lovely! It is the *Ocean Queen*, our yacht;" and of the admiring glances that would be shot out of still more lovely eyes. So we dreamed on through the day, doing our work I fear with but little thought of the interests of Messrs. Doubloon, Dollar, and Co., or of the rights of the Cat and Dog Tax office, sketching fancy yachts and lovely faces on our blotting papers, and looking forward to our cruise with feelings of pride and exultation. At last the offices closed; we were free. We dined hastily; none of us had any appetite; we felt that at such a crisis of our lives we were above eating and drinking. We arrived at Smythe's room all too soon; he was still asleep, and had given strict orders that he was not to be disturbed. We took half an hour's walk and returned; he was still asleep. We took another walk, and again came back; but Smythe slept on. This time we could stand it no longer; we dropped the fire-irons in his sitting room till he turned out in a beastly temper, asking, " What all this infernal row was about?" Little Sturge had the pluck to speak up.

" Look here, old fellow," said he, " you have been spending our money, and we want to know all about it." Fearing this remark would irritate the majestic Smythe, who, we saw, was about to make a sharp reply, we attempted to put matters in a different light. Goggles cried out that he had come to ask him to dine with us, forgetting that we had all pretended to have dined an hour before. He was mollified, accepted, put on his coat, and led the way down stairs. He suggested Simpson's; so in the crowded Strand, where five men can certainly not walk abreast, conversation on the subject nearest our hearts was impossible. When dinner had been ordered and partly eaten, after our curiosity had been baulked a hundred times by Smythe's incessant demand for Worcester sauce, bread, mustard, wine, or some other unnecessary trifle, our plenipotentiary at last consented to tackle the subject in a doubtful manner. "So you have bought the *Ocean Queen* ?" "Yes I have bought her." "What sort of a vessel is it ?" asked Beacon, who was tacitly appointed to be spokesman of the party. "It !" cried Smythe, horrified ; "don't say that anywhere else, or you will be laughed at—a yacht is *she* !" "Very well, what sort of a vessel is she ?" "Well," said Smythe, "she is a very nice boat." "Is she big ?" "N—no, not very big," answered our president ; "you could not expect a very big yacht to be only twenty-eight tons." "Well, but is there plenty of room on board for all of us ?" "Well, of course," replied Smythe, rather hesitatingly, we thought, "you can't expect as much room on board ship as you have on land." "Of course not," we all agreed. "But," continued he, gaining confidence as he spoke, "she is for her size a roomy yacht—a decidedly roomy yacht." We were all much pleased. "How many masts has she ?" asked Beacon. "Masts? Why, of course only one. She is a cutter, and cutters have only one mast." Then, seeing a look of disappointment on our faces, he added, "All good yachts are cutters. They are much faster than any other rig. Schooners are quite going out of fashion." Again a ripple of contentment passed over our faces. Sturge only remained solemn, and said he had reckoned on at least three masts to dazzle Lady Alice F——, with whom he was desperately smitten. The persevering Beacon went on. "Did you have a sail in her?" "How could I?" exclaimed Smythe. "Why, her sails are not bent!" "What does it matter whether they are bent or straight?" asked Beacon. Tired of being questioned Smythe proposed an adjournment to cigars and coffee, when, soothed by a huge regalia, which Goggles offered him, he at last condescended to give us a continuous narrative. The fact was, he told us, we had been expecting rather too much for our three hundred pounds. "300*l.*" we all exclaimed; "why! we only agreed to 200*l.*" "But I have given 300*l.* for the *Ocean Queen*, and she is dirt cheap at the money. I know how to buy a yacht, I can tell you;" and as he said this he glared fiercely around, challenging contradiction. Little Sturge was not to be beaten. "That makes sixty pounds apiece, which is more than we can manage; you had no right to go beyond the limit." We all nodded assent. "Very well," said Smythe grandly, "if you fellows haggle over a paltry twenty pounds, I shall pay for her myself, and sell her at a profit when I bring her round to the island—unless, indeed," concluded he reflectively, "I prefer to keep her. Perhaps I shall." This was taking the bull by the horns indeed. Here was a man willing to take the whole huge responsibility on himself, and talking of sailing the *Ocean Queen* alone in his glory, while we wretches were craning at a miserable contribution of twenty pounds. We consulted each other by glances—they were sufficient. Sturge only looked doubtful, hardly knowing how to raise the sum in question. " Very well," said Beacon, " we agree to pay sixty pounds each; now tell us all about the yacht." " You see," began Smythe again, obviously more communicative as soon as the ticklish money question was settled, " good yachts, I find, fetch from 20*l.* to 30*l.* per ton.   Now I have bought this boat at twelve pounds; she wants a few shillings —quite a trifle—spent on her; then, after we have had our cruise, we can easily sell her for much more than we gave. But, as I told you before, we expected rather too much." " She is very fast," interrupted Beacon, who had been study- ing the record of regattas past. " Has she won the Queen's Cup at Cowes ? "   " Not quite that.   I understand she has won a prize in the Orkneys, and another in the Isle of Skye, but I don't think she would be quite fast enough for the Squadron regatta ; besides, she does not belong to the club. But," he added hastily, seeing our disappointment, " there is no telling ; she looks very quick, and may win many races for us.   She has two berths in the main cabin, two in the ladies cabin."   At this we pricked up our ears. She must be a very grand boat indeed to have a " ladies " cabin !   Why, there were few houses in London containing sitting rooms exclusively for ladies.   " And one forward for the steward, but of course we shall use that for ourselves, as we don't want a steward." We nodded, not knowing what else to do. "She is not fitted out; yachts never are in winter, but I have seen all her inventory, and it is very complete." This was about all Smythe could tell us. Each of us purchased Hunt's list. We looked out the *Ocean Queen*, and found that she had been built twenty years ago, so she was decidedly old ; but Smythe told us there was nothing like a good old-fashioned boat. So we took his word for it. Now we had to become members of a yacht club. Smythe proposed Goggles at the Barnacle, getting a chance acquaintance to second him. Then all were elected in due course, except little Sturge, who resolutely refused to add five guineas to the 60*l.* already spent for the yacht. But as we all liked him, and could ill spare his obligingness and his sound common sense, we used to take him into the Barnacle turn and turn about, till the porter let him pass without question, and he became *de facto* if not *de jure*, member of the club. We could not think of fitting out the *Ocean Queen* till summer, and the time passed wearily. " Why not beg an additional day or two at Whitsuntide, get the yacht fitted out, and sail to Cowes with her ? " We did so. We got a crew, but determined to do much of the work ourselves. Two men were therefore considered sufficient. We were to start from town on Friday evening, and the morning brought the welcome news that she was ready. So we wandered off to Leadenhall Street, and each purchased pilot coats, to which the club buttons were sewn in our presence, and at 8 P.M. we all met in sailor hats and deck shoes at King's Cross, ready to start for the north, and eager to inspect our new purchase, to inhale ocean breezes, and to try our "sea legs."

CHAPTER IV.

WE found it very cold on our way to Glasgow. To sleep comfortably in a railway carriage there ought not to be more than four persons in it—one in each corner. Now we were five, and Sturge, being the smallest, did not get a corner, and was unmercifully kicked by Smythe and Beacon, besides being growled at for always getting in the way. Of course we had second-class tickets, and fondly hoped that the looks of surprise with which the porters and guards noticed our sailor hats and seafaring "get up" denoted admiration. Perhaps they did, although at Newcastle in the early dawn we heard some disagreeable fellow in a rough jersey talk to one of the officials about horse-marines. After this, sleep fled from my eyelids and from those of little Sturge. While the others snored he told me about Lady Alice, and poured into my sympathising ears his tale of constant affection. She was kind to him, said he, but not otherwise than to her pug dog. She let him fetch and carry for her, and took all his little attentions as a matter of course. When she wanted an escort she sent for Sturge, but when she found one she liked better she sent him away again. There had been a party at Mrs. Erthoyle's, the rich American, a few nights ago. Lady Alice was there, and Sturge asked for a dance. He was graciously allowed to put his name down. But when he came to claim it, his partner was engaged in an animated conversation with Colonel Wildauk of the Guards, and said, "Oh, Mr. Sturge, go and dance with poor Miss Wallflower; she has not found a single partner yet. I want to talk to Colonel Wildauk," and dismissed him without even a glance of compassion. In vain did he hang about door-ways all the evening to obtain but a few moments from Lady Alice. One partner after another claimed her, and his cup of misery was filled by seeing her "sit out" three dances with that abominable colonel in the conservatory. "I think I shall flirt," concluded Sturge, "with Clara Meadows. I know they hate each other; perhaps she will notice it."

Poor Sturge! The notion of his flirting desperately with any one! "Suppose we invite Clara Meadows on board the *Ocean Queen*," I suggested. "The very thing!" cried Sturge; "Lady Alice will get savage, and then perhaps she may remember that I am not quite a worm." "But we should have to ask that terrible Mrs. Meadows too," said I, "unless we got her brother to chaperone her

—he is a nice lad." "So we might," he assented; "you fellows must try and help me."

Old Seabag, who was awake by this time and had heard the conversation, promised his support, and we relapsed into sleepy silence, which was only interrupted by the ticket-collector at Glasgow.

We were too impatient to go to an hotel for beds and breakfast, so instantly took train for Greenock, chartered a cab, and drove off to the Clyde. We found the builder's yard after a very long drive and some trouble. The gates were just being opened, and one or two sleepy men were dropping in to work. On the left of the gate was a little wooden office, then a shed full of old ropes, blocks, bits of wood of curious shapes, and a quantity of rubbish. In front of us was a muddy bank sloping down to the dirty river. On the bank two clumsy-looking boats were drawn up; they appeared about the size of a Brighton wherry. On the right a larger vessel was in the water, with a rickety plank as a gangway. The whole place looked seedy in the chill, cloudy morning, the vessels appeared disreputable, the men hardly recovered from a night's carouse. We asked for Mr. Carvel. He was not expected for a couple of hours. We then inquired for the *Ocean Queen*. "*Ocean Queen*," repeated the man, dubiously; "I don't know her. Andrew," he called out, "which is the *Ocean Queen?*" "Why, here she is," answered the second man, "straight before you," pointing to the smaller of the two very ill-looking boats on the mud. "The—the *Ocean Queen*," we all exclaimed; "impossible! Why, that is a nasty, ugly, little fishing boat." So we turned inquiringly to Smythe, who had, however, unaccountably disappeared. Andrew grinned. "That is the *Ocean Queen*, to be sure," he said. "Would the gentlemen like to go on board?—we can rig up a gangway directly."

Although still convinced that there must be some mistake, we agreed, and looked for Smythe, while the two men were dragging some planks and a ladder down the mud. We found him pretending to be very busy lighting his pipe in the far corner of the shed. "What is this?" we all howled; "surely you do not mean to say that horrid, clumsy little cockle-shell is the *Ocean Queen?* You don't mean to say you paid 300*l.* for that thing? Why our Thames boat was longer than that!" Smythe looked guilty, but attempted to cover his confusion under the cloak of audacity. "You do not know anything about it," said he; "she is a very nice vessel, and looks very different in the water." "That is all very well," said Beacon, "but she will not grow any bigger when she is in the water, and any fool can see that she is not worth 300*l.* I never would have bought such a thing. Why we sha'n't all be able to get on board her ourselves, still less can we ask any one! Now if you had given 300*l.* for that other vessel on the right, we might perhaps have been satisfied," and he pointed to the larger one, whose fine taper masts and slender rigging had pleased us. "Perhaps we could get her." "Perhaps so," agreed Smythe; "we will inquire." We walked down to the men who had just placed a ladder against the *Ocean Queen's* side, and asked about the vessel that had taken our fancy. "That is one of the steamers that runs down the river; she is having new boilers put in." "What do you think she is worth?" continued Beacon, determined to get to the bottom of it. "A'm sure a don't know," replied the man; "perhaps 5,000*l.*, perhaps 6,000*l.*" "Five thousand pounds!" we exclaimed. "Ay, to be sure," he answered. "Why, she is barque rigged, more than 200 feet long, and has powerful big engines." We were quite shut up. Little Sturge was the first to climb on board our new purchase. He stepped aside from the ladder and looked round silently. We all carefully followed; but our captain was in too great a hurry. In his desire to display his familiarity with all things nautical, he ascended the ladder as if he had been running up stairs at home. It first shook, then swayed violently from side to side, and finally the foot, slipping off the plank which gave it a bearing, fell into the mud. We were standing on the deck of the *Ocean Queen* looking on in dismay. There was Smythe sitting in the ooze, dazed, but apparently not hurt. The slime was gradually rising round the hole his fall had made; we saw it ascending up his beautiful navy blue trousers, while a huge splash of green mud disfigured that irreproachable sailor's knot, which after the night's journey had been carefully adjusted with the help of a pocket-mirror. The mud had carried off his new sailor hat, which was bobbing up and down on the brown waters of the Clyde, evidently leaking, notwithstanding its oilskin cover, and likely to founder unless very-soon picked up. Several men now rushed to the rescue; he was evidently more affected by the unexpected change in his appearance than by the fall itself. He was helped off to the little office, to be made as presentable as possible, while we examined the yacht. Now that Smythe was out of the way, we felt no hesitation in giving vent to our exasperated feelings, which were hardly modified when we looked round the tiny craft. We had dreamt of walking up and down the quarter-deck on stormy nights, occasionally giving stern orders to the man at the wheel. There was, as far as we could see, no quarter-deck to walk on; nothing but a narrow strip of clean white planking between the side of the ladder and the steep which led "down stairs" (we could say "down stairs" in peace and comfort now, as Smythe was safe in the wooden office being cleaned). There was certainly no wheel, only an iron bar like a pump handle turned sideways. This, we presumed, was the tiller. There could be no walking up and down on stormy nights, as a step either way would take one into

the sea, and walking lengthways appeared equally impossible, for there were a lot of windows, ropes, sticks, and
other impediments in the way. Besides, there was nothing
but quite a low ledge to prevent one falling overboard
with the slightest motion. Sturge, and perhaps others,
had thought of cosy flirtations in quiet corners, concealed
by a friendly sail. Why, there was not a corner on the
Ocean Queen, and every bit of her was in full view. As
to a quiet flirtation, such a thing could not be dreamt
of, for she looked quite crowded already with no one on
board except ourselves. It took us all our time even now
not to get into each other's way, and to avoid following
Smythe's example of falling into the mud. We were
thoroughly disgusted. However, we proceeded to go
" down stairs." Sturge, being the smallest, crawled down
first, but old Seabag, who followed him, knocked his head
violently against something or other, and disappeared with
a run and a subdued but powerful exclamation. The
third man followed sideways, and Beacon finished by
backing down carefully doubled up. We landed in a
little cabin with a sofa on each side and a table in the
middle. We all cautiously remained in crouching posi-
tions, as there was no room to stand upright. There
were no silk hangings, no beautifully painted panels,
and only one wretched little looking-glass. The sides
were coarsely grained in imitation oak. The sofas were
covered with faded chintz. We collapsed on them, two

on each side; there was a dead silence for a few minutes. At last Sturge spoke. "Damn!" said he. "This *is* a sell," remarked Beacon. "Confound that fellow Smythe," added Seabag. "Call this a yacht!" cried Goggles, "why, there is not room to turn round." "How can five fellows sleep here?" asked Sturge again. "Let us look; there must be more room than this," said Beacon. We looked. There was. We found a door on each side of the fire-place. Neither of these doors would open. But on returning to the deck and looking through the skylight we made out two more small cabins, each with one berth. Nothing could possibly be plainer and less attractive than the decorations of the *Ocean Queen*. We crept down a square hole into the sailors' part of the yacht (called the four xl), and found a close stuffy little place, with a thing like a doll's stove against one side. We passed into the two cabins, observing, however, a cupboard full of dishes and glasses. Leaning against the doors we butted them open, and thus reached the "drawing-room" once more, where we sat down in mute despair. "What on earth are we to do?" asked Seabag. "You mean what are to do on the water," said Beacon, who thought he was a wit. "Don't talk nonsense," said Sturge; "now we have paid for the ship we must make the best of it." "Of her," corrected Goggles. "Very well, of her—we must try and make the best of her." "I suppose we must," we assented.

"It will take a long time to get used to this wretched little cabin." "It is not quite so bad when you come to look closer," said Goggles; "see, that fire-place, with its encaustic tiles, is really pretty." "And look," added Sturge, who had been investigating matters, "what a lot of cupboards there are in all sorts of places. It is really quite convenient." "But where shall we sleep?" asked Beacon. "I have not the slightest idea," old Seabag replied. "D——n that fellow Smythe." "He shall sleep on deck," suggested Beacon. "Of course he must," we all cried; "he got us into the mess and he must suffer for it." "But I am very hungry," suggested Sturge. "Suppose we drive to an hotel to breakfast?" We all jumped up, and bumped our heads violently against the ceiling. However, we crawled on deck. Just as Beacon was going to slip down the ladder Sturge stopped him. "I say, you fellows, we must call this wretched boat something else. We should only make asses of ourselves if we keep her present name. Every one would laugh at us." "So they would," we all agreed. "We will think of another name less ambitious—say the *Moonshine*." Which was adopted by acclamation. Thus we got on shore, fetched the dirty and now very silent Smythe, and drove off to the hotel.

CHAPTER V.

A START.

IT was a cold raw morning such as is not unusual in
Scotland at the end of May, and we were glad of a warm
breakfast after our disturbed night and unsatisfactory
inspection of the late *Ocean Queen*. A certain feeling of *géne*
prevailed among our party. We all felt profoundly dis-
satisfied with Smythe, and yet we did not know what to
do next. We were obliged to continue to consult him,
although we felt we had been grossly misled by his advice.
If trial cruise there was to be, we were bound to start
that very day; yet how were we to do everything that was
bound to be done before we could go? We had no idea of
what was wanted, and the only thing that we were sure of
was that we five would find it very awkward for any length
of time on board the *Moonshine*. Still, having come all the
way from London for a cruise, we were ashamed to turn back
and sell the boat. Sturge whispered to me that he did not
dare to retire from the position he had taken up. Old
Seabag had been bragging about "our yacht" all over

London; Smythe had astonished a number of his fellow clerks with accounts of the perils of the ocean. All of us had "made the running" with partners at sundry small dances, and had talked big of our yachting during the summer. The favourite dodge was to ask the young lady where she was going after the season. This inevitably led to the counter question, " What are you going to do ?" " Oh " was the equally inevitable reply, " I suppose we shall be about Cowes and Ryde a good deal. We are going yachting; we have a vessel called the *Ocean Queen*. Perhaps we shall go over to France, or we may possibly just run across to Norway." To resign the halo prematurely assumed, and to appear in the character of an ordinary braggart, who had said he was going to sail and then did not; to lay oneself open to the well-founded suspicion of never having had a yacht at all, and to be put down as an impostor, was a catastrophe none of us would face. Of two evils choose the least. We felt we were in for it, and must go to sea in the *Moonshine*, small though she was and uncomfortable. All this was not said aloud. Our breakfast was remarkably silent. But no doubt such thoughts occupied all our minds. We had engaged a room for our ablutions. After breakfast Sturge said, " I am going to fetch my pipe ; come along, Beacon." The others followed shortly, except Smythe, who felt himself tacitly sent to Coventry, and accepted his position with a resignation which would have been touching if it had not been irritating. We felt that the man who had got us into the mess should make some effort to get us out of it, and not sit there silently and eat his breakfast calmly as if it were not his fault. He ought to have been up and doing, though what he ought to have done, and how he ought to have done it, none of us could have told. However, we all assembled in the washing room. Beacon sat down on a portmanteau, Sturge made vain efforts to light his pipe. Old Seabag stretched himself on the bed, with a cigar in his mouth, regardless of his dirty boots. The place was littered with towels, pea-jackets, glazed hats, soap, open travelling-bags, newspapers, cigar boxes, and books on yachting. "We must really make up our minds," began little Sturge. "This is a most miserable position."

"Better give it up and go home," suggested old Seabag. "It would be the best plan," admitted Goggles. "But," said Beacon, "I asked my mother and sisters to come out yachting with us this summer." Goggles pricked up his ears. Beacon had two nice-looking sisters. "We shall be miserable on board that cockle-shell," said Seabag. "Why, there is not room to stretch one's legs." "I don't think it will be so bad when we get used to it," remarked Sturge, his mind full of Lady Alice, "besides, we need not always sleep on board." "No more we need," said Goggles, "we can rough it a little at first, but in the summer we can always get a bed at an hotel in the Island." "What island?" asked Seabag. "The Wight, of course," replied Goggles, who had evidently kept his ears open at the Barnacle Club. "Oh," acquiesced Seabag. "But it will be expensive," remarked Beacon. "*You* need not complain," said Sturge; "your people will always put you up. Besides, we shall lose all our trouble, and perhaps a lot of money, if we try to sell the *Ocean Queen*. I don't believe we should get 300*l.* for her." "No one would be such a fool except Smythe," said Goggles. "But, then, what is to be done?" asked Beacon. "Get a crew and go to sea," answered little Sturge firmly. "It is all very well to say get a crew and go to sea, but how are we to do it?" "Smythe must do it." "Smythe is an infernal fool," growled Seabag from the bed. No one ventured to oppose this assertion, which seemed self-evident. "But we shall want something to eat," remarked Beacon. "And to drink," added Goggles. "And to smoke," added Seabag. "Well, we had better make haste," said Sturge, who was evidently taking the lead. "Let us go and tell Smythe that he must set to work." "I sha'n't," grumbled Seabag sulkily. "I should like to kick him." "So should I," we all chimed in cheerfully. "But we want him." "Well," admitted Beacon "if we go, we do." "And the fact is," said Sturge, who was never afraid of speaking out, "we have all been bragging so much about our yachting that we can't afford to go home." "I have not bragged," contradicted Seabag. "Yes, you have," asserted Beacon; "you are an old fool. Perhaps you have not been bragging to the women, but you have taken it out with the men. You have been coaching up the nautical dictionary for months." "At any rate," retorted Seabag, "I have not made an ass of myself by asking a lot of girls to sail in a beastly little boat like this."

But Sturge had practically won. Seabag's position was felt to be a matter of form only. We were all deeply compromised, and we knew it. None of us could afford to go back, so we all agreed to go on. Sturge knocked the ashes out of his pipe and said resolutely, "Let us go back to the coffee-room and speak to Smythe." Some one suggested that the coffee-room was too public, so it was resolved to call Smythe, and Sturge volunteered to fetch him. Soon the culprit appeared. Seabag, who had not moved from the bed, greeted him with the remark that he was a stupid blunderer. "I am not," answered the accused. " None of you fellows know any-thing about it. I have made a capital bargain for you, and now you are all grumbling because I did not buy an ocean steamer for 300*l.*" "She is a great deal too small for us," said Goggles. "Then you should have given me more money," said Smythe. "You said she would suit us exactly," said Beacon. "So she will," answered Smythe, "when you get used to her; you cannot be as comfort-able on board ship as on shore." "We have asked no end of people for the summer," remarked Sturge; "where are we to put them?" "I did not tell you to ask them," was the answer. This was true. We felt we were getting the worst of it. We found that recriminations would be worse than useless. So Goggles continued: "We have determined to go on." "Of course," said Smythe, "whoever thought of going back?" "I did," growled Seabag, "I am tired of the whole thing already." "Then go," said Smythe. "Pay me back my money and I will." This was felt to be impossible, so Sturge interrupted—"Now, don't get quarrelling. Look here, we all want to sail the ship round and enjoy ourselves. Let us work together, and not begin fighting." We grumbled assent. "So," continued he, "we had better get a crew, and plenty to eat and drink." This being agreed on we settled down more calmly to discuss details. It was arranged that Smythe was to look out for the three men who would be necessary, as he had been informed, to navigate the vessel. Three, as we were told, were sufficient. "We ought to have four," said he; "but of course we shall be our own skippers." We all felt the nautical spirit coming over us again. "Of course," we assented. Smythe would also look after the various necessaries for sailing, such as charts, flags, and so on. Beacon was to see our things brought on board, and the cabins made tidy. Goggles was to purchase drinkables. Seabag was to provide food. Sturge would be mate and general *aide-de-camp*. Thus we broke up in harmony, paid our bills, and departed.

As the day wore on we found a number of minor difficulties cropping up. The *Moonshine* was on the mud, and could not be floated till the afternoon. The men had to be hunted up in all sorts of back slums. We never found one at the address given us, which was in itself not easy to find. He was always either out fishing, or doing an odd job at some dock three miles off, or, at least, in the public-house round the corner. When they were at last found they hesitated about going at all. One was engaged for Monday; another had some lobster-pots at Dunoon he was obliged to look after; a third was obliged to go to kirk on Sunday. In short, we had to discover and converse with ten at least before we found three who agreed to start on what appeared to us ex-orbitant terms; but we were assured that they were usual on the Clyde. Towards four in the afternoon we got them on board. Their appearance was anything but prepossessing. One named Andrew was a sandy-haired, weather-beaten, thick-set fellow, who came in his shirt-sleeves, with a ragged old waterproof over his arm, one brace torn, locks unkempt, and a very dirty grey night-cap drawn over his eyes. The second, Bob, was tall, dark, lanky, silent, sullen. He was a little cleaner than Andrew, but never removed a horrible cutty pipe from his mouth, and steadily spat in every direction. The third, Jim, was not to be found for a long time. He had "signed articles," as he himself expressed the consent he appeared to have

P

given most unwillingly, but did not come at the time appointed. We all went to look for him, and as none of us had ever seen him before except Smythe, it was no easy matter to find him. We went into every public-house and inquired whether there was a man of the name of Jim who had engaged to join the *Ocean Queen*. In some establishments we met with a sulky but unanimous growl. In others one more inclined to chaff than the rest would ask us sundry questions about Jim and the *Ocean Queen*. Was the man we were looking for hump-backed, with a wooden leg? Was it James Macfarlane, who had sailed formerly with the *Flying Dutchman?* Was the *Ocean Queen* a man-of-war, and were we admirals of the fleet? At a sailors' boarding-house a man volunteered to say where Jim was. He told Goggles to take the second turning to the right, then the third to the left, then go straight on till he saw a church, then the fourth to the right over a railway bridge, then the fifth house on the left was Jim's. If not at home we should find him in Davy Jones's locker, "for," added the informant, "Tim was always very fond of Davy Jones." Poor Goggles carefully put down all these directions in his note-book, and read them over to the man before starting on his errand. "The fourth to the right over the railway bridge?" he inquired. "That's it," agreed his informant. Goggles started, and when at last Jim was discovered by the builder's foreman, and brought to the yard in a condition I should be sorry to qualify as "half seas over," for he appeared to me not half, but entirely drunk, Goggles was nowhere to be found. Of course there was fresh delay, more searching and more growling, during which the delinquent Jim fell fast asleep on the cabin sofa. Goggles at last turned up in a cab. He had not gone far when he found himself in a blind alley, so that he was unable to carry out the directions given him. He had inquired for "Davy Jones's locker," upon which a pugnacious Scotchman had threatened to knock him down. Another swore at him, and walked off. So he was afraid to make further inquiries, and after walking many miles had hailed the first cab he saw.

At last, then, everything was ready. The *Moonshine* was fastened somehow to something floating in the river near the boat-builder's yard. We all got on board by successive trips in her boat, which appeared to be a most unsafe and dangerous little thing for the sea. But we were used to outriggers, and did not mind a crank craft as long as we were in the river. Seabag rushed off to fetch some forgotten article of food, and soon reappeared with a huge ham in one hand and a cold roast leg of mutton in the other. He had been sharper than we should have expected; for seeing the disorder which prevailed, he doubted our being able to cook any dinner on the first night, and had provided accordingly. An important question was now put by Andrew. "Who is the captain?" asked he. "Which of you gentlemen is going to sail her?" We looked at Smythe. None of us felt competent to undertake the office, and yet Smythe was silent. "Mr. Smythe, of course," answered Beacon, pointing to him; "that is the captain." Smythe said hesitatingly, "Really, some one else had better." "Nonsense," interrupted Goggles, "of course you are the only one of us that knows anything about it." "Well, I will do my best," acquiesced Smythe. Andrew had been looking on with one eye screwed up. "Do you want to get under way, sir?" asked he. "Certainly," said Smythe. "Very well, sir, then we had better get the foresail up before we let go our moorings, otherwise we shall run foul of some of this shipping." "All right," said Smythe. The foresail was got up somehow. "Now," said Andrew, "take the helm and keep her well into the wind, sir, while I let go. Bob, stand by the main halyard. That Jim, sir," added he, "ain't no manner of use." Nor was he, for Goggles had been busy putting the eatables away in the cabin, and had attempted to rouse him from the sofa. Jim had not even condescended to open his eyes, but had simply declared that he would pitch any (expletive) body overboard who did not leave him alone. So Goggles had wisely left him alone, postponing further action until reinforced from the deck. Meanwhile, we were watching Andrew. He let go something or other, and we saw a barrel bobbing just under the *Ocean Queen's* bowsprit. Then somehow we went all over on one side. Andrew shouted out, " Luff, sir, luff, or the crutch will be overboard ! "

But Smythe did not appear to understand, for the ship seemed to turn round quickly and fly through the water. The next moment a great heavy thing came crashing over, knocked Smythe on the shoulder violently, and sent him flying into the water on one side, while some bits of wood which had held it up flew over on the other. We all shouted. Smythe rose to the surface spluttering ; of course we all knew he could swim, so there was no particular danger. But meanwhile the yacht seemed to be flying away from him. Andrew rushed to the tiller. " Get the fore sheet over," shouted he. " Out of the way, gentlemen ! "

The vessel very soon stopped, and Andrew called out to Bob to take the tiller. It was all the work of but a few minutes. But Smythe seemed to be drifting further and further away. Sturge and Beacon had both got their coats off ready for a plunge when Andrew called out, " Hold on, gents, don't jump in; I'll get him with the boat." The dirty old fellow jumped into the boat, and in a minute more was pulling to where we saw poor Smythe battling with the tide, and making vain efforts to approach the vessel. Long before Andrew got up to him a shore boat had hauled him in. He was brought on alongside, very wet, but otherwise unhurt. " Did not you see the boom a coming over ? " asked Andrew, as he helped him on board. " Any fool must have known that it must come over to leeward when you was letting her fall off that way." " Five shillings, please, sir," said the boat-man who had rescued him. " Please pay," said Smythe disconsolately to Sturge ; " I have not got a sixpence left." And then he resigned the office of captain to Andrew, whom we unanimously confirmed in that capacity.

CHAPTER VI.

THE FIRST CRUISE.

"There is but a light air from the easterly," said Andrew, "and if you gentlemen want to get out to sea to-night we had better look sharp."

We proceeded to help Bob at some horrible rope which broke our nails and took the skin off our hands. "One gentleman aft!" cried Andrew. Of course we did not know what he meant. "One gentleman aft!" shouted he again. No one moved.

"If there's a sailor amongst you," he cried at last in despair, "let him come here and get the peak clear of the topping lifts."

This appeal was more effectual than any former ones. For although there certainly was not a sailor amongst us, Beacon suddenly guessed that he wanted some one at the back part of the ship, and rushed there. He soon found out what was wanted. Meanwhile a great row was going on in the cabin. Smythe wanted to change his wet clothes, and Jim was resting his weary head on our ex-captain's dressing-bag. He tried to draw it away from under the sleeper's head. Jim growled. He tried again, upon which Jim half rose and threatened to knock the "drowned rat" down. The wet chief assumed a posture of self-defence, which was sorely disturbed by the vessel heeling over to the wind (the sails being now set) so that Smythe's head went straight into Jim's chest. Jim shook him off, and composed himself to sleep again. Smythe picked himself up and made another dart at the bag, upon which the sailor reluctantly got up, saying, "Well, if you are determined to fight you shall have it!" (I omit the verbal ornaments) and hitting poor Smythe straight between the eyes, sent him crashing over the table on to the opposite sofa with a great bang, which brought us all below. Jim was sitting on the sofa ready for anything.

"Why," expostulated he in a drunken voice, "don't you let a fellow alone? I ain't doing no harm. Let a man have his sleep when he wants it; if you don't, by —— it will be worse for you."

We none of us cared to have a fight in the cabin. It was very low, and we constantly kept knocking our heads against the beams. It was full of bags, portmanteaus, bottles, and tins; so there was no chance of a fair field. Besides, the ship was heeling over very much, and none of us felt quite safe on his feet. We therefore retired, and appealed to our new captain, poor Smythe meanwhile shivering all over, getting more miserable every moment.

"Won't get off the sofa, won't he?" said Andrew. "Ah well, you must not be too hard upon him. A sailor's life is a very hard one, gentlemen, and he is bound to take a drop of spirits now and then."

"But we want our things," expostulated Sturge, "and we can't have that drunken fellow in the cabin."

"He don't seem partickler drunk," said Andrew, "only a bit sleepy-like. I'll see what I can do with him. Will one of you gentlemen take the helm? Keep her free, and mind you don't run into any of those vessels."

Beacon took the helm, nervously indeed, but still he took it. He was not quite devoid of intelligence. He looked at the brass box containing the compass. It pointed north-west. "Now," said he, "one of you fellows keep looking at the compass and tell me if I am right. I must keep the same course."

Sturge undertook the office. Beacon kept shifting the tiller a little to the right or left according as Sturge directed him. But meanwhile we had forgotten another danger. Bob, who had I suppose been putting his things to rights, suddenly appeared on deck and shouted out, "Port, sir, port; that barque will run into you." And sure enough there was a great three-masted ship close to us, which we had never noticed, so busy were we learning to steer. Beacon ported; he had presence of mind to guess what was the right thing in time, but only just, for in another moment we were close alongside the great clumsy merchant vessel, which seemed to tower ever so high above our little boat. Bob quickly held some fenders overboard, while the crew of the merchantman abused us for a lot of land-lubbers, saying that as they were close hauled and we were going free we ought to have kept out of their way. This was of course quite beyond us, but we were much relieved when Andrew came up and said he had coaxed Jim into his " bunk "—whatever that was. Jim had at last disappeared, and Smythe finding one of the small cabins too cramped for his toilet, was busy changing his wet clothes in the " drawing-room." By this time we had found out that Smythe knew no more than we did, and were, therefore, inclined to be rather hard on him. From the position of chief he had formerly held he had fallen to be a butt and a scapegoat. Not even his sound wetting could induce us to look on him kindly.

" What do you mean by messing about the cabin with your wet clothes ! " growled Scabag.

" You had no business to undress here," cried Beacon.

" Go into your own cabin," halloed Goggles.

" But which is my cabin ? " asked Smythe piteously.

Which indeed ? Here was a question. There were, including the sofas, but four sleeping-places for five of us. We could not seriously make Smythe sleep on deck after he had been half drowned twice in one day. We could not " make up a bed on the floor," after the manner of seaside lodgings, as there was no floor available to make up a bed on. While Smythe was dressing we discussed the question. No one was inclined to try the "forecastle" with drunken Jim, dirty Andrew, and spitting Bob; besides, there was no spare bed there. At last Beacon said—

"*One of us must keep watch.*"

"But who?"

"Oh, we must toss. Or is there a pack of cards?" No one had brought any cards. But after some trouble we found a pencil, and having written five numbers on bits of paper, Beacon screwed them up, shook them in his hat, and the others drew. No. 1 was to have the choice of what Smythe, who had now recovered his spirits with his dry clothes, nautically called watches. The night was divided into five parts of two hours each, from ten to eight, and one of us was to be on deck during each of these sets. Sturge drew No. 1, and chose from six to eight in the morning. Smythe, poor fellow, was further punished by No. 5; so he had to take from two till four, which had been left to the last. While all this was going on we were dropping down the Clyde fast. Evening was approaching, and our appetites increasing. Jim was snoring in the forecastle, Bob lying on his stomach on deck, lifting his head up occasionally to look out; the captain was at the helm. We were really sailing. But now arose a difficulty. Andrew could not steer all night, that was clear. None of us would trust Smythe, and Beacon declined the responsibility. Andrew called down into the cabin while we were all trying to tidy up and prepare for supper, and asked "whether we had a glass of spirits, as he was beginning to feel cold." We found a bottle of whiskey, but no corkscrew and no glass. At last we prized it open and gave him the cup of Goggle's flask.

Having drunk it down in one gulp he said, "The tide is running very slack, gentlemen; we had better think of anchoring soon."

"Why anchor?" we exclaimed.

"Because, if we don't, the flood will take us back pretty near as far as we have come, the wind being so light."

"But, if we anchor every night, we shall be a week getting round to the Isle of Wight," said Smythe.

"Well," asked the captain, "you surely don't expect to get all round England in less time than that?"

"We do though," answered Goggles. "I have got to be at my office on Wednesday."

"And I must be at the bank by Thursday at latest," added Sturge.

"Then you had better get ashore, and go by train," said Andrew. "If you was to get fair winds all the way, you couldn't get round in much less than five days."

This was a tremendous blow. We all turned on Smythe fiercely.

"Why, you said we could sail round in four days."

"So we ought," answered he. "We ought to sail six

miles an hour at least. I have measured the distance on the map, and it is less than 600 miles. So we ought to do it in less than 100 hours."

"You can't reckon that way, governor," corrected Andrew. "The yacht ain't a steamer. Some days we might run 100 miles or more, and other days we might not do forty."

Here Smythe was wrong again; this time awfully and unpardonably wrong.

"You ought to have known better," we said.

"I am sure we can get round in four or five days," he maintained stoutly, "if we don't anchor at night. That fellow," continued he *sotto voce*, "only wants to stop because he is lazy and prefers a quiet night's rest. Make him go on, and I am sure we shall get to the Isle of Wight by Wednesday."

But we had had enough of Smythe's advice. We determined, by a large majority, to do as the captain suggested, and in a very few minutes the rattle of the chain told us that the day's cruise was ended. Notwithstanding our various misfortunes we all felt jolly. The vessel rose and fell gently with the incoming tide. There was hardly a breath of wind, but what there was was charged with sea salt and ozone—health-giving and hungry. Twilight stole over us gently. The cabin was getting dark. Goggles, who had been appointed to attend the cuisine, shouted for a light. We all re-echoed the call. There were hanging candle-lamps in the cabins, but no candles in them.

"Where are the candles?" cried Beacon.

"Somewhere about, I suppose," said Sturge.

We all began hunting in the various cupboards, corners, and shelves. We could find no candles. At last Beacon asked the very pertinent question—

"Did any one buy any?"

"I did not," said Smythe. "I had to attend to the ship and charts."

"Nor did I," said Sturge. "I had to find the crew; and a nice job I had of it."

"Of course *I* did not," said Seabag. "I bought a dozen tins of preserved meat, condensed milk, and cold mutton and ham. I actually got pepper and salt too."

"But no candles," interrupted Beacon.

"Why should I? We don't eat candles."

"I got wine, whiskey, and beer," said Goggles; "but I had nothing to do with candles. That was Beacon's business."

We were all of the same opinion. Beacon had nothing to do but to get our traps on board, so he ought to have provided candles. But he had not done so. Fortunately May nights in Scotland are short, but we could not see to eat our suppers below. The leg of mutton was therefore dragged on deck, and we made a dinner table of the skylight. We drank beer out of the cups of our flasks, and found them too small. We cut huge hunches of bread and used them for plates. We found two knives only on board, and so had to make shift with any weapon that was handy. Andrew came up in the middle of our festivities. He screwed up one eye and looked at us, hitched up his torn brace, and looked again.

"I'm sure I hope you will enjoy your dinner to-morrow."

"Why should we not?" asked Goggles, alarmed, pausing, with a penknife in mid-air, on which a piece of mutton was impaled.

"I dinna ken," answered Andrew; "but I only hope you will." And he screwed up one eye quite tight.

"Confound the fellow!" growled Seabag. "He is quite taking away my appetite. I wish he would remove himself and his dirty night-cap."

"Is it the correct thing," whispered Sturge, "to give the crew something to eat? He looks as if he expected it."

"No," answered Smythe; "they find themselves."

"But he seems very hungry," interceded Sturge; "and he has been steering all day."

"Well," said Beacon, "we can spare some. Here you are, Andrew," he cried out. "Would you like some mutton?"

"Thank ye, sir," said Andrew, pulling a formidable clasp knife out and cutting a huge hole in the proffered leg. "Here's to your good health," as he drank the beer offered.

Goggles took advantage of the skipper having sat down to eat with us to ask—

"Why did you say before that you hoped we should enjoy our dinner to-morrow?"

"Because, to be sure I do hope so," was, however, all he could get out of him,

Either Andrew had no deeper meaning, or he would not admit one. Goggles had to drop the matter; but it preyed on his mind, for before he went to sleep in the little cabin which had fallen to his lot he still called out to us—

"Why did that dirty fellow hope we should enjoy our dinner to-morrow? I am sure he meant something."

"Perhaps he did," answered Smythe, from the main cabin.

"Hold your row!" called out Scabag from the second berth.

"What are you fellows making such a noise about?" asked Beacon from the deck.

So all was still for two short hours as the tide rippled against the sides of the *Moonshine* and lifted her gently up and down. But the time was of short duration.

We were all startled out of our first sleep by a lively altercation between Beacon and Goggles. "Get up, will you!" said Beacon. "I have done my watch. I want to go to bed."

"See you blowed first," answered Goggles turning over to the other side.

"I say, this is not fair!" exclaimed Beacon. "Here have I been shivering on deck since ten o'clock, and now Goggles won't let me go to bed."

"People say 'turn in' on board ship," called out Smythe, though only half awake.

"Well then, make him turn out," returned Beacon.

"Oh, fight it out between yourselves," said another sleepy voice, "and leave us alone."

There was some fierce wrangling, during which Goggles knocked his head against the low ceiling. At last he made room for Beacon, and sneaked up on deck with a number of ulsters and rugs. But the most singular thing was that he began his "watch" by instantly falling asleep, and slept so soundly that he did not call anybody else up all night. Thus we all had a quiet rest till the sun shone in through the skylight and the livelier motion of the ship sent us all out to breathe the brisk morning air.

It was time to be stirring if we ever intended to reach the Channel. So we all thought; but there was no sign of the crew. They were all fast asleep. Sturge roused them out of the smelly close forecastle, and old Andrew came tumbling up, looking dirtier than ever, and trying in vain to secure his braces, which had evidently grown no stronger over night.

CHAPTER VII.

WE were very anxious to be away, to feel the real
" briny " under our feet, to sniff the ocean breeze. As yet
we were almost land-locked, the horizon was not boundless,
and the chimneys of Greenock were still visible in the
north-east just below the sun. But Andrew did not
seem to be in any hurry. His great anxiety was to scrub
the deck, for he evidently cared more about washing
the deck than himself. Very few minutes after the men
had tumbled up they were dashing buckets of water all
about.. Some retired expeditiously, but Sturge and
Beacon, more sensible than the rest, thought that the
ablutions might as well be combined, and performed their
toilet *sub Jove frigido*—pailfuls of brackish water being
capital substitutes for the morning tub. Smythe wanted
to get out in the boat and bathe. " But," expostulated
Goggles, " surely you had enough water yesterday. Don't
make us lose any more time." So he gave it up, and
eventually we all followed the example of the other two,

and got douche baths on deck. To dress, however, proved no easy task. Our things were very much mixed up. Old Seabag's portmanteau was under a mass of tins and biscuit boxes, Beacon's bag was nowhere to be found, and Smythe, having already changed twice on the previous day, had very little left to put on. Sturge slipped into Goggles's lower garments, which were much too large for him, and the owner, never suspecting any one else of taking them, went crashing and banging from one cabin into another, and turning everything topsy-turvy in a vain search for the indispensable article, finally, till Sturge confessed, rolling his legs up in a shawl. When things began to get a little straight everybody clamoured for breakfast, and of course old Seabag, the caterer, was told to look after it, with Sturge to help. Andrew had fortunately not forgotten the fresh water, so while the crew were getting ready to sail, the kettle was filled, and we all set to hunting for breakfast requisites, ultimately succeeding in finding a teapot with a broken handle, a cracked jug, and a number of cups of different patterns and in various stages of decrepitude. To light the fire was the first and apparently most difficult operation, for we heard various growls and grumblings issuing from the forecastle. Meanwhile the whilom Captain Smythe was helping to heave away at the anchor, and Beacon, the only one who had so far shown any sailor-like qualities, was standing by the main halyards. A heel over and a rush of water told that we were at last away, but at the same moment a terrible noise was heard forward. We tumbled through the pantry just in time to see the kettle upset, and the water pouring over the prostrate Seabag in little jets. He was, it appears, just putting it on the painfully lighted fire when the first puff caught the *Moonshine* and upset him; he dropped the kettle, and was punished accordingly. Jim, who was perfectly sober, but painfully haggard, peered into the darkness from above, asking what was the matter. We made him come down to mop up and watch the fire, old Seabag meanwhile retiring in a very bad temper to the recesses of one of the sleeping cabins. But ill humour was soon forgotten as we collected on the deck to see the yacht tearing through the water with a fresh north-easterly breeze on her quarter; the beautiful hills clad in the verdure of early spring on the port bow (we called it "left hand") and a few mountain tops still covered with a sprinkling of snow on the right. It was cool, nay, decidedly cold, and we all felt a yearning for our hot breakfasts. We were rapidly running down with wind and tide in our favour, and Andrew said with a slight twinkle in one eye, "Better get your sea legs ready, gents; there'll be a bit of a toss outside." We all declared that our sea legs were quite ready and were anxious for a bit of a toss—though perhaps we did not feel quite as sanguine as we pretended to be.

Now there was a shout from below, "Tea is ready, gentlemen!" and we found on going down that Jim had turned out the breakfast table in better order than could have been expected from his performances of the previous day. It is true that the table was all on one side, and looked as if everything must slide off, but that was not his fault. Seabag, Smythe, and Beacon chose the right; they had the table about level with their noses, and every now and then seemed to disappear under it. Goggles and Sturge were on the left, with their breakfast somewhere about their knees. Strange to say, a tin opener had not been forgotten. Seabag produced it triumphantly when some one suggested sardines as a welcome addition to our milkless tea, stale bread, and very middling butter. It took a long time, however, to prize the box open, and the table began to rock viciously from side to side. A sudden jerk followed by a big splash made Smythe drop his cup, tea and all, over Beacon, crying out, "We've struck!" He rushed up the steep companion ladder with blanched face and trembling limbs, while we waited with a calmness more apparent than real.

"What has happened?" he cried to Bob, who was steering and spitting.

"Nothing in partickler," answered Bob, cleverly squirting a bit of tobacco over the vessel's side.

"But what was that?"

"What?" asked Bob.

"That shock just now," cried out Smythe, who was holding on to the companion.

"Only a bit of a sea," said the steersman. "Here's another;" and as he spoke we felt another bang and heard another souse; on which Smythe came stumbling down looking wet and white.

"It is a very rough sea," quoth he, "I think I have had enough breakfast," and hastily seizing an ulster he clambered up again, while we who had gradually mastered the sardine tin continued our repast. Every now and then a cup would skate over into some one's lap, or a wily fish elude the grasp of the hungry yachtsman; but we got through our meal somehow, and resumed our conversation on the charms of a cruise, and the delights of an after-breakfast pipe, which of course had always been an institution amongst us. But when breakfast was done no one seemed in a great hurry to begin to smoke. Some ominous sounds came from the deck, and Goggles said "He'd just look and see what was the matter." The ominous sounds increased in intensity, and we then began to look into each other's faces doubtfully, like men on the brink of a great danger. Was it possible—nay, the suggestion was too horrible—was it credible that some one above was seasick? No; surely it must be Bob making more noise than usual over his tobacco. Seabag and Beacon were now on the right, Sturge alone on the left. Little Sturge gradually dropped his head back,

"Old Andrew was at the helm."   Page 231.

reclining, as he said, comfortably "to get a good rest." Then very slowly he drew his legs up, and before long was lying at full length on the sofa, suspiciously silent and thoughtful. The conversation dropped. Beacon slowly pulled his pipe out. He passed the tobacco to old Seabag, who said slowly, "I do not think I shall smoke just now," and leaning his head on his elbow also assumed a pensive attitude.

"Have a pipe, Sturge," said old Beacon, lighting a match; "it will do you good, old boy."

"There's nothing the matter with me," whispered Sturge, "but I am rather sleepy. I wish you would leave me alone."

"All right," answered Beacon, cheerily. "I'll see what's going on on deck."

And on deck he went. Here was a goodly sight. Old Andrew was at the helm again, his eye twinkling more than usual. The vessel was ploughing her way through a bright green sea, the waves were tipped with white, and every now and then a bit of one came over her with a hard rattle as of shot. The bowsprit was bobbing up and down, the deck was wet and slippery, and curled up against the low bulwark lay something wrapped up in an ulster. It was not inanimate for fitful groans and curious noises escaped from the bundle; but it was certainly not lively, for even a green sea which came curling over just then only called forth a slight shudder and a deeper groan. Could this be the noble Smythe, our whilom captain? Hardly; yet it was. On the hatch crouched another figure, also deeply enveloped in the folds of a great coat. Only a portion of a haggard face was visible—the jaw was hanging, the cheeks hollow; and into this ghastly apparition the festive Goggles had in a few short minutes been transformed.

"Sick, are you?" asked Beacon jocosely, digging the prostrate Smythe in the ribs. But even at this supreme time Smythe's audacity did not forsake him. He was still anxious to preserve the prestige which he had in fact lost long before, and answered feebly, "No, I am not sick; I'm only lying down. I'm very bad. Ugh!"

This was too much for the ghastly Goggles. "I'll bet he was!" he exclaimed. "What an awful humbug! He's as sick as a cat, and so am I; you should have seen him just now. Now, leave us alone; and get away with that filthy pipe." Smythe tried still to deny the soft impeachment, but in vain, for inclining his head overboard he took no further interest in the proceedings. Beacon calmly took the helm out of Andrew's hand, saying, "How is her head? South-west by south. All right," and performed a feat at which we all stared in astonishment. He was not only not sea-sick, but he actually steered the *Moonshine* without letting his pipe out. Andrew had become rather sceptical about our seamanship, and for a time busied himself in coiling up ropes and making things what he called "shipshape" on deck, evidently fearful of some catastrophe. But after a time, finding that Beacon apparently knew all about it—which he did not—he disappeared below, the pensive Jim alone lying on his stomach close to the mast, and every now and then raising his head to look out. Little Sturge fell asleep, and in his sleep gradually got used to the motion. Seabag would not admit that he felt queer, but stuck to the sofa on the well-worn plea of fatigue. Goggles and Smythe remained groaning on deck, while Beacon gloated over their miseries, reserving, however, more active chaff for a future occasion.

CHAPTER VIII.

Thus the morning wore on, the toss becoming more and more decided as the wind increased in force and we left the land further behind us—astern, we ought to say. Smythe spent his time in a state of abject misery. Goggles was almost as bad, but still well enough to sneer occasionally. Sturge remained on the lee-side sofa of the main cabin. Old Seabag at first occupied the other sofa, but finding himself shot off on five successive occasions at last also appeared on deck.

"I don't think very much of yachting, after all," he remarked to Beacon, who, having slid over to leeward on the wet deck more than once had resigned the tiller.

"Yachting be blowed!" growled poor Goggles. "I wish I were in town again." "How about lunch?" was the only remark Beacon vouchsafed. "You fellows must be hungry. At any rate I should think Smythe and Goggles must have digested their breakfast by this time."

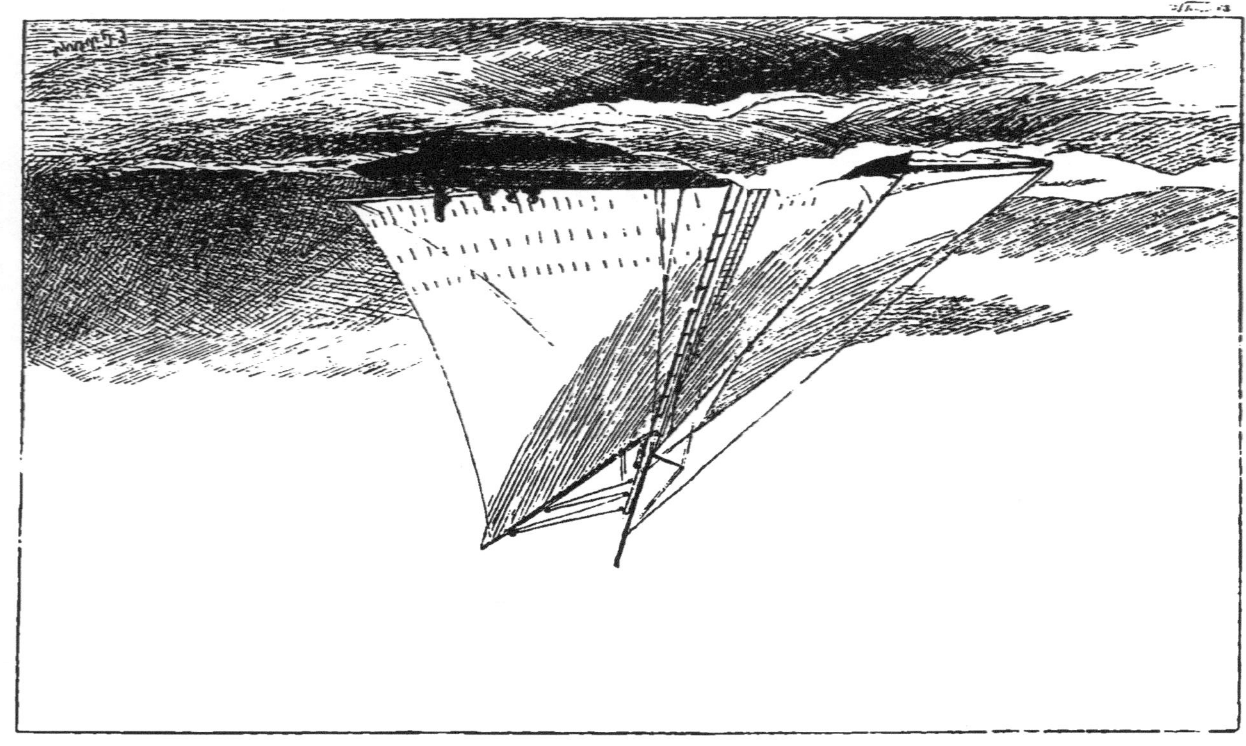

"With all plain sail set we went tearing through the green water at a famous pace."

Page 235.

This was a cruel sneer; but in fact even the sea-sick ones were beginning to feel a certain emptiness which required to be met in some way. Smythe alone was in a state of utter prostration. Finally Beacon had to get lunch, and worked away at opening sundry tins and a bottle of beer with a zeal which made the rest of us almost burst with envy. Easterly winds in May are not particularly balmy in the northern portion of the Irish Channel. Those who were ill were shivering; those who were still well tried to walk up and down the small deck in vain. Yet it was a glorious sight for one not affected by the motion. Our course was now sou'-sou'-west; the wind was therefore well abaft the beam. With all plain sail set we went tearing through the green water at a famous pace. Far on the horizon was a bluish bank of fog: it was the Isle of Man. No other land was in sight; a few distant sails only, glistening in the sunshine, dotted the surface of the heaving deep. But we could not enjoy all this. There was a disagreeable wriggle about the *Moonshine* which seemed to us still worse than any pitching, and when we asked Andrew the cause of it, he said: "She's only trying to shoot up into the wind." We thought she was a great fool for thus trying, and not leaving us alone in peace.

"Let go that lee runner, and ease off the main sheet," shouted Andrew: and Beacon, who was watching intently, helped also to loosen a bundle of ropes—in nautical language he gave her more main sheet. Faster still she went, and still the waves which came after us seemed to grow bigger and bigger.

Evening was drawing on. Beacon resumed the helm; but scarcely had he done so when there came a shout from Jim, who was, as usual, "looking out" forward.

"Take care, sir! she'll gybe. Luff, sir, luff!" And the next moment the big mainsail was all shivering, and with a tremendous bang the boom flew over to the other side. Fortunately Beacon saw the mistake he had made before it was quite too late; he grasped the main sheet like grim death, while both Goggles and Sturge, with a sudden return of energy, took in the slack. Thus the boom did not go far, and the jerk was diminished. But it was sufficient to shake the vessel all through, and to bring up Andrew with curses not loud but deep.

"Bob'll take her, sir," he said. So Beacon retired, and proceeded to prepare for dinner, since no one else could undertake the duties of cook and steward.

The repast was scarcely a merry one. There was some greasy soup out of a tin, some cold mutton, and other *hors d'œuvre*. But our appetites were extremely poor. Only Beacon and Seabag sat down to dinner formally. Old Andrew had not forgotten the gibe. Putting his head down the companion he said, "Didn't I wish ye as good an appetite to-day as ye had yesterday, gentlemen?" Then there was comparative peace for a time, for the wind fell with the sun.

CHAPTER IX.

THE CATASTROPHE.

THERE was a good deal of fuss and commotion in the forecastle towards eight o'clock. First Jim took the tiller, while Andrew and Bob consulted forward. Then Andrew came aft and sent Jim forward. Then, again, Bob took the skipper's place.

"What is the matter?" at last inquired Beacon of the latter.

"I 'canna find the side lights," answered he. "I'm just thinking there are nane on board."

It was some time before we understood the situation. At last it dawned upon us that sailing vessels have to carry a red light on one side and a green on the other when under way at night, and that we had neither, and were therefore infringing the sailing regulations.

"Weel," remarked Andrew at last, the search having proved entirely fruitless, " we must keep a good luik-out; but I dinna like it."

We were all exhausted by the cold or sickness. We

were therefore anxious to turn in. As Smythe refused to move from his position, we covered him up with all the wraps we could spare, and made ourselves comfortable.

"We shall have a fine night, thank heaven," exclaimed Goggles, as he looked around.

"I hope to goodness it won't blow before we have to get up," said Seabag.

But old Andrew did not look quite comfortable. "I wish we had them side lights. There's a sea fog coming on."

Fog or not we were all soon fast asleep, the ship being left entirely in the care of the crew.

Our rest was rudely and suddenly disturbed. We sat up in our "bunks." There was shouting and yelling on deck.

"Port your helm!" screamed one voice.

"She don't see us!" cried another.

"Starboard! Hard a starboard, will you?" cried a third. "Give her another hail!"

And then an unearthly howl from all three brought us all up trembling in our night garments.

There was a thick white mist which seemed to freeze our very bones. One of the men with a foot against the tiller, which was hard-a-starboard, was yelling at the very top of his voice with his hands to his mouth. Three other figures were screaming by his side. We gazed into the white darkness. For a moment we could not make out anything. Then there seemed to be something black, as high as a house, looming over us. A flash of a red light, then a crash, which sent us flying over to the other side of the *Moonshine*, and then suddenly a rush of cold water over our heads, and a blank !

* * * * * *

"Eight of you all told, did you say?" was the first remark heard on our recovering consciousness.

There appeared to be an affirmative grunt from somewhere, and then the cheery observation, "All right; then there's no one lost. But why the d—— had you no lights?" and so on. We had been run into by the good steamer *Merlin*, bound from Douglas for Liverpool. We were at this moment in very comfortable berths. But a few hours ago we had been in imminent danger of our lives. The *Merlin* was, it seems, going dead slow, on account of the fog, otherwise we must all have been drowned. As it was, her tremendous size and weight had sunk our tiny craft, but the men had clung to the rigging, and the steamer did not go right over us. Smythe had seized a rope, and was conscious enough to hold on until he was taken off. Beacon had got hold of the solitary life-buoy. The rest of us were probably knocked insensible, but we were all picked up somehow, and the usual restoratives used with effect. As to the *Moonshine*, she was at the bottom of the sea. We were in a sorry plight; all our clothes and our money had gone down with the ship. Smythe was the only one who had not undressed, and was possessed of eight and sixpence; he, the cause of all our misfortunes, had saved his watch. The captain of the *Merlin*, though very kind, chaffed us most unmercifully.

He took us to Liverpool, where we arrived at noon the next day, and lent us a most curious medley of clothes to go ashore in. We telegraphed to our friends, and had to wait at a third-rate hotel till replies and the necessary funds came. We had to buy clothes at a cheap outfitter's on the Mersey; and our hopes of a summer cruise with the ladies were over. Sturge was particularly doleful: "That beast of a colonel will have it all his own way," he sighed; "there is not a chance of cutting him out now." But we had more serious cares than to bother about Sturge's love affairs: we had to compensate the men for the loss of their outfit. It turned out that the stockings and under garments worn by a sailor are as expensive as those sold by any West-end hosier.

We consoled ourselves with the thought that all this expenditure was only of a temporary nature; that the Insurance Company would repay the whole in full. For little Sturge, (be it said to his credit, he was the only one who thought of it), had insured the vessel for rather more than she had cost before we left London. What was our horror on applying for our money to be told that as we had not complied with the sailing rules we were not entitled to sixpence. So it was; and it appeared that we had had two days' sail, during which time the majority of us were seasick, and no end of trouble, at a cost of not less than £400. We were not inclined to go to law and send good money after bad. We took the paltry £100 the Insurance Company offered us, and swore that we would never trust Smythe again. This was the end of the cruise of the *Moonshine*.

HUNTING FROM TOWN.

HUNTING FROM TOWN.

I.

OLD-FASHIONED sportsmen are rather in the habit of looking down upon the men whom business or pleasure keeps in London during the greater part of the year, and who, if they want to hunt at all, take train from town in the morning and return the same night. They declare that half the pleasure of the sport is lost if you do not belong to the country where you hunt, if you were not almost born and bred there, and if you do not know every squarson and every farmer within a radius of twenty miles of the kennels. No doubt the country gentleman (I speak now of the individual, not of the newspaper, of the name) who was, with the surrounding yeomen, the originator of fox-hunting, still has, to a great extent, the best of it. Every meet becomes for him a festive gathering, a "small and early," without the *gêne* of dress clothes and company manners. His friends are all there, and though some may also be present who are not his friends, he can get out of their way if he likes with much greater facility than he could at a ball or dinner party. It is easy enough to shake off a bore in the field if your heart is in the right place and your horse can jump. But it is not easy to get rid of a tiresome neighbour at a country banquet. The country gentleman too, whether he be young or old, is sure to find what some of the society weeklies call his "lady friends" at the covert side. Even if they do not all ride to hounds, the majority will certainly come out to have a look at them, and if hunting gives plenty of opportunities to get rid of foes, it presents equally good ones for improving one's acquaintance with fair friends, again premising that one has a good horse and a stout heart. Even in a "quick thing" it is so easy to please the adored one by breaking the top bar of a stiff flight of posts and rails, or by holding open an obstinate gate, or by picking up a whip which has dropped, or in many other ways which are familiar enough to the man used to "moving adventures by flood and field." In a slow run, and when sport is poor, the lover who is timid with ladies but bold at his fences has a hundred chances which are never vouchsafed to him whose field is confined to the ball-room. Given a somewhat fidgety horse, or one which the canny rider secretly goads into fidgeting, and there is no limit to the progress which a single afternoon with a provincial pack will enable our swain to make. He can show off his figure, his legs, his seat, his arms, even his head, for he has unlimited opportunities for display; and he

can do all this without appearing to "put any side on."
To jump a five-barred gate when hounds are *not* running,
and there is a good " gallery," may not be very rational, but
it is a *coup* which may very possibly capture the tender
heart of the country beauty. But let him not follow the
example of a rash friend of ours, who, being anxious thus to
obtain the applause of the spectators, especially of one fair
lady, charged a stile, with the result that the horse did
not rise at all, but attempted to gallop through it, and
tumbling head over heels deposited the young hero in
a very dirty road.

But to return from this somewhat long digression, the
man who " hunts from London " will scarcely ever be on
the same pleasant terms of easy familiarity with almost
every one out as he who dwells amongst them. He may
have a few friends who have come down from town like
himself, and will after a few seasons no doubt have
made some in the country. But he is not one of the
family, and as neither his birth, parentage, breeding,
and fortune are known to every farmer like those of the
country squire, he will, even after several years, still
only be Mr. So-and-So from London. Some of the social
pleasures of hunting he will therefore undoubtedly lose,
and it will be many years before he is as familiar with the
country, and knows the probable line of the fox, as well
as the comparatively rough farmer, who turns out on a
powerful horse scarcely in condition, with drab breeches and

gaiters, and a "pot" hat. But *non cuivis contingit adirc Corinthum.* It is not every one who can be born and bred in a hunting country, and live in it all his hunting life. There are many lovers of the chase who would not if they could, and there are still more who could not if they would. Agriculture is scarcely in so blooming a condition as to be able to support the younger sons of country gentlemen in idleness, or even in comparative idleness, and many elder sons, too, have to seek their fortunes in cities. Again, the son of the citizen, the descendant of the man who has made much money in trade and manufacture, naturally, by the process ingrained in every Englishman, strives to emancipate himself from the trammels of town, and to return to the sweet country air whence his ancestors came, perhaps six generations back. He will certainly begin by "hunting from town," and possibly the sport may lead him to settle where he can enjoy it best. Many other classes have within recent years, and thanks to the facilities offered by the railway companies, joined the ranks who "hunt from town." There is the overworked merchant or City man, whom his doctor has warned that if he continues to spend six days a week in his office without exercise, liver complaint will kill him. Somebody suggests hunting, and Crœsus, whose equestrian preformances have hitherto been confined to the Row in the season from 6 to 7 P.M. on a quiet cob, or to the mule ride inseparable from a journey to Switzerland, purchases a couple of horses and tries the noble sport, with the most satisfactory result. There is the successful lawyer who wants to get rid of the cobwebs left by abstruse cases, and to let the winter breezes cool his hot head. There is the biscuit baker, the gelatine man, and the inventor of some non-intoxicating drink, all of whom though perhaps not members of the most aristocratic circles, can ride a little bit; and now that their ingenuity and industry have enabled them to do so without extravagance, resolve to join the cheery crowd who follow hounds. There are the horse-dealers and horse-dealers' sons, who come out on business, but often forget their business in the excitement of a good burst, and thoroughly enjoy their day, even though they have not succeeded in selling a horse dear nor in buying one cheap. There are many worse men than these hard-riding horse-dealers. They are among the best pilots an ambitious stranger can have, for their business prevents them shirking anything, and yet they are anxious not to take too much out of their horses. To ascend a little higher in the scale, we must not forget that the hunting "specials" from town and the "slip" carriages, very frequently carry our legislators, hereditary and elected, whose presence in London affairs of state demand in the evening, but who can afford to spend a few hours of the day in that sport which is, as Mr. Jorrocks says, "The image of war with none of its guilt, and only (what proportion we will leave blank for our readers to fill up) a fraction of its dangers."

It would be idle to assert that these, and many other sets of men we could mention, all hunt for the mere show of the thing, or for health alone. A large number of them love the sport for its own sake—ay, and follow the chase with the same interest and the same knowledge as many a squire who has never left his county. If they have fewer opportunities than he has of studying the habits of the wily fox, the peculiarities of the country, the effect of weather on scent, and many other matters which might appear to be *minutiæ* to the outsider, but are of the utmost importance to one who would hunt as distinguished from him who merely rides to hounds, London men should be pitied for the misfortune which keeps them away from the country for the greater part of the year, rather than chaffed for coming to follow hounds over it whenever they get a chance. Fortunately the prejudice against them is gradually wearing off in most countries. It undoubtedly originated in the circumstance that some years ago, when railway communication was less perfect, a few hard-riding young fellows who knew nothing of hunting, but could afford, or fancied they could afford, to spend any amount of money on their horses, used to train or drive down to certain packs, and ride regardless of hounds and scent ; while others, less wealthy, and in a lower social position, took advantage of Saturday meets near the metropolis to practise on hired hacks which would have been more harmlessly employed in a riding-school. It is during this period that the Old Berkeley

Master ceased advertising his meets, and his example was, unfortunately, followed by a few others, who had less excuse. We say unfortunately, because though no genuine sportsman can rejoice at seeing an unruly rabble surrounding a covert and carefully heading Reynard back every time he tries to get away, yet we find after some years' experience that crowds are apt to be equally uncontrollable whether they collect twenty miles from the metropolis or two hundred. In fact, of the two, we almost prefer the London amateur horseman. He very often knows just enough about hunting to obey orders, while the provincial occasionally thinks he knows more than the Master, or is so keen on the sport that he forgets discipline and order in his anxiety to view the fox or the stag. We therefore think that some of the packs hunting within, say, an hour and a half's ride of London, would not do badly if they, like their neighbours, advertised their meets. Men who will twice or thrice a week get up in the dark and face a long journey down in order to hunt in a favourite country seldom spoil sport. On the contrary, their subscriptions (which they seldom refuse if politely asked for them) would serve materially to promote it. In these periods of agricultural depression many Masters can no longer rely on local support alone, and the majority of London men are very willing to contribute to the expenses of the pack with which they hunt.

THE man who would enjoy both town and country pleasures cannot expect to have quite as easy a time of it as he who is satisfied with one or the other. The country squire who hunts three days a week may, and often has, a long way to drive or ride to covert, but then one transaction covers the whole business. He steps from his hall door into his dog-cart and from the cart on to the back of his hunter. He has probably not had occasion to rise any earlier than usual—certainly not by candle-light, except perhaps for a few mornings about Christmas. The hour of eleven, which is now the usual one for meets all over the country, allows even the most distant sportsmen ample time to dress by daylight, unless they spend an unconscionable time over outward adornment. The squire need but seldom rise before eight. He can breakfast comfortably without being anxious about catching a train, and can smoke his cigar, quietly ensconced in a warm ulster on his cart or on the back of his steady cob. Not so the London man. At the best of times winter mornings in town are dark, and the hour at which he is obliged to rise makes artificial light necessary for many successive weeks. It is very disgusting to have to get up in what appears to be the middle of the night in pursuit of pleasure, and those who do it regularly—particularly after a heavy dinner party or a long rubber on the previous evening—may be credited with genuine love of sport. London servants are not generally early risers, and their temper is scarcely improved by having to get bath, hot water, and breakfast for their masters before the cold gloomy dawn of a winter morning. There will almost certainly be sundry little domestic obstacles raised in the best-conducted establishments. Perhaps the wife does not sympathise, and then the case is serious indeed, for it is ten to one that the choice will be between train and breakfast. If you eat the latter you will miss the former, and if you determine to catch the former you must do without the latter. A resolute will and persistence in hunting, notwithstanding every inconvenience, will alone bring the lady round to a more wholesome frame of mind, and convince her that she had better make the best of a bad job and assist her husband to get away comfortably, since go he will. But it is possible that Nimrod is a bachelor, and then, unless blessed with one of those model servants often told of in novels but seldom met with in real life, his chance of finding everything ready for him when he wakes, and when, his toilet completed, he yearns for breakfast, is small indeed.

The toast will not appear until the cab is at the door, and as the baker has not yet gone his rounds there will be nothing but stale bread; the water did not boil when the tea was made, and the result is a tepid fluid scarcely coloured; the milkman has not made his call, and the cat (?) lapped up what was put by for the morning. One tiny trouble after another crops up, until our poor friend is almost disheartened, and feels inclined to go to bed again, postponing sport to another day. However, bolder thoughts prevail, and at last he climbs into a hansom, which is probably the last of the night cabs, and which the tired horse can scarcely drag. He reaches the station barely in time, and it is quite likely that in the scramble his creamy tops have been splashed, or the mirror-like surface of his boots dulled by the rude contact of a cab-wheel. However, he just manages to bundle into a first-class carriage, which is probably occupied by persons strongly objecting to smoke. There was no time for selection, and it is a blessing to have caught the train at all. His spirits are as low as they well can be. It is scarcely light yet; everything looks dull, black and dreary. He feels as if he had had only half the necessary quantity of sleep, and no breakfast at all. There is a deep consciousness of misery, not untempered by indigestion, discomfort, and damp. It is cold, and the foot-warmers do not deserve the name; in the hurry of starting, too, the warm rug was forgotten. The solace of tobacco is denied, and to sleep is impossible, as the carriage is crowded, and the boots

must be carefully preserved immaculate. In short, he who
hunts from town is not unlikely to consider the whole thing
a huge mistake. If he has had to "box" his horse as well
(a proceeding which we would warn our friends to get done
for them whenever they can) his feet will probably be still
colder, and his temper worse.

The train stops at the great junction on the outskirts
of the Metropolis, and then speeds along till it fairly
reaches the open country. The scene changes, the black
fog is left behind, the lamp above drags out a lingering
competition with the increasing daylight, green fields
appear, and at last a bright ray of real sunshine lights up
the river over which the train is speeding. The sportsman
wakes from the uneasy slumber into which he had sunk,
and sees wide pastures, cattle munching the short grass,
sheep scudding away as the train passes, and trees glowing
in all the varying shades of brown, red, and yellow. A
subdued, but bright enough light is cast over the whole
from the sun, struggling as it is with thin mists which are
curling up from the reeds by yonder stream, and are still
settled motionless in the hollow, over which the train
rattles on the iron viaduct. See, yonder, a huge waggon,
with four burly horses, toiling up the ascent, and as we
mark their gallant efforts the train plunges into a tunnel
underneath the hill they are striving to climb. Once
emerged, and all traces of the great city are left behind.
The sun has at last conquered the autumn mists, and his

slanting rays fall on the white chalk slope of the railway cutting. They fall, too, on the closed window of the carriage, which some one at last puts down, admitting the mild yet bracing air, and letting out the London fog which had filled it. A new spirit comes over the man who " hunts from London." He looks out eagerly, calculating how he would get over that brook if he had to face it, or how he would avoid that wire-bound hedge, if hounds ran through it. His thoughts no longer dwell on his disturbed night's rest, nor on his scanty breakfast. " We shall make it up at the Royal George," he thinks, and indeed this hostelry is always full of chops, eggs, or toast, or devilled kidneys. Or if there is no inn handy, there is sure to be some friendly squire or hospitable farmer *en route*, who will gladly make up for the deficiencies of a London household. - " What a jolly morning ! scent is sure to be good. I wonder which covert we shall draw first ? Will it be Langton Spinney or Squire Braxton's Wood ? Will he run up to the wolds, where we are sure to have a run over light ploughs and small fences, or will he make for the big woodlands at Wheatley, and give us no end of trouble to rout him out ? But then, when he does go, he is sure to make for the vale, and the grass, and the big oxers." Such are the thoughts which now flit across his brain, no longer troubled with London cobwebs. The train slackens speed, and at last pulls up at the well-known platform. " Hullo, Jack, are you there ? Just look after my traps, will you?" he calls out, as he sees the son of mine host of the Royal George assisting his father's customers to alight. Outside the station a number of horses are fidgeting, pricking their anxious ears at the sound of the engine's whistle. "Has Mr. Smith come down?" "How are you, Brown?" "Nice morning, isn't it, Jones?" "Steady, man!" "Steady, old woman!" "Fresh, is she?" "Never mind, she'll have enough to do before the day is over." "Jack, what has your father got for breakfast?" Such or such like are the interjective remarks which our whilom silent, dull London man utters quickly and in the height of good spirits. Away, then, to the Royal George, where something substantial and the presence of sympathising friends make all past troubles disappear entirely from memory. But there is no time to be wasted over breakfast: it is five miles to covert, and the squire is punctual. So away all go, cantering along the side of the road, the only ones who tarry being those who keep a "galloping hack" and have sent their two on. The very birds seem to greet the worker weary of London noise and London smoke, as they chirrup in the boughs above him. One friend after another comes up, and is greeted with waves of the hand or jovial threats of the hunting-whip, and in a short time a few black spots are seen bobbing over the distant hedge. "There are the hounds!" cries one, as the horses of all break from a jog-trot into a canter, and as they come up to the cross-roads,

Harry the second whip, is holding the gate open for the beauties, who rush through with eager noses and waving sterns, recognising the old favourite covert whence they have so· often driven their fox into the open to die a victim to their scent and speed.

Seeing him, then, at the meet, who shall say that the "man who hunts from town" has the worst of the bargain?

November mornings in London are often dark—even in the country they are sometimes dark, too. It is one of the darkest of November mornings in London. The servant comes in at eight o'clock and opens the shutters and draws the blinds, but he lets in no sunshine, though the sun should rise at half-past seven; no light, though the window looks south-east. There is a brown expanse to gaze on, with a near chimney-pot, looming black through it, as if it were the Monument half a mile off; the view goes no further. It surely cannot be a hunting morning; what a fool the fellow is to lay out all the riding clothes, and to place the top-boots by the fire he has just lighted! This must be one of those days on which the keenest sportsman feels that an extra half hour in bed is justifiable, for hounds would surely not come out in such a fog! And if they did, no one could see them.

"Past eight o'clock, sir," says the man at last, finding that his manœuvres, which generally suffice to rouse you into the liveliest motions, have not so far produced any effect whatever, " and the train starts at 9.15, sir ! "

Still half-asleep you are just about to turn over for another doze, and mutter, "Sha'n't hunt ; no use."

But scarcely are the words spoken when memory, or perhaps a dream, recalls a similar morning last winter, when, driving up to the station in a fog black as ink, you felt a fool for your pains, and would have returned home had it not been for the persuasions of some friends booted for the same apparently bootless errand. On that day it was difficult to get out of bed, and the prospect seemed more hopeless than even to-day; yet, ten miles out, the sun was shining brightly, and you had the best run you can remember—forty minutes, the latter part of it very fast, killed in the open, and cut down your field. Why should not a similar reward await you to-day? From bed to tub is a short distance, and can be quickly accomplished ; but the water is undoubtedly most disagreeable this morning. It is getting late, too : no time to dally over a parting, or to dwell lovingly over the fold of a tie. Only twenty minutes left for breakfast and the drive to Euston : call a cab, sharp, or your efforts will have been vain. Under such circumstances eating with any satisfaction to yourself is impossible; besides, that final brandy-and-soda last night, and those strong cigars in the small hours, do not improve the morning's appetite. After an evening begun at a dinner of twenty people, and finished in the Club smoking-room, a late, calm, and thoughtful breakfast is the natural consequence, not a hurried scramble like this. The tea is too hot, the broiled kidney not hot enough; there is no cayenne to help it down.

"The cab is at the door, please, sir." Away you go, a bit of toast in one hand and a pair of gloves in the other, while the servant stuffs in a railway rug—very necessary on a nasty raw morning like this. The streets are greasy, the horse is slow, and the cabman cross. Perhaps he has been out all night, or perhaps he also has been to a "swarry" among his pals, and has wound up the previous evening with tobacco and strong liquors. Surely, if his liver were not out of order, he would not decline to urge on his steed for a "fare" who promises an extra shilling. But he does, and the cab crawls up to the station in time to hear the guard whistling off the train. You plunge out, and dart up the platform, forgetting to pay the cabman. The 9.15 is moving, but a carriage door is still open, and you take a run in, landing with a jerk on the toes of an elderly gentleman who has just made himself comfortable, and, with laudable self-control, abstains from bad language. Bad language, however, is audible on the platform, down which runs breathless a man encumbered with a huge many-caped coat, a metal badge flying behind him. It is the Jehu! "Stop that swindler!" he cries, using very strong expressions; "'e ain't paid me;

and he promised me an extra bob!" You tread on the old gentleman's toes again in your attempt to protrude your body from the window, and just in time you succeed in throwing two florins on the platform—double the man's fare, even allowing for "the extra bob;" but there was no time to think, and you did not want your fellow-passenger, who already regards you with undisguised aversion, to consider you an immoral rogue as well as an ill-mannered cub. Before you can find your proper seat the train has plunged under Primrose Hill, but the feeble light shows that you have entered a second-class compartment. Never mind, it will do as far as Willesden. The train moves slowly on account of the fog. Willesden at last is reached. "First smoking? Look sharp, sir; going on directly; late already," and you are hustled into a carriage which is *not* a smoking compartment, and where the occupiers, on inquiry, strongly object to the fragrant weed. Settling down without the consolation of a cigarette, and not even possessing a newspaper, you notice a horrible streak of mud all down one boot, top and all—probably a mark of the cab-wheel—and your thoughts become dismal. Nor are they made more cheerful by the white mist which hangs over the country like a veil. The *Standard* can be procured at the next station, but a penny will not remove that cold, wet fog which penetrates into the carriage and makes you shiver under your rug. At Mugford, your destination, there is no one to meet you on the platform, nor does a single one of your usual companions emerge from the train.

"Hardly expected you this morning, sir," your groom says, touching his cap, as you enter the stables. "A'most too thick, we thought."

However, The Knight is soon saddled, and you start on your way to Beech Grove, a trysting-place not often fixed on, but which you suppose to be about six miles off. The fog has not cleared. White, cloud-like masses lie in the centre of the meadows; fringes, like sails blown into tatters, float from the hedgerows; the few wayfarers you meet emerge suddenly close to your horse's head before you suspected their approach; the sound of the infrequent cart-wheels is deadened, and you have to be careful not to miss your road. It seems little short of insanity to think of hunting on a morning like this; if you had not come all the way from town, of course you would turn back. But there is no up train till two, so the day is lost at any rate; you may as well go on. Still jogging on through the fog, you reflect on the disadvantages of hunting from London, and wish you could manage to live in the country so as not to be entrapped into such a fool's errand. Your thoughts are rudely interrupted by The Knight's stumbling very nearly down on his head, on a loose stone. Never was such a beastly bad hack as The Knight; he pushes the same stone along for twenty yards and then tumbles over it. "Hold up, you brute!" and you punish the poor Knight with a dig of the spurs. He is a good-tempered animal, but this rouses him, and he begins to pull, and will neither walk nor trot, but insists on dancing along the road sideways, under the impression that hounds are running just the other side of that fence. *He* can't see them on account of the fog, but no doubt you can, being higher up and a clever man ; while he (so he thinks to himself) is only a stupid horse. But you see no hounds —you wish you did ; and you begin to think that you ought to be near the lane which they told you leads to Beech Grove. There is no doubt that you have passed Oxley Heath ; then you recollect that there ought to be a turning to the left, but you did not notice it in the fog, and cannot remember whether you passed it or not. You must ask some one. But whom ? There is no one to ask. On you go, yearning for a human being or a sign-post—the latter for choice. It is past eleven, and there ought to be some indication of hounds, some life about the neighbourhood. Yet all appears still as death, and the mist is thicker than ever. You fancy you know the country fairly well ; but all landmarks are hidden in the mist. At last there is a welcome scrunch of wheels. A butcher's cart flashes out of the fog and passes you at full trot ; you shout an inquiry, the man nods, points in a vague way to the right with his whip, and disappears in the cotton-like atmosphere. Still on, for what appears to be another mile or so. It is very cold and disagreeable; your feet are like icicles, and your boots dull as ditch-water—splashed, too, as well, for you can't avoid puddles on a morning like this. Hurrah! a gleam of sunshine breaks down from the sky. The mist does not clear, but it is lighter and more transparent. There, too, hanging almost overhead, is an undoubted public-house sign. A halloa brings the landlady out, "Beech Grove? You have passed it a mile and a half back. Just past Squire Horn's house, through the gate to the left."

There is another weary trudge, and The Knight, thinking he is going home, pulls and fidgets. But the mist is gradually clearing off the ground and condensing into cold clouds higher up, so you make out your way, and a road-mender shows you the line of gates. They are all closed, and you cannot open the rusty latches. You have to get off your horse, and, as he stands over sixteen hands and is rather fresh, it is a job to get on again; besides, the ground is poached at every gate, and your boots are soon one mass of mud. At last you reach a wood, apparently a large one. The lane leads through it; on the left is a gate, against which leans a young man, half squire, half farmer. "Is this Beech Grove?' you ask.

"Beech Grove is just over there," he replies; "but the hounds are sure to draw this way. You can't do better than wait here."

You are thankful indeed, and soon a couple of hounds emerge into the lane, and then more, carefully hunting through the underwood. The welcome scarlet of the huntsman gleams through the withered leaves of the oaks, and then some of the field come squelching up the wet ride. The boughs are shedding heavy drops, and the dried foliage is dripping under the weight of the water that has settled on it. But hounds are hunting, and you follow up one ride and down another, squelching like the rest of them, and more than once covered with a perfect downpour from the branches. At last the welcome notes strike the ear. They are on a fox, and pretty close to him, as it appears. Away then to the right, through the wood you force your way, The Knight almost pulling you out of your saddle. Bang! goes your hat against the branch of a tree, and you feel a little cool stream of water trickling down your neck, while you replace the injured head-gear and struggle to make the horse go *your* pace and not his. The scent fails. "Back, back!" cries the huntsman; back it is, through underwood, up the rides to the lane again, then into the covert, across some more squelchy and boggy ground. Thus matters go on for an hour; the fox will not break, and yet the hounds are on him, so there is nothing for it but patience. Gradually you weary of tearing through the underwood, scratching you face, knocking your hat about, bumping against trunks, and blundering over roots. You return to the lane to wait on events, and hope that the fox will break at last. Several others are also sick of covert hunting, and walk up and down as gently as their horses will let them. After a couple of false alarms, in one of which The Knight shies at a pheasant which rockets up from under his forefeet, and nearly crushes your leg against a tree, you resolve to bide your time and not be tempted again. Having had no breakfast to speak of, you feel hungry, and open your sandwich case, but take The Knight into a quiet corner, out of sight of the other horses, to keep him from fidgeting. When you come back there is no one in sight, but you hear the horn in a distant part of the wood. Down a ride you go at full gallop, and after a scamper of five minutes are delighted to see a horseman turning the next corner in front. After him, for your life! He takes a bend to the right; you also; you see another man in front of *him*, you catch them up, and the first question they ask is, "Where are the hounds?"

Where, indeed! The wood is large and straggling, and you have no idea on which side the fox broke, if indeed he has broken at all. It is no use stopping here, at any rate; so on you go. The ride brings you to the end of the wood, and there is a nasty-looking stile between you and the open. Before trying it you may as well be sure that you are not galloping away from the hounds instead of towards them. Hark! there is the horn in the distance; at any rate you are going in the right direction. There must be no hesitation now. One of your companions turns his horse and hops over; you follow, and find yourself in a low-lying meadow beneath a steep, grass-covered hill. You both tear up as hard as you can go. It is a long pull, and the horses are pretty well blown before at last you reach the ridge. There is a wide expanse of country before you ; a formidable post and rails separates you from the next field. You look, but see nothing of hounds. Your companion looks; he also sees nothing at first. At last he raises his arm and points away to the far distance. There, a couple of miles off, you can dimly make out a number of dots moving rapidly across a wide plough. There are many fields and a deep valley between you and them. You do not know what may have to be crossed before you get to them, and you are sure to lose sight of even these dots the moment you leave your exalted position.

"Is it any use going after them ? " you ask despairingly.

"Not a bit," replies your friend. " That's an old fox, to be sure. He's bound for Morton's Hollow I expect, right the other side of the country. We can't get over those rails. Come this way."

And you turn to the left through a farmyard, follow your leader at a gallop down one lane and up another, through some gates, and into the road. Here he pulls up. "I am going home," he says; "my little mare has lost a shoe. If you want to catch them, keep along the road."

You do; first at a gallop, then at a canter, and finally at a trot. At last you give it up, and pull The Knight into a walk. The few people you meet ask *you* where the hounds are. You ride slowly and sadly back to Mugford, ten miles off. While waiting for the train two friends ride up. "Best run I can remember," cries one; "splendid country, capital scent, and a kill at the end."

" Fifty minutes, and only two short checks," says the other.

" Weren't you in it, old chap?" asks the first. "Sorry for you !"

" No," you say decisively, "I wasn't in it. Hunting from town is a fraud."

"YES, we have two good nags," remarked Wetherall, as we were smoking our cheroots in the verandah after mess, "but I don't see my way to getting any price about either."

"It's very awkward," I answered. "The whole cantonment knows all about it if you only take a morning gallop."

"Yes," said Wetherall; "and the worst of it is, that every fellow in the town knows it as well. Do you remember our Derby last year?"

"Rather," said I; "and a good win it was, too. Why you had them all beaten at the distance, and Rocket pulled up fresh as paint."

"I did not mean the race itself," remarked my friend, confederate, and jockey (for Wetherall was all three), "but the lotteries and the betting. Why, they ran him up to such a price at the Assembly-rooms that you could not think of giving it! That junior partner in Smith, Wells, and Co.'s bought the ticket for five hundred!"

"And," I chimed in, "they wanted me to lay seven to four on him a week before the race." ·

" Seven to four on an untried one in a field of a dozen !" sneered Wetherall. "As if any owner would be such an ass ! How much did you win in bets after all ? "

" About a hundred and fifty rupees," I replied.

" And I won eighty ! " exclaimed he. " A nice lot, to be sure. Not enough to pay the syce's wages nor the gram for the horses. Why, the clerks at the Bank of Beloochistan made more than that. What is the use of racing on those terms ? "

" Not much, except for the honour and glory of the thing," I replied. " We must try and keep things darker this time."

" How ? " asked Wetherall.

" Is there not a bit of grass somewhere in the jungle where we can train them ? " I inquired.

" Not enough for a gallop anywhere," answered my friend. " I have been riding all over the country to find a place, but there is not room for a hundred yards' sprint. Nothing but paddy-fields or thick jungle. There's nothing but the race-course, and you know how that's watched."

I did indeed, by bitter experience. Ten months ago I had had a promising colt for the local Derby, which was annually competed for by untried horses only. Of course I wanted to find out whether he was really any good, and so Wetherall and I had waited for an opportunity of having a private trial. In the early morning the race-course was always occupied by trainers, horses, and syces, and surrounded by natives looking on at the gallops. In the evening there were people driving and riding, and just as many natives as in the morning. So we had gone there at tiffin-time—two o'clock—with a blazing tropical sun pouring down on the Maidan. We secured our solar topees tightly on our heads, for fear of sunstroke, and prepared to ride the Derby course. Wetherall was on an old crock who was an infallible trial horse; he had won handicaps and minor plates for us at every meeting, and we knew his form to an ounce. This animal, named Catastrophe, carried the Derby weight of ten stone. I was mounted on the untried one, and pulled just eleven. We were to start by consent. Before doing so Wetherall rose in his stirrups and looked round. It was fearfully hot, and the distance was quivering in the sunshine. Not a soul was to be seen. "All right," said he; "away we go." And away we went. Catastrophe made the running at first, but I kept my colt close to his quarters. When half the course was covered I let Rocket have his head a little, and crept to the front. At the distance I looked over my shoulder and saw Wetherall raising his whip. Then I put my hands down and shot forward. It was not a race at all. Rocket won as he liked, though he was giving a stone. We were delighted, and turned for home in high spirits. We pulled up for a minute under the big trees by the grand stand to take breath and wipe our foreheads, when Wetherall caught sight of two white-robed figures dodging round the corner of the building. He was off in a second to find out who they were. Joining me afterwards, he swore that he had recognised one as the syce of Agabeg, a rich Armenian ; but I pooh-poohed the idea. However, he must have been right, for when I wanted to back my nomination for the Derby on that very evening, I could only get six to four at the club, and next day Rocket was at evens. We were entirely forestalled ; there was not a chance of getting any odds at all, and it was evident that the trial had been watched from end to end.

Now in England there is a chance for an owner to pull off several races, because there are plenty of meetings ; but the Junghabad folks had only one annual three days' racing, and a couple of smaller meetings in the Mofussil. The sport could not therefore be at all profitable ; in fact it was bound to result in loss, however good one's horses, unless an occasional "long shot" could be obtained. How to keep the stable secrets from the ubiquitous natives was a puzzle which cost Wetherall and myself many an anxious hour. You can't train horses on a hard road, nor round a compound of half an acre. The parade-ground and the race-course were the only available open spaces, and both were equally public. We pondered and talked over the matter without arriving at any definite result. I had two untried ones for the approaching meeting. The "Derby" was run on the

Wednesday, and the "St. Leger" on Friday in the same week. A winner of the Derby carried a stone extra in the Leger, the second seven pounds extra. My entries for these races were, I believed, good ones—both pure-bred Arabs, and likely to make an example of the cocktail tattoos which were generally produced as maidens. One, "Wanderer," was a long, low grey, with sloping shoulders and capital legs, but rather poor behind; the other, "Rajah," was a more compact horse, with the most perfect quarters I have ever seen even in an Arab. He had the broad forehead, projecting eyes, and fine coat characteristic of his race, and he was a bright bay. Wanderer had been seen about in the cantonment, for of course we could not keep the horses perpetually in the stable; but Rajah was persistently lame, and had done no work up to within four weeks of the races.

Our only vet. in Junghabad was a frightful gossip, so we had not dared to consult him about Rajah. Had we done so, the points of the horse would have been all over the place in twenty-four hours. So Wetherall and I tried some amateur doctoring. We failed to detect the seat of the lameness, beyond that it was somewhere in the off foreleg. We bandaged, we fomented, we rubbed his legs with embrocation—all to no purpose. There was no apparent heat nor pain anywhere, and yet Rajah was as lame as a cat. One evening, after we had spent an hour at the stables as usual, and had done no good, I was pondering over a cigar and the prospects, while Wetherall turned over the leaves of *Youatt on the Horse.*

Suddenly he jumped up and threw the book down. "I've got it," he cried, and then shouting "*Qui hye!*" he ordered the bearer to bring a lantern.

"What is it all about?" I asked. "What is the matter?"

"I think I know," he answered. "What fools we have been! But I won't tell you till I see whether I am right. Come on to the stables."

We went. Rajah was comfortable enough in his box, chewing the last of his evening grain, but resting the off fore-leg as usual.

"Hold the lantern, please," said Wetherall. "Cast the light on the ground if you can. Steady, old boy, hold up."

Suiting the action to the words he picked up the horse's fore-leg, and carefully examined the foot by the light of the lantern.

"I'm right, by Jove!" he exclaimed at last. "It's thrush."

"Thrush?" I asked in wonderment.

"Yes," he replied, "nothing else. Rajah has been for weeks in that dirty shed of the Barracootan chap you bought him of, and they never cleaned out the place nor looked after his feet. What owls we have been, to be sure!"

Owls, indeed, to worry the poor horse with bandages, and ointments, and applications of every nostrum under the sun, and never to look at his feet! But what could be expected of two youngsters whose united ages did not exceed fifty? Of course we thought we knew everything concerning horses; but then most men of that age think so also. However, the difficulty was now practically at an end. We studied Youatt together, and at once applied the recommended remedies But the horse's complaint suggested a method of getting round the touts, and of thus obtaining a chance of a few satisfactory bets.

Next morning just before sunrise our string was out as usual on the race-course. There was Wanderer, and last year's Derby winner, Rocket, and a sharp little pony in training for the dwarf races, and old Dowager, the tall, leggy, steeple-chase mare preparing for the cross-country events. But this time Rajah was also brought out, though he was so lame that he could scarcely hobble on to the course. While I led Wanderer's gallop on Rocket, a curious crowd surrounded the bay, whose first appearance it was. "Kabardah!" cried his syce, when any one came too near the horse, "he kicks, sahib." This was an innocent ruse to prevent outsiders investigating his condition too closely. When Wetherall and I came back from our gallop there was a little chaff about the Arab. Sandy, an enterprising young Scotch merchant, who was the Leviathan bookmaker at Junghabad, several bank clerks, and a number of other civilians and soldiers interested in sport, were standing round, or riding up and down, and watching the various canters.

"He's too fat," said Wetherall, "and I'm afraid he's not quite sound. We are going to give him a breather. Please make room."

Rajah was saddled over his clothes, and Wetherall mounted. The poor beast cantered on three legs, and made, of course, a miserable exhibition. Wetherall soon pulled up to a walk, and while the Arab was hobbling round the course I was exposed to a good deal of chaff.

"I don't think much of your second string, old man," said Sandy. "Wanderer's a good one, but this poor beast will never be able to gallop a yard."

"I'm afraid not," I sighed.

"Do you want to back him for the Derby?" asked Sandy.

"What odds will you lay? I'll take a hundred to one in gold mohurs on the off chance."

"Too much," answered Sandy; "he might get sound after all."

"Anything is possible," remarked Mr. Powis, a middle-aged civilian, "but I don't think it's probable."

A good deal of this sort of talk went on, and at last Sandy, encouraged by the sarcastic observations of my brother officers on our "second string," laid me five hundred rupees to ten about the horse for the Derby, and the same for the Leger. When Wetherall joined us the excitement grew, for he at once asked what price any one would lay him about Wanderer. In fact we both made a great show of wanting to back the grey, and our anxiety to do so convinced all that we did not think much of Rajah's chance. But we could not get anything better than even money, so a single small bet of fifty rupees for the Derby was all the business we really did, although others backed him more warmly.

During the next few days the remedies began to produce a satisfactory result, and Rajah improved rapidly. We did not, however, allow him to gallop on the race-course; had we done so the bubble would at once have burst, and his price in the lottery would have been absurd. Yet it was indispensable to try him, otherwise we might make some fearful mistake. And it was just as indispensable to train him. Walking exercise would not get him into proper condition for the races. But how? The puzzle was still as puzzling as before.

At last one evening I had a literally luminous idea. I was sitting on the verandah about nine o'clock, gazing vacantly into the compound, which was lighted up in patches by the almost horizontal rays of a moon in her first quarter. A number of our men were about, and several strangers also, so I had the discretion to hold my peace for the moment. But later on I took Wetherall aside and informed him of my plan. Next evening we both dined quietly at my bungalow, getting off mess, and at eight o'clock we sneaked down to the stables. We saddled Rajah, who was now quite sound, and old Dowager, and rode off to the race-course, keeping as much as possible in the shadow of the big jack-trees. The great maidan was sparkling in the moonlight, but absolutely deserted. The Europeans were still at dinner, the natives cooking their curries for supper. Along the road which fringed the course-side a hired gharry was occasionally heard to rumble, but this we did not mind, as the sharpest gharry wallah would, in the fickle moon-beams, have failed to recognise a horse galloping over the race-course half a mile off. We set them both going, and gave Rajah, who was now quite sound, a good doing. Next day, the moon being of course later, we dined at mess as usual, and sneaked off afterwards. In order not to attract attention I let Wetherall take the horse to the course alone, and returned to the mess-room as soon as I had helped to saddle him—for of course at that hour the syces were in their own huts and not at all likely to appear in the stable. This we continued for ten days, and our pet Rajah improved rapidly. He could now gallop the Derby course at a fair pace without distress, and we thought it about time to try him. Meanwhile we had brought him out nearly every morning with the others, his off fore-leg being still bandaged very carefully. We did not remove his clothes, but walked him gently round the course. His "doing" over-night had generally been sufficient to take any superfluous steam out of him, so he was quiet enough, and nobody suspected that he was daily becoming more and more fit to go. On the contrary, while the odds we were asked to lay *on* Wanderer gradually expanded to two to one, we could have had almost any price about the bay. But we were afraid to bet any more until we knew something about his speed ourselves.

It was three days after full moon, and within five of the races. We left the mess-room at ten o'clock, and turned in at once. I, for one, was too excited to sleep. I heard the clock strike each successive hour till two; then I woke Wetherall. We donned our wide breeches and loose boots, and sneaked off to the stable. We could hear the syces snoring in their huts. We had taken care that dogs should be tied up, and they made no noise. Wanderer and Rajah were quickly saddled and led out of the compound with cloths over their noses for fear they should whinny after the manner of Arabs. We rode along the ditch behind each other, so that the patrol might not see us. Until we reached the course we were able to keep entirely in the shadow. There, of course, we had to face the plain all bathed in the glorious white light of a tropical moon. We could have read the smallest print without difficulty, and every object stood out clear and distinct. I swept the plain with my race-glass. There was no one visible except the distant sentry at the powder magazine, a long way off. So we rode to the starting point, myself on Rajah, Wetherall on Wanderer. In a low voice I asked my friend whether he was ready. Receiving an affirmative reply, I said in a whisper, " Go ! " and away he went at full tear. I found no difficulty in keeping Rajah within hail, and we began to breast the hill, about one-third of the way round, almost together. Here I took a pull on account of the bay's backward condition, but as soon as we reached the top I set him going again, and closed with Wanderer at the turn for home. " Don't punish him," I hastily whispered to Wetherall; " you might spoil his temper for next Wednesday." My friend just nodded. We neither of us had spurs, but we pressed the flanks of the horses with our heels. Both did their best, and raced from the distance in earnest. I believe Wanderer won by about half a length, but as I was giving nearly a stone, we came to the conclusion that Rajah was quite as good as the grey. On our return home we separated. I was hailed by the patrol, but on being recognised, the sergeant probably thought that I had been " on the spree " somewhere, and no questions were asked. Wetherall got back unnoticed. Next day our commissioner—a half caste who had the *entrée* of most of the best Mogul houses—was told to get all the money he could about Rajah both for the Derby and the Leger. He laid out about a thousand rupees, but the average was only about fifteen to one, and we had reason to suspect that he was not running quite straight. Still, the English community had no notion of what was going on. At the lotteries on the first night of the races it was customary to make a declaration for the Derby if a man had more than one horse entered. I declared to win with Wanderer, and to make things comfortable, put the pen through Rajah's name.

" You may as well scratch him for the Leger at once," suggested Mr. Powis.

There was a laugh. Our secret had, so far, been evidently well kept. We did not buy in the grey for the Derby, as his chance was run up to seven hundred rupees by the keen bidding of the young merchants and enterprising Moguls. So we made up our mind to lose money by the Derby. As a fact we did, for we had backed Rajah so heavily for both races that the bets we lost almost equalled the value of the stakes, which Wanderer won in a common canter.

He was at once installed favourite for the St. Leger, notwithstanding his overweight. Neither Wetherall nor

I backed him for sixpence. At the assembly rooms on the Thursday evening I was asked for my declaration. I at once announced Rajah as the Simon Pure of the stable, and there was a general howl.

" We have all backed Wanderer," shouted one.

" You have sold us," cried another ; " it is not fair."

" Then the horse's lameness is a do," said another.

" I call it a swindle," remarked Sandy, who was celebrated for his sharp practice.

" Listen, gentlemen," I said, when the hubbub had somewhat subsided, " I have swindled no one. You backed the horse you thought the best on your own judgment. I have never said that Rajah was lame."

" No," interrupted Sandy, " but you acted an untruth, if you did not tell one."

" Perhaps I played a little comedy on you, gentlemen, which I had a perfect right to do, considering how my horses have been watched and spied on day after day. I have a right to do as I please with my own. But I tell you what. Nobody shall have a right to complain. Both horses shall run on their merits. I believe Wanderer has no chance of carrying the extra stone against his stable companion, but he shall win if he can."

" How do we know that he will be fairly ridden ? " asked some one.

" You shall have a chance of doing what no owner has

allowed any one to do before," I answered. "You shall select a committee among yourselves, and the committee shall pick out a rider—a gentleman-rider, of course, as no others are accepted. The selected one shall have the horse brought to his own stable at once, so that you may be sure that there is no foul play, and he shall ride the public favourite for the public money."

"That's fair!" cried one.

"Bravo!" said another.

My success intoxicated me. In a hasty moment of fervour I added—

"And look here! To satisfy all of you, Rajah shall put up fourteen pounds extra, just as if he had won the Derby."

"You must be screwed, or mad," whispered Wetherall to me. "He will never do it. You are throwing forty thousand rupees away."

"All right, old man," I said, "I will pay your losses if we can't pull it off. Are you afraid to ride him?"

"I can't win," answered Wetherall, "not, at least, under these conditions."

"Then I will ride him myself," I replied, "and you will see who is right."

Mr. Burgess, a lieutenant in the gallant 126th, was selected as the popular champion. He was undoubtedly one of the best riders in the station, and willingly gave up his mount on an outsider to steer the favourite, who was immediately transferred to his stables. Burgess, I believe, sat up all night with the horse, so fearful was he lest some trick might be played. As to myself, as soon as I reached my bungalow I bitterly repented my hasty offer. To lose all my own bets would be bad enough ; to pay Wetherall's losses as I had promised would mean almost ruin. And how could I expect to beat the fast grey at even weights ? It appeared very unlikely, particularly with so good a man on his back as Burgess.

The eventful afternoon drew on, and the bell was rung for the St. Leger. The occurrence of the previous evening had of course become generally known, and the declaration of fourteen pounds overweight for Rajah was stuck up on the board. Never had there been such a crowd on the Junghabad race-course. We had some difficulty in making our way through it when we came out of the saddling inclosure. Wanderer looked a picture, but he laid his ears back and kicked occasionally in an unpleasant manner. His temper was never of the sweetest, and he hated crowds. Possibly, too, he was by this time rather sick of the race-course. Rajah, on the contrary, was as gentle and quiet as a lamb. We got off to a good start, a little chestnut called Alompra, who had been second in the Derby, making the running for Burgess. I kept well forward, so as not to get messed up by one or other of the fourteen competitors, and rode as steadily as I could, while my heart went pit-a-pat, pit-a-pat. Going up the hill several fell back, and when he had breasted it Alompra was still leading, a weedy brown was doing his best to keep the second place, I followed, and Burgess was on my quarters. At the second or upper turn, when a mile had been covered, the brown shut up entirely and Alompra fell back, while Wanderer crept up on the inside. I still sat as quiet as I could, and stole a glance at Burgess's pale, determined face as we galloped neck and neck. At the turn for home Wanderer, with the inside berth, went to the front, and led about half a length. I gave Rajah one touch with the whip, and closed up again. When we reached the distance we reached the crowd as well, which was leaning forward in serried masses to see the finish. I began riding in earnest, but did not use the whip nor the spurs. I just managed to keep Rajah's head level with Burgess's knee, but I feared that I could do no more. There was a tremendous yell from the crowd as we neared the grand stand. Wanderer seemed to falter, and Burgess raised his whip. I heard the hissing cuts close to my ear, and then I saw the grey's ears laid back, and heard a deep curse from Burgess's lips. In another second Rajah had won by a length.

I hardly knew how it had happened, but Wetherall, who seized both my hands when the clerk of the scales said "All right," told me that Wanderer had probably been frightened by the crowd, and had bored into the rails, nearly smashing Burgess's leg.

This was how we sold the spies.

THE END.

LONDON: R. CLAY, SONS, AND TAYLOR, PRINTERS.

11, *Henrietta Street, Covent Garden, W.C.*
(*Late* 193, *Piccadilly, W.*)

March, 1884.

CATALOGUE OF BOOKS

PUBLISHED BY

CHAPMAN & HALL,

LIMITED,

INCLUDING

DRAWING EXAMPLES, DIAGRAMS, MODELS, INSTRUMENTS, ETC.

ISSUED UNDER THE AUTHORITY OF

THE SCIENCE AND ART DEPARTMENT, SOUTH KENSINGTON,

FOR THE USE OF SCHOOLS AND ART AND SCIENCE CLASSES.

MILITARY BIOGRAPHIES.

Messrs. CHAPMAN & HALL are preparing for publication a Series of Volumes dedicated to the Lives of Great Military Commanders.

The volumes are designed to form a set of critical Biographies, illustrative of the operations and the art of war, by writers of distinction in the profession of arms, whose competence to weigh the military qualities and deeds of the Chiefs can be accepted. Maps will, when necessary, accompany the volumes, for the convenience of students.

The aim of these volumes is to be both popular and scientific, combining the narrative of the most romantic and instructive of human lives with a clear examination of the genius of the soldier.

The first volume, "FREDERICK THE GREAT," by Col. C. B. BRACKENBURY, containing Maps, will appear in March.

"MARSHAL LOUDON," by Col. MALLESON, C.S.I., will follow it; the two Lives presenting the opposing aspects of the Seven Years' War.

BOOKS
PUBLISHED BY
CHAPMAN & HALL, LIMITED.

ABBOTT (EDWIN), formerly Head Master of the Philological School—
A CONCORDANCE OF THE ORIGINAL POETICAL
WORKS OF ALEXANDER POPE. Medium 8vo, 21s.

ADAMS (FRANCIS)—
HISTORY OF THE ELEMENTARY SCHOOL CON-
TEST IN ENGLAND. Demy 8vo, 6s.

BADEN-POWELL (GEORGE)—
STATE AID AND STATE INTERFERENCE. Illus-
trated by Results in Commerce and Industry. Crown 8vo, 9s.

BARTLEY (G. C. T.)—
A HANDY BOOK FOR GUARDIANS OF THE POOR.
Crown 8vo, cloth, 3s.
THE PARISH NET: HOW IT'S DRAGGED AND
WHAT IT CATCHES. Crown 8vo, cloth, 7s. 6d.
THE SEVEN AGES OF A VILLAGE PAUPER. Crown
8vo, cloth, 5s.

BAYARD: HISTORY OF THE GOOD CHEVALIER,
SANS PEUR ET SANS REPROCHE. Compiled by the LOYAL SERVITEUR;
translated into English from the French of Loredan Larchey. With over 200
Illustrations. Royal 8vo, 21s.

BEESLEY (EDWARD SPENCER)—
CATILINE, CLODIUS, AND TIBERIUS. Large crown
8vo, 6s.

BELL (DR. JAMES), Principal of the Somerset House Laboratory—
THE CHEMISTRY OF FOODS. With Microscopic
Illustrations.
PART I. TEA, COFFEE, SUGAR, ETC. Large crown 8vo, 2s. 6d.
PART II. MILK, BUTTER, CEREALS, PREPARED STARCHES, ETC.
Large Crown 8vo, 3s.

BENNET (WILLIAM) The Late—
KING OF THE PEAK: a Romance. With Portrait.
Crown 8vo, 6s.

BENSON (W.)—
MANUAL OF THE SCIENCE OF COLOUR. Coloured
Frontispiece and Illustrations. 12mo, cloth, 2s. 6d.
PRINCIPLES OF THE SCIENCE OF COLOUR. Small
4to, cloth, 15s.

BINGHAM (CAPT. THE HON. D.)—
NAPOLEON'S DESPATCHES. 3 vols. demy 8vo. [*In the Press.*

BIRDWOOD (SIR GEORGE C. M.), C.S.I.—
THE INDUSTRIAL ARTS OF INDIA. With Map and
174 Illustrations. New Edition. Demy 8vo, 14s.

BLACKIE (JOHN STUART) F.R.S.E.—
ALTAVONA: FACT AND FICTION FROM MY LIFE
IN THE HIGHLANDS. Third Edition. Crown 8vo, 6s.

BLAKE (EDITH OSBORNE)—
THE REALITIES OF FREEMASONRY. Demy 8vo, 9s.

BLATHERWICK (DR.)—
PERSONAL RECOLLECTIONS OF PETER STONNOR,
Esq. With Illustrations by JAMES GUTHRIE and A. S. BOYD. Crown 8vo, 6s.

BOYLE (FREDERICK)—
ON THE BORDERLAND—BETWIXT THE REALMS
OF FACT AND FANCY. Crown 8vo, 10s. 6d.
BRADLEY (THOMAS), of the Royal Military Academy, Woolwich—
ELEMENTS OF GEOMETRICAL DRAWING. In Two
Parts, with Sixty Plates. Oblong folio, half bound, each Part 16s.
BRAY (MRS.)—
AUTOBIOGRAPHY OF (born 1789, died 1883).
Author of the "Life of Thomas Stothard, R.A.," "The White Hoods," &c.
Edited by JOHN A. KEMPE. With Portraits. Crown 8vo, 10s. 6d.

MRS. BRAY'S NOVELS AND ROMANCES.

New and Revised Editions, with Frontispieces.

THE WHITE HOODS; a Romance of Flanders.
DE FOIX; a Romance of Bearn.

THE TALBA; or, The Moor of Portugal.
THE PROTESTANT; a Tale of the Times of Queen Mary.

NOVELS FOUNDED ON TRADITIONS OF DEVON AND CORNWALL.

FITZ OF FITZFORD; a Tale of Destiny.
HENRY DE POMEROY.
TRELAWNY OF TRELAWNE.

WARLEIGH; or, The Fatal Oak.
COURTENAY OF WALREDDON.
HARTLAND FOREST AND ROSE-TEAGUE.

MISCELLANEOUS TALES.
A FATHER'S CURSE AND A DAUGHTER'S SACRIFICE.
TRIALS OF THE HEART.

BROADLEY (A. M.)—
HOW WE DEFENDED ARABI AND HIS FRIENDS.
A Story of Egypt and the Egyptians. Illustrated by FREDERICK VILLIERS.
Second Edition. Demy 8vo. 12s.
BUCKLAND (FRANK)—
LOG-BOOK OF A FISHERMAN AND ZOOLOGIST.
Third Edition. With numerous Illustrations. Crown 8vo, 5s.
BURCHETT (R.)—
DEFINITIONS OF GEOMETRY. New Edition. 24mo,
cloth, 5d.
LINEAR PERSPECTIVE, for the Use of Schools of Art.
Twenty-first Thousand. With Illustrations. Post 8vo, cloth, 7s.
PRACTICAL GEOMETRY: The Course of Construction
of Plane Geometrical Figures. With 137 Diagrams. Eighteenth Edition. Post
8vo, cloth, 5s.
BURNAND (F. C.). B.A., Trin. Coll. Camb.—
THE "A. D. C.;" being Personal Reminiscences of the
University Amateur Dramatic Club, Cambridge. Second Edition. Demy 8vo, 12s.
CAMPION (J. S.).—
ON THE FRONTIER. Reminiscences of Wild Sports,
Personal Adventures, and Strange Scenes. With Illustrations. Second Edition.
Demy 8vo, 16s.
ON FOOT IN SPAIN. With Illustrations. Second Edition.
Demy 8vo, 16s.
CARLYLE (THOMAS)—See pages 18 and 19.
CARLYLE BIRTHDAY BOOK (THE). Prepared by
Permission of Mr. THOMAS CARLYLE. Small crown, 3s.
CHAMPEAUX (ALFRED)—
TAPESTRY. With Woodcuts. Cloth, 2s. 6d.
CHRISTIANITY AND COMMON SENSE. A Plea for the
Worship of our Heavenly Father, and also for the Opening of Museums and
Galleries on Sundays. By a BARRISTER. Demy 8vo, 7s. 6d.

CHURCH (A. H.), M.A., Oxon.—
PLAIN WORDS ABOUT WATER. Illustrated. Large crown 8vo, sewed, 6d.

FOOD : A Short Account of the Sources, Constituents, and Uses of Food. Large crown 8vo, cloth, 3s.

PRECIOUS STONES : considered in their Scientific and Artistic Relations. With Illustrations. Large crown 8vo, 2s. 6d.

CLINTON (R. H.)—
A COMPENDIUM OF ENGLISH HISTORY, from the Earliest Times to A.D. 1872. With Copious Quotations on the Leading Events and the Constitutional History, together with Appendices. Post 8vo, 7s. 6d.

COBDEN, RICHARD, LIFE OF. BY JOHN MORLEY. With Portrait. In 2 vols., demy 8vo, 32s.

New Edition. Portrait. Large crown 8vo, 7s. 6d.

Popular Edition, with Portrait, sewed, 1s.; cloth, 2s.

CHAPMAN & HALL'S SIX SHILLING NOVELS:
New and Cheaper Editions of Popular Novels.

FAUCIT OF BALLIOL. By HERMAN MERIVALE.
AYALA'S ANGEL. By ANTHONY TROLLOPE.
THE VICAR'S PEOPLE. By G. MANVILLE FENN.
AUNT HEPSY'S FOUNDLING. By MRS. LEITH ADAMS.
AN AUSTRALIAN HEROINE. By MRS. CAMPBELL PRAED.
FASHION AND PASSION, OR LIFE IN MAYFAIR. By the DUKE DE POMAR.
HARD LINES. By HAWLEY SMART.

COLENSO (FRANCES E.)—
HISTORY OF THE ZULU WAR AND ITS ORIGIN. Assisted in those portions of the work which touch upon Military Matters by Lieut.-Colonel EDWARD DURNFORD. Demy 8vo, 18s.

COOKERY—
OFFICIAL HANDBOOK FOR THE NATIONAL TRAINING SCHOOL FOR COOKERY. Containing Lessons on Cookery; forming the Course of Instruction in the School. Compiled by "R. O. C." Tenth Thousand. Large crown 8vo, 8s.

HOW TO COOK FISH. A Series of Lessons in Cookery, from the Official Handbook to the National Training School for Cookery, South Kensington. Compiled by "R. O. C." Crown 8vo, sewed. 3d.

SICK-ROOM COOKERY. From the Official Handbook for the National School for Cookery, South Kensington. Compiled by "R. O. C." Crown 8vo, sewed, 6d.

CRAIK (GEORGE LILLIE)—
ENGLISH OF SHAKESPEARE. Illustrated in a Philological Commentary on his Julius Cæsar. Sixth Edition. Post 8vo, cloth, 5s.

OUTLINES OF THE HISTORY OF THE ENGLISH LANGUAGE. Ninth Edition. Post 8vo, cloth, 2s. 6d.

CRAWFORD (F. MARION)—
TO LEEWARD. New Edition. Crown 8vo, 5s.

CRIPPS (WILFRED)—
COLLEGE AND CORPORATION PLATE. With numerous Illustrations. Large crown 8vo, cloth, 2s. 6d.

DAME TROT AND HER PIG (The Wonderful History of). With Coloured Illustrations. Crown 4to, 3s. 6d.

DAUBOURG (E.)—
INTERIOR ARCHITECTURE. Doors, Vestibules, Staircases, Anterooms, Drawing, Dining, and Bed Rooms, Libraries, Bank and Newspaper Offices, Shop Fronts and Interiors. Half-imperial, cloth, £2 12s. 6d.

DAVIDSON (ELLIS A.)—
PRETTY ARTS FOR THE EMPLOYMENT OF
LEISURE HOURS. A Book for Ladies. With Illustrations. Demy 8vo, 6s.

THE AMATEUR HOUSE CARPENTER: a Guide in
Building, Making, and Repairing. With numerous Illustrations, drawn on Wood
by the Author. Royal 8vo, 10s. 6d.

DAVISON (THE MISSES)—
TRIQUETI MARBLES IN THE ALBERT MEMORIAL
CHAPEL, WINDSOR. A Series of Photographs. Dedicated by express permission to Her Majesty the Queen. The Work consists of 117 Photographs, with
descriptive Letterpress, mounted on 49 sheets of cardboard, half-imperial. £10 10s.

DAY (WILLIAM)—
THE RACEHORSE IN TRAINING, with Hints on
Racing and Racing Reform, to which is added a Chapter on Shoeing. Fourth
Edition. Demy 8vo, 12s.

D'HAUSSONVILLE (VICOMTE)—
SALON OF MADAME NECKER. Translated by H. M.
TROLLOPE. 2 vols. Crown 8vo, 18s.

DE KONINCK (L. L.) and DIETZ (E.)—
PRACTICAL MANUAL OF CHEMICAL ASSAYING,
as applied to the Manufacture of Iron. Edited, with notes, by ROBERT MALLET.
Post 8vo, cloth, 6s.

DICKENS (CHARLES)—See pages 20-24.
THE LETTERS OF CHARLES DICKENS. Edited
by his Sister-in-Law and his Eldest Daughter. Two vols. uniform with " The
Charles Dickens Edition " of his Works. Crown 8vo, 8s.

THE CHARLES DICKENS BIRTHDAY BOOK.
Compiled and Edited by his Eldest Daughter. With Five Illustrations by his
Youngest Daughter. In a handsome fcap. 4to volume, 12s.

DIXON (W. HEPWORTH)—
BRITISH CYPRUS. With Frontispiece. Demy 8vo, 15s.

DRAYSON (LIEUT.-COL. A. W.)—
THE CAUSE OF THE SUPPOSED PROPER MOTION
OF THE FIXED STARS. Demy 8vo, cloth, 10s.

THE CAUSE, DATE, AND DURATION OF THE
LAST GLACIAL EPOCH OF GEOLOGY. Demy 8vo, cloth, 10s.

PRACTICAL MILITARY SURVEYING AND
SKETCHING. Fifth Edition. Post 8vo, cloth, 4s. 6d.

DYCE'S COLLECTION. A Catalogue of Printed Books and Manuscripts
bequeathed by the REV. ALEXANDER DYCE to the South Kensington Museum.
2 vols. Royal 8vo, half-morocco, 14s.

A Collection of Paintings, Miniatures, Drawings, Engravings,
Rings, and Miscellaneous Objects, bequeathed by the REV. ALEXANDER DYCE
to the South Kensington Museum. Royal 8vo, half-morocco, 6s. 6d.

DYCE (WILLIAM), R.A.—
DRAWING-BOOK OF THE GOVERNMENT SCHOOL
OF DESIGN; OR, ELEMENTARY OUTLINES OF ORNAMENT. Fifty
selected Plates. Folio, sewed, 5s.; mounted, 18s.
Text to Ditto. Sewed, 6d.

EGYPTIAN ART—
A HISTORY OF ART IN ANCIENT EGYPT. By
G. PERROT and C. CHIPIEZ. Translated by WALTER ARMSTRONG. With over
600 Illustrations. 2 vols. Royal 8vo, £2 2s.

ELLIOT (FRANCES)—
PICTURES OF OLD ROME. New Edition. Post 8vo,
cloth, 6s.

ELLIS (CAPTAIN A. B.)—
THE LAND OF FETISH. Demy 8vo. 12s.

ENGEL (CARL)—
A DESCRIPTIVE AND ILLUSTRATED CATALOGUE OF THE MUSICAL INSTRUMENTS in the SOUTH KENSINGTON MUSEUM, preceded by an Essay on the History of Musical Instruments. Second Edition. Royal 8vo, half-morocco, 12s.

MUSICAL INSTRUMENTS. With numerous Woodcuts. Large crown 8vo, cloth, 2s. 6d.

ESCOTT (T. H. S.)—
PILLARS OF THE EMPIRE : Short Biographical Sketches. Demy 8vo, 10s. 6d.

EWALD (ALEXANDER CHARLES), F.S.A.—
REPRESENTATIVE STATESMEN : Political Studies. 2 vols. Large crown 8vo, £1 4s.

SIR ROBERT WALPOLE. A Political Biography, 1676-1745. Demy 8vo, 18s.

FANE (VIOLET)—
QUEEN OF THE FAIRIES (A Village Story), and other Poems. Crown 8vo, 6s.

ANTHONY BABINGTON : a Drama. Crown 8vo, 6s.

FEARNLEY (W.)—
LESSONS IN HORSE JUDGING, AND THE SUM-MERING OF HUNTERS. With Illustrations. Crown 8vo, 4s.

FITZ-PATRICK (W. J.)—
LIFE OF CHARLES LEVER. 2 vols. Demy 8vo, 30s.

FLEMING (GEORGE), F.R.C.S.—
ANIMAL PLAGUES : THEIR HISTORY, NATURE, AND PREVENTION. 8vo, cloth, 15s.

PRACTICAL HORSE-SHOEING. With 37 Illustrations. Second Edition, enlarged. 8vo, sewed, 2s.

RABIES AND HYDROPHOBIA : THEIR HISTORY, NATURE, CAUSES, SYMPTOMS, AND PREVENTION. With 8 Illustrations. 8vo, cloth, 15s.

A MANUAL OF VETERINARY SANITARY SCIENCE AND POLICE. With 33 Illustrations. 2 vols. Demy 8vo, 36s.

FORSTER (JOHN), M.P. for Berwick—
THE CHRONICLE OF JAMES I., KING OF ARAGON, SURNAMED THE CONQUEROR. Written by Himself. Translated from the Catalan by the late JOHN FORSTER, M.P. for Berwick. With an Historical Introduction by DON PASCUAL DE GAYANGOS. 2 vols. Royal 8vo, 28s.

FORSTER (JOHN)—
THE LIFE OF CHARLES DICKENS. With Portraits and other Illustrations. 15th Thousand. 3 vols. 8vo, cloth, £2 2s.

THE LIFE OF CHARLES DICKENS. Uniform with the Illustrated Library Edition of Dickens's Works. 2 vols. Demy 8vo, £1 8s.

THE LIFE OF CHARLES DICKENS. Uniform with the Library Edition. Post 8vo, 10s. 6d.

THE LIFE OF CHARLES DICKENS. Uniform with the "C. D." Edition. With Numerous Illustrations. 2 vols. 7s.

THE LIFE OF CHARLES DICKENS. Uniform with the Household Edition. With Illustrations by F. BARNARD. Crown 4to, cloth, 5s.

WALTER SAVAGE LANDOR : a Biography, 1775-1864. With Portrait. A New and Revised Edition. Demy 8vo, 12s.

FORTNIGHTLY REVIEW—
　　FORTNIGHTLY REVIEW.—First Series, May, 1865, to
　　Dec. 1866. 6 vols. Cloth, 13s. each.
　　New Series, 1867 to 1872. In Half-yearly Volumes. Cloth,
　　13s. each.
　　From January, 1873, to the present time, in Half-yearly
　　Volumes. Cloth, 16s. each.
　　CONTENTS OF FORTNIGHTLY REVIEW. From
　　the commencement to end of 1878. Sewed, 2s.

FORTNUM (C. D. E.)—
　　A DESCRIPTIVE AND ILLUSTRATED CATALOGUE
　　OF THE BRONZES OF EUROPEAN ORIGIN in the SOUTH KEN-
　　SINGTON MUSEUM, with an Introductory Notice. Royal 8vo, half-morocco,
　　£1 10s.
　　A DESCRIPTIVE AND ILLUSTRATED CATALOGUE
　　OF MAIOLICA, HISPANO-MORESCO, PERSIAN, DAMASCUS, AND
　　RHODIAN WARES in the SOUTH KENSINGTON MUSEUM. Royal
　　8vo, half-morocco, £2.
　　MAIOLICA. With numerous Woodcuts. Large crown
　　8vo, cloth, 2s. 6d.
　　BRONZES. With numerous Woodcuts. Large crown
　　8vo, cloth, 2s. 6d.

FRANCATELLI (C. E.)—
　　ROYAL CONFECTIONER: English and Foreign. A
　　Practical Treatise. New and Cheap Edition. With Illustrations. Crown 8vo, 5s.

FRANKS (A. W.)—
　　JAPANESE POTTERY. Being a Native Report. Nume-
　　rous Illustrations and Marks. Large crown 8vo, cloth, 2s. 6d.

GALLENGA (ANTONIO)—
　　IBERIAN REMINISCENCES. Fifteen Years' Travelling
　　Impressions of Spain and Portugal. With a Map. 2 vols. Demy 8vo, 32s.
　　A SUMMER TOUR IN RUSSIA. With a Map.
　　Demy 8vo, 14s.
　　DEMOCRACY ACROSS THE CHANNEL. Crown
　　8vo, 3s.

GORST (J. E.), Q.C., M.P.—
　　An ELECTION MANUAL. Containing the Parliamentary
　　Elections (Corrupt and Illegal Practices) Act, 1883, with Notes. Crown 8vo, 2s. 6d.

GRIFFITHS (MAJOR ARTHUR), H.M. Inspector of Prisons—
　　CHRONICLES OF NEWGATE. Illustrated. New
　　Edition in 1 vol. Demy 8vo. 　　　　　　　　　　　　　　[In March.

HALL (SIDNEY)—
　　A TRAVELLING ATLAS OF THE ENGLISH COUN-
　　TIES. Fifty Maps, coloured. New Edition, including the Railways, corrected
　　up to the present date. Demy 8vo, in roan tuck, 10s. 6d.

HARDY (LADY DUFFUS)—
　　DOWN SOUTH. Demy 8vo. 14s.
　　THROUGH CITIES AND PRAIRIE LANDS. Sketches
　　of an American Tour. Demy 8vo, 14s.

HATTON (JOSEPH) and HARVEY (REV. M.)—
　　NEWFOUNDLAND. The Oldest British Colony. Its
　　History, Past and Present, and its Prospects in the Future. Illustrated from
　　Photographs and Sketches specially made for this work. Demy 8vo, 18s.
　　TO-DAY IN AMERICA. Studies for the Old World and
　　the New. 2 vols. Crown 8vo, 18s.

HEAPHY (MUSGRAVE)—
　　GLIMPSES AND GLEAMS. Crown 8vo, 5s.

HILDEBRAND (HANS)—
INDUSTRIAL ARTS OF SCANDINAVIA IN THE
PAGAN TIME. Illustrated. Large crown 8vo, 2s. 6d.

HILL (MISS G.)—
THE PLEASURES AND PROFITS OF OUR LITTLE
POULTRY FARM. Small crown 8vo, 3s.

HITCHMAN (FRANCIS)—
THE PUBLIC LIFE OF THE EARL OF BEACONS-
FIELD. 2 vols. Demy 8vo, £1 12s.

HOLBEIN—
TWELVE HEADS AFTER HOLBEIN. Selected from
Drawings in Her Majesty's Collection at Windsor. Reproduced in Autotype, in
portfolio. £1 16s.

HOLLINGSHEAD (JOHN)—
FOOTLIGHTS. Crown 8vo. 7s. 6d.

HOVELACQUE (ABEL)—
THE SCIENCE OF LANGUAGE: LINGUISTICS,
PHILOLOGY, AND ETYMOLOGY. With Maps. Large crown 8vo, cloth, 5s.

HOW I BECAME A SPORTSMAN. By "AVON." Illustrated. Crown
8vo. 6s.

HUMPHRIS (H. D.)—
PRINCIPLES OF PERSPECTIVE. Illustrated in a
Series of Examples. Oblong folio, half-bound, and Text 8vo, cloth, £1 1s.

IRON (RALPH)—
THE STORY OF AN AFRICAN FARM. New Edition.
Crown 8vo, 5s.

JAMES I., KING OF ARAGON (THE CHRONICLE OF),
SURNAMED THE CONQUEROR. Written by Himself. Translated from
the Catalan by the late JOHN FORSTER, M.P. for Berwick. With an Historical
Introduction by DON PASCUAL DE GAYANGOS. 2 vols. Royal 8vo. 28s.

JARRY (GENERAL)—
OUTPOST DUTY. Translated, with TREATISES ON
MILITARY RECONNAISSANCE AND ON ROAD-MAKING. By Major-
Gen. W. C. E. NAPIER. Third Edition. Crown 8vo, 5s.

JEANS (W. T.)—
CREATORS OF THE AGE OF STEEL. Memoirs of
Sir W. Siemens, Sir H. Bessemer, Sir J. Whitworth, Sir J. Brown, and other
Inventors. Crown 8vo, 7s. 6d.

JOHNSON (DR. SAMUEL)—
LIFE AND CONVERSATIONS. By A. MAIN. Crown
8vo, 10s. 6d.

JONES (CAPTAIN DOUGLAS), R.A.—
NOTES ON MILITARY LAW. Crown 8vo, 4s.

JONES COLLECTION (HANDBOOK OF THE) IN THE SOUTH
KENSINGTON MUSEUM. Illustrated. Large crown 8vo, 2s. 6d.

KEMPIS (THOMAS Ã)—
OF THE IMITATION OF CHRIST. Four Books.
Beautifully Illustrated Edition. Demy 8vo, 16s.

KENT (CHARLES)—
HUMOUR AND PATHOS OF CHARLES DICKENS,
WITH ILLUSTRATIONS OF HIS MASTERY OF THE TERRIBLE
AND PICTURESQUE. Portrait. Crown 8vo. 6s.

KLACZKO (M. JULIAN)—
TWO CHANCELLORS: PRINCE GORTCHAKOF AND
PRINCE BISMARCK. Translated by MRS. TAIT. New and cheaper Edition, 6s.

LACORDAIRE'S CONFERENCES. JESUS CHRIST, GOD,
AND GOD AND MAN. New Edition in 1 vol. Crown 8vo, 6s.

LAVELEYE (EMILE DE)—

THE ELEMENTS OF POLITICAL ECONOMY.
Translated by W. POLLARD, B.A., St. John's College, Oxford. Crown 8vo, 6s.

LEFÈVRE (ANDRÉ)—

PHILOSOPHY, Historical and Critical. Translated, with
an Introduction, by A. W. KEANE, B.A. Large crown 8vo, 7s. 6d.

LETOURNEAU (DR. CHARLES)—

SOCIOLOGY. Based upon Ethnology. Translated by
HENRY M. TROLLOPE. Large crown 8vo, 10s.

BIOLOGY. Translated by WILLIAM MacCALL. With Illus-
trations. Large crown 8vo, 6s.

LILLY (W. S.)—

ANCIENT RELIGION AND MODERN THOUGHT.
One vol. demy 8vo.   *[In the Press.*

LOW (C. R.)—

SOLDIERS OF THE VICTORIAN AGE. 2 vols. Demy
8vo, £1 10s.

LUCAS (CAPTAIN)—

THE ZULUS AND THE BRITISH FRONTIER.
Demy 8vo, 16s.

CAMP LIFE AND SPORT IN SOUTH AFRICA.
With Episodes in Kaffir Warfare. With Illustrations. Demy 8vo. 12s.

LYTTON (ROBERT, EARL)—

POETICAL WORKS—
FABLES IN SONG. 2 vols. Fcap. 8vo, 12s.
THE WANDERER. Fcap. 8vo, 6s.
POEMS, HISTORICAL AND CHARACTERISTIC. Fcap. 6s.

MACEWEN (CONSTANCE)—

ROUGH DIAMONDS: OR, SKETCHES FROM REAL
LIFE. Crown 8vo, 3s. 6d.

MALLET (DR. J. W.)—

COTTON: THE CHEMICAL, &c., CONDITIONS OF
ITS SUCCESSFUL CULTIVATION. Post 8vo, cloth, 7s. 6d.

MALLET (ROBERT)—

PRACTICAL MANUAL OF CHEMICAL ASSAYING,
as applied to the Manufacture of Iron. By L. L. DE KONINCK and E. DIETZ.
Edited, with notes, by ROBERT MALLET. Post 8vo, cloth. 6s.

GREAT NEAPOLITAN EARTHQUAKE OF 1857.
First Principles of Observational Seismology, as developed in the Report to the
Royal Society of London. Maps and numerous Illustrations. 2 vols. Royal 8vo,
cloth, £3 3s.

MASKELL (WILLIAM)—

A DESCRIPTION OF THE IVORIES, ANCIENT AND
MEDIÆVAL, in the SOUTH KENSINGTON MUSEUM, with a Preface.
With numerous Photographs and Woodcuts. Royal 8vo, half-morocco, £1 1s.

IVORIES: ANCIENT AND MEDIÆVAL. With nume-
rous Woodcuts. Large crown 8vo, cloth, 2s. 6d.

HANDBOOK TO THE DYCE AND FORSTER COL-
LECTIONS. With Illustrations. Large crown 8vo, cloth, 2s. 6d.

McCOAN (J. CARLILE)—

OUR NEW PROTECTORATE. TURKEY IN ASIA: ITS
GEOGRAPHY, RACES, RESOURCES, AND GOVERNMENT. With Map. 2 vols.
Large crown 8vo, £1 4s.

MEREDITH (GEORGE)—
  MODERN LOVE AND POEMS OF THE ENGLISH
  ROADSIDE, WITH POEMS AND BALLADS. Fcap. cloth, 6s.

MERIVALE (HERMAN CHARLES)—
  BINKO'S BLUES. A Tale for Children of all Growths.
  Illustrated by EDGAR GIBERNE. Small crown 8vo. [*In the Press.*

  THE WHITE PILGRIM, and other Poems. Crown 8vo, 9s.

  FAUCIT OF BALLIOL. Crown 8vo, 6s.

MOLESWORTH (W. NASSAU)—
  HISTORY OF ENGLAND FROM THE YEAR 1830
  TO THE RESIGNATION OF THE GLADSTONE MINISTRY, 1874. 3 vols.
  Crown 8vo, 18s.

  ABRIDGED EDITION. Large crown, 7s. 6d.

MORLEY (HENRY)—
  ENGLISH WRITERS. Vol. I. Part I. THE CELTS
  AND ANGLO-SAXONS. With an Introductory Sketch of the Four Periods of
  English Literature. Part II. FROM THE CONQUEST TO CHAUCER.
  (Making 2 vols.) 8vo, cloth, £1 2s.

  Vol. II. Part I. FROM CHAUCER TO DUNBAR.
  8vo, cloth, 12s.

  TABLES OF ENGLISH LITERATURE. Containing
  20 Charts. Second Edition, with Index. Royal 4to, cloth, 12s.
    In Three Parts. Parts I. and II., containing Three Charts, each 1s. 6d.
    Part III., containing 14 Charts, 7s. Part III. also kept in Sections, 1, 2, and 5.
    1s. 6d. each ; 3 and 4 together, 3s. *₊* The Charts sold separately.

MORLEY (JOHN)—
  LIFE OF RICHARD COBDEN. With Portrait. Popular
  Edition. 4to, sewed, 1s. Bound in cloth, 2s.

  LIFE AND CORRESPONDENCE OF RICHARD
  COBDEN. Fourth Thousand. 2 vols. Demy 8vo, £1 12s.

  DIDEROT AND THE ENCYCLOPÆDISTS. 2 vols.
  Demy 8vo, £1 6s.

NEW UNIFORM EDITION.

  LIFE OF RICHARD COBDEN. With Portrait. Large
  crown 8vo, 7s. 6d.

  VOLTAIRE. Large crown 8vo, 6s.

  ROUSSEAU. Large crown 8vo, 9s.

  DIDEROT AND THE ENCYCLOPÆDISTS. Large
  crown 8vo, 12s.

  CRITICAL MISCELLANIES. First Series. Large crown
  8vo, 6s.

  CRITICAL MISCELLANIES. Second Series. [*In the Press.*

  ON COMPROMISE. New Edition. Large crown 8vo, 3s. 6d.

  STRUGGLE FOR NATIONAL EDUCATION. Third
  Edition. Demy 8vo, cloth, 3s.

MUNTZ (EUGÈNE), From the French of—
  RAPHAEL : HIS LIFE, WORKS, AND TIMES.
  Edited by W. ARMSTRONG. Illustrated with 155 Wood Engravings and 41 Full-
  page Plates. Imperial 8vo, 36s.

MURPHY (J. M.)—
   RAMBLES IN NORTH - WEST AMERICA. With
   Frontispiece and Map. 8vo, 16s.
MURRAY (ANDREW), F.L.S.—
   ECONOMIC ENTOMOLOGY. APTERA. With nume-
   rous Illustrations. Large crown 8vo, 7s. 6d.
NAPIER (MAJ.-GEN. W. C. E.)—
   TRANSLATION OF GEN. JARRY'S OUTPOST DUTY.
   With TREATISES ON MILITARY RECONNAISSANCE AND ON
   ROAD-MAKING. Third Edition. Crown 8vo, 5s.
NECKER (MADAME)—
   THE SALON OF MADAME NECKER. By VICOMTE
   D'HAUSSONVILLE. Translated by H. M. TROLLOPE. 2 vols. Crown 8vo, 18s.
NESBITT (ALEXANDER)—
   GLASS. Illustrated. Large crown 8vo, cloth, 2s. 6d.
NEVINSON (HENRY)—
   A SKETCH OF HERDER AND HIS TIMES. With
   a Portrait. Demy 8vo, 14s.
NEWTON (E. TULLEY), F.G.S.—
   THE TYPICAL PARTS IN THE SKELETONS OF
   A CAT, DUCK, AND CODFISH, being a Catalogue with Comparative
   Description arranged in a Tabular form. Demy 8vo, cloth, 3s.
NORMAN (C. B.), late of the 90th Light Infantry and Bengal Staff Corps—
   TONKIN ; OR, FRANCE IN THE FAR EAST. Demy
   8vo, with Maps, 14s.
OLIVER (PROFESSOR), F.R.S., &c.—
   ILLUSTRATIONS OF THE PRINCIPAL NATURAL
   ORDERS OF THE VEGETABLE KINGDOM, PREPARED FOR THE
   SCIENCE AND ART DEPARTMENT, SOUTH KENSINGTON. With
   109 Plates. Oblong 8vo, plain, 16s. ; coloured, £1 6s.
PERROT (GEORGES) and CHIPIEZ (CHARLES)—
   CHALDÆA AND ASSYRIA, A HISTORY OF ART IN.
   Translated by WALTER ARMSTRONG, B.A. Oxon. With 452 Illustrations. 2 vols.
   Demy 8vo. Uniform with "Ancient Egyptian Art." 42s.
   ANCIENT EGYPT, A HISTORY OF ART IN. Trans-
   lated from the French by W. ARMSTRONG. With over 600 Illustrations. 2 vols.
   Imperial 8vo, 42s.
POLLEN (J. H.)—
   ANCIENT AND MODERN FURNITURE AND
   WOODWORK IN THE SOUTH KENSINGTON MUSEUM. With an
   Introduction, and Illustrated with numerous Coloured Photographs and Woodcuts.
   Royal 8vo, half-morocco, £1 1s.
   GOLD AND SILVER SMITH'S WORK. With nume-
   rous Woodcuts. Large crown 8vo, cloth, 2s. 6d.
   ANCIENT AND MODERN FURNITURE AND
   WOODWORK. With numerous Woodcuts. Large crown 8vo, cloth, 2s. 6d.
POLLOK (LIEUT.-COLONEL)—
   SPORT IN BRITISH BURMAH, ASSAM, AND THE
   CASSYAH AND JYNTIAH HILLS. With Notes of Sport in the Hilly Dis-
   tricts of the Northern Division, Madras Presidency. With Illustrations and 2
   Maps. 2 vols. Demy 8vo, £1 4s.
POYNTER (E. J.), R.A.—
   TEN LECTURES ON ART. Second Edition. Large
   crown 8vo, 9s.
PRAED (MRS. CAMPBELL)—
   AN AUSTRALIAN HEROINE. Cheap Edition. Crown
   8vo, 6s.
   NADINE. Cheap Edition. Crown 8vo, 5s.
   MOLOCH. Cheap Edition.   [*In the Press.*

PRINSEP (VAL), A.R.A.—

IMPERIAL INDIA. Containing numerous Illustrations and Maps made during a Tour to the Courts of the Principal Rajahs and Princes of India. Second Edition. Demy 8vo, £1 1s.

PUCKETT (R. CAMPBELL), Ph.D., Bonn University—

SCIOGRAPHY; or, Radial Projection of Shadows. Third Edition. Crown 8vo, cloth, 6s.

RAMSDEN (LADY GWENDOLEN)—

A BIRTHDAY BOOK. Illustrated. Containing 46 Illustrations from Original Drawings, and numerous other Illustrations. Royal 8vo, 21s.

REDGRAVE (GILBERT)—

PRE-CHRISTIAN ORNAMENTATION. Translated from the German and edited. With numerous Illustrations. Crown 8vo.
[*In the Press.*

REDGRAVE (GILBERT R.)—

MANUAL OF DESIGN, compiled from the Writings and Addresses of RICHARD REDGRAVE, R.A. With Woodcuts. Large crown 8vo, cloth, 2s. 6d.

REDGRAVE (RICHARD)—

MANUAL AND CATECHISM ON COLOUR. 24mo, cloth, 9d.

REDGRAVE (SAMUEL)—

A DESCRIPTIVE CATALOGUE OF THE HISTORICAL COLLECTION OF WATER-COLOUR PAINTINGS IN THE SOUTH KENSINGTON MUSEUM. With numerous Chromo-lithographs and other Illustrations. Royal 8vo, £1 1s.

RENAN (ERNEST)—

RECOLLECTIONS OF MY YOUTH. Translated from the original French by C. B. PITMAN, and revised by MADAME RENAN. Crown 8vo, 8s.

RIANO (JUAN F.)—

THE INDUSTRIAL ARTS IN SPAIN. Illustrated. Large crown 8vo, cloth, 4s.

ROBINSON (JAMES F.)—

BRITISH BEE FARMING. Its Profits and Pleasures. Large crown 8vo, 5s.

ROBINSON (J. C.)—

ITALIAN SCULPTURE OF THE MIDDLE AGES AND PERIOD OF THE REVIVAL OF ART. With 20 Engravings. Royal 8vo, cloth, 7s. 6d.

ROBSON (GEORGE)—

ELEMENTARY BUILDING CONSTRUCTION. Illustrated by a Design for an Entrance Lodge and Gate. 15 Plates. Oblong folio, sewed, 8s.

ROBSON (REV. J. H.), M.A., LL.M.—

AN ELEMENTARY TREATISE ON ALGEBRA. Post 8vo, 6s.

ROCK (THE VERY REV. CANON), D.D.—

ON TEXTILE FABRICS. A Descriptive and Illustrated Catalogue of the Collection of Church Vestments, Dresses, Silk Stuffs, Needlework, and Tapestries in the South Kensington Museum. Royal 8vo, half-morocco, £1 11s. 6d.

TEXTILE FABRICS. With numerous Woodcuts. Large crown 8vo, cloth, 2s. 6d.

ROLAND (ARTHUR)—

FARMING FOR PLEASURE AND PROFIT. Edited
by WILLIAM ABLETT. 8 vols. Large crown 8vo, 5s. each.
DAIRY-FARMING, MANAGEMENT OF COWS, &c.
POULTRY-KEEPING.
TREE-PLANTING, FOR ORNAMENTATION OR PROFIT.
STOCK-KEEPING AND CATTLE-REARING.
DRAINAGE OF LAND, IRRIGATION, MANURES, &c.
ROOT-GROWING, HOPS, &c.
MANAGEMENT OF GRASS LANDS.
MARKET GARDENING.

RUSDEN (G. W.), for many years Clerk of the Parliament in Victoria—

A HISTORY OF AUSTRALIA. With a Coloured Map.
3 Vols. Demy 8vo, 50s.

A HISTORY OF NEW ZEALAND. 3 vols. Demy 8vo.
with Maps, 50s.

SALUSBURY (PHILIP H. B.)—

TWO MONTHS WITH TCHERNAIEFF IN SERVIA.
Large crown 8vo, 9s.

SCOTT-STEVENSON (MRS.)—

ON SUMMER SEAS. Including the Mediterranean, the
Ægean, the Ionian, and the Euxine, and a voyage down the Danube. With a
Map. Demy 8vo, 16s.

OUR HOME IN CYPRUS. With a Map and Illustrations. Third Edition. Demy 8vo, 14s.

OUR RIDE THROUGH ASIA MINOR. With Map.
Demy 8vo, 18s.

SIMMONDS (T. L.)—

ANIMAL PRODUCTS: their Preparation, Commercial
Uses, and Value. With numerous Illustrations. Large crown 8vo, 7s. 6d.

SMART (HAWLEY)—

SALVAGE. A Collection of Stories. Crown 8vo, 10s. 6d.

HARD LINES. 1 vol. Crown 8vo, 6s.

SMITH (MAJOR R. MURDOCK), R.E.—

PERSIAN ART. Second Edition, with additional Illustrations. Large crown 8vo, 2s.

ST. CLAIR (S. G. B.)—

TWELVE YEARS' RESIDENCE IN BULGARIA.
Revised Edition. Crown 8vo, 9s.

STORY (W. W.)—

ROBA DI ROMA. Seventh Edition, with Additions and
Portrait. Crown 8vo, cloth, 10s. 6d.

CASTLE ST. ANGELO. With Illustrations. Crown
8vo, 10s. 6d.

SUTCLIFFE (JOHN)—

THE SCULPTOR AND ART STUDENT'S GUIDE
to the Proportions of the Human Form, with Measurements in feet and inches of
Full-Grown Figures of Both Sexes and of Various Ages. By Dr. G. SCHADOW,
Member of the Academies, Stockholm, Dresden, Rome, &c. &c. Translated by
J. J. WRIGHT. Plates reproduced by J. SUTCLIFFE. Oblong folio, 31s. 6d.

TANNER (PROFESSOR), F.C.S.—

HOLT CASTLE; or, Threefold Interest in Land. Crown
8vo, 4s. 6d.

JACK'S EDUCATION; OR, HOW HE LEARNT
FARMING. Second Edition. Crown 8vo, 3s. 6d.

TOPINARD (DR. PAUL)—

ANTHROPOLOGY. With a Preface by Professor PAUL
BROCA. With numerous Illustrations. Large crown 8vo, 7s. 6d.

TRAILL (H. D.)—
THE NEW LUCIAN. Being a Series of Dialogues of the
Dead. Demy 8vo, 12s.

TROLLOPE (ANTHONY)—
AYALA'S ANGEL. Crown 8vo. 6s.
LIFE OF CICERO. 2 vols. 8vo. £1 4s.
THE CHRONICLES OF BARSETSHIRE. A Uniform
Edition, in 8 vols., large crown 8vo, handsomely printed, each vol. containing
Frontispiece. 6s. each.

THE WARDEN and BAR- CHESTER TOWERS. 2 vols.	THE SMALL HOUSE AT ALLINGTON. 2 vols.
DR. THORNE.	LAST CHRONICLE OF
FRAMLEY PARSONAGE.	BARSET. 2 vols.

TROLLOPE (MR. and MRS. THOMAS ADOLPHUS)—
HOMES AND HAUNTS OF ITALIAN POETS. 2 vols.
Crown 8vo, 18s.

UNIVERSAL—
UNIVERSAL CATALOGUE OF BOOKS ON ART.
Compiled for the use of the National Art Library, and the Schools of Art in the
United Kingdom. In 2 vols. Crown 4to, half-morocco, £2 2s.
Supplemental Volume to Ditto.

VERON (EUGENE)—
ÆSTHETICS. Translated by W. H. ARMSTRONG. Large
crown 8vo, 7s. 6d.

WALE (REV. HENRY JOHN), M.A.—
MY GRANDFATHER'S POCKET BOOK, from 1701 to
1796. Author of "Sword and Surplice." Demy 8vo, 12s.

WATSON (ALFRED E. T.)
SKETCHES IN THE HUNTING FIELD. Illustrated
by JOHN STURGESS. Cheap Edition. Crown 8vo, 6s.

WESTWOOD (J. O.), M.A., F.L.S., &c.—
CATALOGUE OF THE FICTILE IVORIES IN THE
SOUTH KENSINGTON MUSEUM. With an Account of the Continental
Collections of Classical and Mediæval Ivories. Royal 8vo, half-morocco, £1 4s.

WHEELER (G. P.)—
VISIT OF THE PRINCE OF WALES. A Chronicle of
H.R.H.'s Journeyings in India, Ceylon, Spain, and Portugal. Large crown 8vo, 12s.

WHITE (WALTER)—
HOLIDAYS IN TYROL: Kufstein, Klobenstein, and
Paneveggio. Large crown 8vo, 14s.
A MONTH IN YORKSHIRE. Post 8vo. With a Map.
Fifth Edition. 4s.
A LONDONER'S WALK TO THE LAND'S END, AND
A TRIP TO THE SCILLY ISLES. Post 8vo. With 4 Maps. Third Edition. 4s.

WILDFOWLER—
SHOOTING, YACHTING, AND SEA-FISHING TRIPS,
at Home and on the Continent. Second Series. By "WILDFOWLER," "SNAP-
SHOT." 2 vols. Crown 8vo, £1 1s.

SHOOTING AND FISHING TRIPS IN ENGLAND,
FRANCE, ALSACE, BELGIUM, HOLLAND, AND BAVARIA. New
Edition, with Illustrations. Large crown 8vo, 8s.

WILL-O'-THE-WISPS, THE. Translated from the German
of Marie Petersen by CHARLOTTE J. HART With Illustrations. Crown 8vo,
7s. 6d.

WORNUM (R. N.)—
   ANALYSIS OF ORNAMENT: THE CHARACTER-
ISTICS OF STYLES. An Introduction to the Study of the History of Orna-
mental Art. With many Illustrations. Ninth Edition. Royal 8vo, cloth, 8s.

WORSAAE (J. J. A.)—
   INDUSTRIAL ARTS OF DENMARK, FROM THE
EARLIEST TIMES TO THE DANISH CONQUEST OF ENGLAND.
With Maps and Illustrations. Crown 8vo, 3s. 6d.

WYLDE (ATHERTON)—
   MY CHIEF AND I; OR, SIX MONTHS IN NATAL
AFTER THE LANGALIBALELE OUTBREAK. With Portrait of Colonel
Durnford, and Illustrations. Demy 8vo, 14s.

YEO (DR. J. BURNEY)—
   HEALTH RESORTS AND THEIR USES: BEING
Vacation Studies in various Health Resorts. Crown 8vo, 8s.

YOUNGE (C. D.)—
   PARALLEL LIVES OF ANCIENT AND MODERN
HEROES. New Edition. 12mo, cloth, 4s. 6d.

SOUTH KENSINGTON MUSEUM DESCRIPTIVE AND ILLUSTRATED CATALOGUES.

Royal 8vo, half-bound.

BRONZES OF EUROPEAN ORIGIN. By C. D. E. Fortnum.
£1 10s.

DYCE'S COLLECTION OF PRINTED BOOKS AND
MANUSCRIPTS. 2 vols. 14s.

DYCE'S COLLECTION OF PAINTINGS, ENGRAVINGS,
&c. 6s. 6d.

FURNITURE AND WOODWORK, ANCIENT AND
MODERN. By J. H. Pollen. £1 1s.

GLASS VESSELS. By A. Nesbitt. 18s.

GOLD AND SILVER SMITH'S WORK. By J. G. Pollen.
£1 6s.

IVORIES, ANCIENT AND MEDIÆVAL. By W. Maskell.
21s.

IVORIES, FICTILE. By J. O. Westwood. £1 4s.

MAIOLICA, HISPANO-MORESCO, PERSIAN, DAMAS-
CUS AND RHODIAN WARES. By C. D. E. Fortnum. £2.

MUSICAL INSTRUMENTS. By C. Engel. 12s.

SCULPTURE, ITALIAN SCULPTURE OF THE MIDDLE
AGES. By J. C. Robinson. Cloth, 7s. 6d.

SWISS COINS. By R. S. Poole. £2 10s.

TEXTILE FABRICS. By Rev. D. Rock. £1 11s. 6d.

WATER-COLOUR PAINTING. By S. Redgrave. £1 1s.

UNIVERSAL CATALOGUE OF WORKS OF ART. 2 vols.
Small 4to, £1 1s. each.

UNIVERSAL CATALOGUE OF WORKS OF ART. Supple-
mentary vol.

SOUTH KENSINGTON MUSEUM SCIENCE AND ART HANDBOOKS.

Published for the Committee of the Council on Education.

ART IN RUSSIA. Forming a New Volume of the South Kensington Art Handbooks. With numerous Illustrations. Crown 8vo. [*In the Press.*

FRENCH POTTERY. Forming a New Volume of the South Kensington Art Handbooks. With Illustrations. Crown 8vo. [*In the Press.*

INDUSTRIAL ARTS OF DENMARK. From the Earliest Times to the Danish Conquest of England. By J. J. A. WORSAAE, Hon. F.S.A., M.R.I.A., &c. &c. With Map and Woodcuts. Large crown 8vo, 3s. 6d.

INDUSTRIAL ARTS OF SCANDINAVIA IN THE PAGAN TIME. By HANS HILDEBRAND, Royal Antiquary of Sweden. Woodcuts. Large crown 8vo, 2s. 6d.

PRECIOUS STONES. By PROFESSOR CHURCH. With Illustrations. Large crown 8vo, 2s. 6d.

INDUSTRIAL ARTS OF INDIA. By Sir GEORGE C. M. BIRDWOOD, C.S.I. With Map and 174 Illustrations. Demy 8vo, 14s.

HANDBOOK TO THE DYCE AND FORSTER COLLECTIONS. By W. MASKELL. With Illustrations. Large crown 8vo, 2s. 6d.

INDUSTRIAL ARTS IN SPAIN. By JUAN F. RIANO. Illustrated. Large crown 8vo, 4s.

GLASS. By ALEXANDER NESBITT. Illustrated. Large crown 8vo, 2s. 6d.

GOLD AND SILVER SMITH'S WORK. By JOHN HUNGERFORD POLLEN. With numerous Woodcuts. Large crown 8vo, 2s. 6d.

TAPESTRY. By ALFRED CHAMPEAUX. With Woodcuts. 2s. 6d.

BRONZES. By C. DRURY E. FORTNUM, F.S.A. With numerous Woodcuts. Large crown 8vo, 2s. 6d.

PLAIN WORDS ABOUT WATER. By A. H. CHURCH, M.A., Oxon. Illustrated. Large crown 8vo, sewed, 6d.

ANIMAL PRODUCTS: their Preparation, Commercial Uses, and Value. By T. L. SIMMONDS. With numerous Illustrations. Large crown 8vo, 7s. 6d.

FOOD: A Short Account of the Sources, Constituents, and Uses of Food; intended chiefly as a Guide to the Food Collection in the Bethnal Green Museum. By A. H. CHURCH, M.A., Oxon. Large crown 8vo, 3s.

SCIENCE CONFERENCES. Delivered at the South Kensington Museum. 2 vols. Crown 8vo, 6s. each.
VOL. I.—Physics and Mechanics.
VOL. II.—Chemistry, Biology, Physical Geography, Geology, Mineralogy, and Meteorology.

ECONOMIC ENTOMOLOGY. By ANDREW MURRAY, F.L.S. APTERA. With numerous Illustrations. Large crown 8vo, 7s. 6d.

JAPANESE POTTERY. Being a Native Report. Edited by A. W. FRANKS. Numerous Illustrations and Marks. Large crown 8vo, 2s. 6d.

HANDBOOK TO THE SPECIAL LOAN COLLECTION of Scientific Apparatus. Large crown 8vo, 3s.

INDUSTRIAL ARTS: Historical Sketches. With 242 Illustrations. Large crown 8vo, 3s.

TEXTILE FABRICS. By the Very Rev. DANIEL ROCK, D.D. With numerous Woodcuts. Large crown 8vo, 2s. 6d.

JONES COLLECTION IN THE SOUTH KENSINGTON MUSEUM. With Portrait and Illustrations. Large crown 8vo, 2s. 6d.

SOUTH KENSINGTON MUSEUM SCIENCE & ART HANDBOOKS—*Continued.*

COLLEGE AND CORPORATION PLATE. By WILFRED CRIPPS. With numerous Illustrations. Large crown 8vo, cloth, 2s. 6d.

IVORIES: ANCIENT AND MEDIÆVAL. By WILLIAM MASKELL. With numerous Woodcuts. Large crown 8vo, 2s. 6d.

ANCIENT AND MODERN FURNITURE AND WOOD-WORK. By JOHN HUNGERFORD POLLEN. With numerous Woodcuts. Large crown 8vo, 2s. 6d.

MAIOLICA. By C. DRURY E. FORTNUM, F.S.A. With numerous Woodcuts. Large crown 8vo, 2s. 6d.

THE CHEMISTRY OF FOODS. With Microscopic Illustrations. By JAMES BELL, Principal of the Somerset House Laboratory. Part I.—Tea, Coffee, Cocoa, Sugar, &c. Large crown 8vo, 2s. 6d. Part II.—Milk, Butter, Cereals, Prepared Starches, &c. Large crown 8vo, 2s. 6d.

MUSICAL INSTRUMENTS. By CARL ENGEL. With numerous Woodcuts. Large crown 8vo, 2s. 6d.

MANUAL OF DESIGN, compiled from the Writings and Addresses of RICHARD REDGRAVE, R.A. By GILBERT R. REDGRAVE. With Woodcuts. Large crown 8vo, 2s. 6d.

PERSIAN ART. By MAJOR R. MURDOCK SMITH, R.E. Second Edition, with additional Illustrations. Large crown 8vo, 2s.

FREE EVENING LECTURES. Delivered in connection with the Special Loan Collection of Scientific Apparatus, 1876. Large crown 8vo, 8s.

CARLYLE'S (THOMAS) WORKS.
CHEAP AND UNIFORM EDITION.
In 23 vols., Crown 8vo, cloth, £7 5s.

THE FRENCH REVOLUTION: A History. 2 vols., 12s.

OLIVER CROMWELL'S LETTERS AND SPEECHES, with Elucidations, &c. 3 vols., 18s.

LIVES OF SCHILLER AND JOHN STERLING. 1 vol., 6s.

CRITICAL AND MISCELLANEOUS ESSAYS. 4 vols., £1 4s.

SARTOR RESARTUS AND LECTURES ON HEROES. 1 vol., 6s.

LATTER-DAY PAMPHLETS. 1 vol., 6s.

CHARTISM AND PAST AND PRESENT. 1 vol., 6s.

TRANSLATIONS FROM THE GERMAN OF MUSÆUS, TIECK, AND RICHTER. 1 vol., 6s.

WILHELM MEISTER, by Göthe. A Translation. 2 vols., 12s.

HISTORY OF FRIEDRICH THE SECOND, called Frederick the Great. 7 vols., £2 9s.

LIBRARY EDITION COMPLETE.
Handsomely printed in 34 vols., demy 8vo, cloth, £15:

SARTOR RESARTUS. The Life and Opinions of Herr Teufelsdröckh. With a Portrait, 7s. 6d.

THE FRENCH REVOLUTION. A History. 3 vols., each 9s.

CARLYLE'S (THOMAS) WORKS—*Continued.*

LIFE OF FREDERICK SCHILLER AND EXAMINATION OF HIS WORKS. With Supplement of 1872. Portrait and Plates, 9s.

CRITICAL AND MISCELLANEOUS ESSAYS. With Portrait. 6 vols., each 9s.

ON HEROES, HERO WORSHIP, AND THE HEROIC IN HISTORY. 7s. 6d.

PAST AND PRESENT. 9s.

OLIVER CROMWELL'S LETTERS AND SPEECHES. With Portraits. 5 vols., each 9s.

LATTER-DAY PAMPHLETS. 9s.

LIFE OF JOHN STERLING. With Portrait, 9s.

HISTORY OF FREDERICK THE SECOND. 10 vols., each 9s.

TRANSLATIONS FROM THE GERMAN. 3 vols., each 9s.

EARLY KINGS OF NORWAY; ESSAY ON THE POR-TRAITS OF JOHN KNOX; AND GENERAL INDEX. With Portrait Illustrations. 8vo, cloth, 9s.

EARLY KINGS OF NORWAY: also AN ESSAY ON THE PORTRAITS OF JOHN KNOX. Crown 8vo, with Portrait Illustrations, 7s. 6d.

PEOPLE'S EDITION.

In 37 vols., small Crown 8vo. Price 2s. each vol., bound in cloth ; or in sets of 37 vols. in 19, cloth gilt, for £3 14s.

SARTOR RESARTUS.

FRENCH REVOLUTION. 3 vols.

LIFE OF JOHN STERLING.

OLIVER CROMWELL'S LET-TERS AND SPEECHES. 5 vols.

ON HEROES AND HERO WORSHIP.

PAST AND PRESENT.

CRITICAL AND MISCELLA-NEOUS ESSAYS. 7 vols.

LATTER-DAY PAMPHLETS.

LIFE OF SCHILLER.

FREDERICK THE GREAT. 10 vols.

WILHELM MEISTER. 3 vols.

TRANSLATIONS FROM MU-SÆUS, TIECK, AND RICHTER. 2 vols.

THE EARLY KINGS OF NOR-WAY ; Essay on the Portraits of Knox ; and General Index.

SIXPENNY EDITION.

4to, sewed.

SARTOR RESARTUS. Eightieth Thousand.

HEROES AND HERO WORSHIP.

ESSAYS: BURNS, JOHNSON, SCOTT, THE DIAMOND NECKLACE.

The above are also to be had in 1 vol., 2s. 6d.

B 2

DICKENS'S (CHARLES) WORKS.

ORIGINAL EDITIONS.

In Demy 8vo.

THE MYSTERY OF EDWIN DROOD. With Illustrations by S. L. Fildes, and a Portrait engraved by Baker. Cloth, 7s. 6d.

OUR MUTUAL FRIEND. With Forty Illustrations by Marcus Stone. Cloth, £1 1s.

THE PICKWICK PAPERS. With Forty-three Illustrations by Seymour and Phiz. Cloth, £1 1s.

NICHOLAS NICKLEBY. With Forty Illustrations by Phiz. Cloth, £1 1s.

SKETCHES BY "BOZ." With Forty Illustrations by George Cruikshank. Cloth, £1 1s.

MARTIN CHUZZLEWIT. With Forty Illustrations by Phiz. Cloth, £1 1s.

DOMBEY AND SON. With Forty Illustrations by Phiz. Cloth, £1 1s.

DAVID COPPERFIELD. With Forty Illustrations by Phiz. Cloth, £1 1s.

BLEAK HOUSE. With Forty Illustrations by Phiz. Cloth, £1 1s.

LITTLE DORRIT. With Forty Illustrations by Phiz. Cloth, £1 1s.

THE OLD CURIOSITY SHOP. With Seventy-five Illustrations by George Cattermole and H. K. Browne. A New Edition. Uniform with the other volumes, £1 1s.

BARNABY RUDGE: a Tale of the Riots of 'Eighty. With Seventy-eight Illustrations by George Cattermole and H. K. Browne. Uniform with the other volumes, £1 1s.

CHRISTMAS BOOKS: Containing—The Christmas Carol; The Cricket on the Hearth; The Chimes; The Battle of Life; The Haunted House. With all the original Illustrations. Cloth, 12s.

OLIVER TWIST and TALE OF TWO CITIES. In one volume. Cloth, £1 1s.

OLIVER TWIST. Separately. With Twenty-four Illustrations by George Cruikshank. Cloth, 11s.

A TALE OF TWO CITIES. Separately. With Sixteen Illustrations by Phiz. Cloth, 9s.

**** *The remainder of Dickens's Works were not originally printed in Demy 8vo.*

DICKENS'S (CHARLES) WORKS—*Continued.*

LIBRARY EDITION.

In Post 8vo. With the Original Illustrations, 30 vols., cloth, £12.

			s.	d.
PICKWICK PAPERS	43 Illustrns., 2 vols.		16	0
NICHOLAS NICKLEBY	39 ,, 2 vols.		16	0
MARTIN CHUZZLEWIT	40 ,, 2 vols.		16	0
OLD CURIOSITY SHOP & REPRINTED PIECES	36 ,, 2 vols.		16	0
BARNABY RUDGE and HARD TIMES	36 ,, 2 vols.		16	0
BLEAK HOUSE	40 ,, 2 vols.		16	0
LITTLE DORRIT	40 ,, 2 vols.		16	0
DOMBEY AND SON	38 ,, 2 vols.		16	0
DAVID COPPERFIELD	38 ,, 2 vols.		16	0
OUR MUTUAL FRIEND	40 ,, 2 vols.		16	0
SKETCHES BY "BOZ"	39 ,, 1 vol.		8	0
OLIVER TWIST	24 ,, 1 vol.		8	0
CHRISTMAS BOOKS	17 ,, 1 vol.		8	0
A TALE OF TWO CITIES	16 ,, 1 vol.		8	0
GREAT EXPECTATIONS	8 ,, 1 vol.		8	0
PICTURES FROM ITALY & AMERICAN NOTES	8 ,, 1 vol.		8	0
UNCOMMERCIAL TRAVELLER	8 ,, 1 vol.		8	0
CHILD'S HISTORY OF ENGLAND	8 ,, 1 vol.		8	0
EDWIN DROOD and MISCELLANIES	12 ,, 1 vol.		8	0
CHRISTMAS STORIES from "Household Words," &c.	14 ,, 1 vol.		8	0

THE LIFE OF CHARLES DICKENS. By JOHN FORSTER. With Illustrations.
Uniform with this Edition. 1 vol. 10s. 6d.

THE "CHARLES DICKENS" EDITION.

In Crown 8vo. In 21 vols., cloth, with Illustrations, £3 16s.

		s.	d.
PICKWICK PAPERS	8 Illustrations	4	0
MARTIN CHUZZLEWIT	8 ,,	4	0
DOMBEY AND SON	8 ,,	4	0
NICHOLAS NICKLEBY	8 ,,	4	0
DAVID COPPERFIELD	8 ,,	4	0
BLEAK HOUSE	8 ,,	4	0
LITTLE DORRIT	8 ,,	4	0
OUR MUTUAL FRIEND	8 ,,	4	0
BARNABY RUDGE	8 ,,	3	6
OLD CURIOSITY SHOP	8 ,,	3	6
A CHILD'S HISTORY OF ENGLAND	4 ,,	3	6
EDWIN DROOD and OTHER STORIES	8 ,,	3	6
CHRISTMAS STORIES, from "Household Words"	8 ,,	3	6
SKETCHES BY "BOZ"	8 ,,	3	6
AMERICAN NOTES and REPRINTED PIECES	8 ,,	3	6
CHRISTMAS BOOKS	8 ,,	3	6
OLIVER TWIST	8 ,,	3	6
GREAT EXPECTATIONS	8 ,,	3	6
TALE OF TWO CITIES	8 ,,	3	0
HARD TIMES and PICTURES FROM ITALY	8 ,,	3	0
UNCOMMERCIAL TRAVELLER	4 ,,	3	0
THE LIFE OF CHARLES DICKENS. Numerous Illustrations.	2 vols.	7	0
THE LETTERS OF CHARLES DICKENS	2 vols.	8	0

DICKENS'S (CHARLES) WORKS—*Continued.*

THE ILLUSTRATED LIBRARY EDITION.

Complete in 30 Volumes.　Demy 8vo, 10s. each; or set, £15.

This Edition is printed on a finer paper and in a larger type than has been employed in any previous edition. The type has been cast especially for it, and the page is of a size to admit of the introduction of all the original illustrations.

No such attractive issue has been made of the writings of Mr. Dickens, which, various as have been the forms of publication adapted to the demands of an ever widely-increasing popularity, have never yet been worthily presented in a really handsome library form.

The collection comprises all the minor writings it was Mr. Dickens's wish to preserve.

SKETCHES BY "BOZ." With 40 Illustrations by George Cruikshank.

PICKWICK PAPERS. 2 vols. With 42 Illustrations by Phiz.

OLIVER TWIST. With 24 Illustrations by Cruikshank.

NICHOLAS NICKLEBY. 2 vols. With 40 Illustrations by Phiz.

OLD CURIOSITY SHOP and REPRINTED PIECES. 2 vols. With Illustrations by Cattermole, &c.

BARNABY RUDGE and HARD TIMES. 2 vols. With Illustrations by Cattermole, &c.

MARTIN CHUZZLEWIT. 2 vols. With 4 Illustrations by Phiz.

AMERICAN NOTES and PICTURES FROM ITALY. 1 vol. With 8 Illustrations.

DOMBEY AND SON. 2 vols. With 40 Illustrations by Phiz.

DAVID COPPERFIELD. 2 vols. With 40 Illustrations by Phiz.

BLEAK HOUSE. 2 vols. With 40 Illustrations by Phiz.

LITTLE DORRIT. 2 vols. With 40 Illustrations by Phiz.

A TALE OF TWO CITIES. With 16 Illustrations by Phiz.

THE UNCOMMERCIAL TRAVELLER. With 8 Illustrations by Marcus Stone.

GREAT EXPECTATIONS. With 8 Illustrations by Marcus Stone.

OUR MUTUAL FRIEND. 2 vols. With 40 Illustrations by Marcus Stone.

CHRISTMAS BOOKS. With 17 Illustrations by Sir Edwin Landseer, R.A., Maclise, R.A., &c. &c.

HISTORY OF ENGLAND. With 8 Illustrations by Marcus Stone.

CHRISTMAS STORIES. (From "Household Words" and "All the Year Round.") With 14 Illustrations.

EDWIN DROOD AND OTHER STORIES. With 12 Illustrations by S. L. Fildes.

DICKENS'S (CHARLES) WORKS—*Continued.*

HOUSEHOLD EDITION.

Complete in 22 Volumes.　Crown 4to, cloth, £4 8s. 6d.

MARTIN CHUZZLEWIT, with 59 Illustrations, cloth, 5s.
DAVID COPPERFIELD, with 60 Illustrations and a Portrait, cloth, 5s.
BLEAK HOUSE, with 61 Illustrations, cloth, 5s.
LITTLE DORRIT, with 58 Illustrations, cloth, 5s.
PICKWICK PAPERS, with 56 Illustrations, cloth, 5s.
OUR MUTUAL FRIEND, with 58 Illustrations, cloth, 5s.
NICHOLAS NICKLEBY, with 59 Illustrations, cloth, 5s.
DOMBEY AND SON, with 61 Illustrations, cloth, 5s.
EDWIN DROOD; REPRINTED PIECES; and other Stories, with 30 Illustrations, cloth, 5s.
THE LIFE OF DICKENS. By JOHN FORSTER. With 40 Illustrations. Cloth, 5s.
BARNABY RUDGE, with 46 Illustrations, cloth, 4s.
OLD CURIOSITY SHOP, with 32 Illustrations, cloth, 4s.
CHRISTMAS STORIES, with 23 Illustrations, cloth, 4s.
OLIVER TWIST, with 28 Illustrations, cloth, 3s.
GREAT EXPECTATIONS, with 26 Illustrations, cloth, 3s.
SKETCHES BY "BOZ," with 36 Illustrations, cloth, 3s.
UNCOMMERCIAL TRAVELLER, with 26 Illustrations, cloth, 3s.
CHRISTMAS BOOKS, with 28 Illustrations, cloth, 3s.
THE HISTORY OF ENGLAND, with 15 Illustrations, cloth, 3s.
AMERICAN NOTES and PICTURES FROM ITALY, with 18 Illustrations, cloth, 3s.
A TALE OF TWO CITIES, with 25 Illustrations, cloth, 3s.
HARD TIMES, with 20 Illustrations, cloth, 2s. 6d.

MR. DICKENS'S READINGS.

Fcap. 8vo, sewed.

CHRISTMAS CAROL IN PROSE. 1s.

CRICKET ON THE HEARTH. 1s.

CHIMES: A GOBLIN STORY. 1s.

STORY OF LITTLE DOMBEY. 1s.

POOR TRAVELLER, BOOTS AT THE HOLLY-TREE INN, and MRS. GAMP. 1s.

A CHRISTMAS CAROL, with the Original Coloured Plates, being a reprint of the Original Edition. Small 8vo, red cloth, gilt edges, 5s.

DICKENS'S (CHARLES) WORKS—*Continued.*

THE POPULAR LIBRARY EDITION
OF THE WORKS OF
CHARLES DICKENS,

In 30 Vols., large crown 8vo, price £6; separate Vols. 4s. each.

An Edition printed on good paper, containing Illustrations selected from the Household Edition, on Plate Paper. Each Volume has about 450 pages and 16 full-page Illustrations.

SKETCHES BY "BOZ."	OLD CURIOSITY SHOP AND REPRINTED PIECES. 2 vols.
PICKWICK. 2 vols.	BARNABY RUDGE. 2 vols.
OLIVER TWIST.	UNCOMMERCIAL TRAVELLER.
NICHOLAS NICKLEBY. 2 vols.	GREAT EXPECTATIONS.
MARTIN CHUZZLEWIT. 2 vols.	TALE OF TWO CITIES.
DOMBEY AND SON. 2 vols.	CHILD'S HISTORY OF ENGLAND.
DAVID COPPERFIELD. 2 vols.	EDWIN DROOD AND MISCELLANIES.
CHRISTMAS BOOKS.	PICTURES FROM ITALY AND AMERICAN NOTES.
OUR MUTUAL FRIEND. 2 vols.	
CHRISTMAS STORIES.	
BLEAK HOUSE. 2 vols.	
LITTLE DORRIT. 2 vols.	

The Cheapest and Handiest Edition of

THE WORKS OF CHARLES DICKENS.

The Pocket-Volume Edition of Charles Dickens's Works.
In 30 Vols. small fcap. 8vo, £2 5s.

New and Cheap Issue of

THE WORKS OF CHARLES DICKENS.

In pocket volumes.

PICKWICK PAPERS, with 8 Illustrations, cloth, 2s.
NICHOLAS NICKLEBY, with 8 Illustrations, cloth, 2s.
OLIVER TWIST, with 8 Illustrations, cloth, 1s.
SKETCHES BY "BOZ," with 8 Illustrations, cloth, 1s.
OLD CURIOSITY SHOP, with 8 Illustrations, cloth, 2s.
BARNABY RUDGE, with 16 Illustrations, cloth, 2s.
AMERICAN NOTES AND PICTURES FROM ITALY, with 8 Illustrations, cloth, 1s.6d.
CHRISTMAS BOOKS, with 8 Illustrations, cloth, 1s. 6d.

SIXPENNY REPRINTS.

(I.)

A CHRISTMAS CAROL AND THE HAUNTED MAN.

By CHARLES DICKENS. Illustrated.

(II.)

READINGS FROM THE WORKS OF CHARLES DICKENS.

As selected and read by himself and now published for the first time. Illustrated.

(III.)

THE CHIMES: A GOBLIN STORY, AND THE CRICKET ON THE HEARTH.

Illustrated.

List of Books, Drawing Examples, Diagrams, Models, Instruments, etc.,

INCLUDING

THOSE ISSUED UNDER THE AUTHORITY OF THE SCIENCE AND ART DEPARTMENT, SOUTH KENSINGTON, FOR THE USE OF SCHOOLS AND ART AND SCIENCE CLASSES.

CATALOGUE OF MODERN WORKS ON SCIENCE AND TECHNOLOGY. 8vo, sewed, 1s.

BENSON (W.)—

PRINCIPLES OF THE SCIENCE OF COLOUR. Small 4to, cloth, 15s.

MANUAL OF THE SCIENCE OF COLOUR. Coloured Frontispiece and Illustrations. 12mo, cloth, 2s. 6d.

BRADLEY (THOMAS), of the Royal Military Academy, Woolwich—

ELEMENTS OF GEOMETRICAL DRAWING. In Two Parts, with 60 Plates. Oblong folio, half-bound, each part 16s.
Selections (from the above) of 20 Plates, for the use of the Royal Military Academy, Woolwich. Oblong folio, half-bound, 16s.

BURCHETT—

LINEAR PERSPECTIVE. With Illustrations. Post 8vo, 7s.

PRACTICAL GEOMETRY. Post 8vo, 5s.

DEFINITIONS OF GEOMETRY. Third Edition. 24mo, sewed, 5d.

CARROLL (JOHN)—

FREEHAND DRAWING LESSONS FOR THE BLACK BOARD. 6s.

CUBLEY (W. H.)—

A SYSTEM OF ELEMENTARY DRAWING. With Illustrations and Examples. Imperial 4to, sewed, 8s.

DAVISON (ELLIS A.)—

DRAWING FOR ELEMENTARY SCHOOLS. Post 8vo, 3s.

MODEL DRAWING. 12mo, 3s.

THE AMATEUR HOUSE CARPENTER: A Guide in Building, Making, and Repairing. With numerous Illustrations, drawn on Wood by the Author. Demy 8vo, 10s. 6d.

DELAMOTTE (P. H.)—
PROGRESSIVE DRAWING-BOOK FOR BEGINNERS.
12mo, 3s. 6d.

DYCE—
DRAWING-BOOK OF THE GOVERNMENT SCHOOL
OF DESIGN : ELEMENTARY OUTLINES OF ORNAMENT. 50 Plates.
Small folio, sewed, 5s. : mounted, 18s.

INTRODUCTION TO DITTO. Fcap. 8vo, 6d.

FOSTER (VERE)—
DRAWING-BOOKS :
(*a*) Forty-two Numbers, at 1d. each.
(*b*) Forty-six Numbers, at d. each. The set *b* includes the subjects in *a*.
DRAWING-CARDS :
Freehand Drawing : First Grade, Sets I., II., III., price 1s. each.
Second Grade, Set I., price 2s.

HENSLOW (PROFESSOR)—
ILLUSTRATIONS TO BE EMPLOYED IN THE
PRACTICAL LESSONS ON BOTANY. Prepared for South Kensington
Museum. Post 8vo, sewed, 6d.

JACOBSTHAL (E.)—
GRAMMATIK DER ORNAMENTE, in 7 Parts of 20
Plates each. Price, unmounted, £3 13s. 6d. ; mounted on cardboard, £11 4s.
The Parts can be had separately.

JEWITT—
HANDBOOK OF PRACTICAL PERSPECTIVE. 18mo,
cloth, 1s. 6d.

KENNEDY (JOHN)—
FIRST GRADE PRACTICAL GEOMETRY. 12mo, 6d.
FREEHAND DRAWING-BOOK. 16mo, 1s.

LINDLEY (JOHN)—
SYMMETRY OF VEGETATION : Principles to be
Observed in the Delineation of Plants. 12mo, sewed, 1s.

MARSHALL—
HUMAN BODY. Text and Plates reduced from the large
Diagrams. 2 vols., £1 1s.

NEWTON (E. TULLEY), F.G.S.—
THE TYPICAL PARTS IN THE SKELETONS OF A
CAT, DUCK, AND CODFISH, being a Catalogue with Comparative De-
scriptions arranged in a Tabular Form. Demy 8vo, 3s.

OLIVER (PROFESSOR)—
ILLUSTRATIONS OF THE VEGETABLE KINGDOM.
109 Plates. Oblong 8vo, cloth. Plain, 16s.; coloured, £1 6s.

POYNTER (E. J.), R.A., issued under the superintendence of—
ELEMENTARY, FREEHAND, ORNAMENT :
Book I. Simple Geometrical Forms, 6d.
  „   II. Conventionalised Floral Forms, &c., 6d.

POYNTER (E. J.), R.A.—Continued.

FREEHAND—FIRST GRADE:

Book I. Simple Objects and Ornament, 6d.
  „   II. Various Objects, 6d.
  „   III. Objects and Architectural Ornaments, 6d.
  „   IV. Architectural Ornament, 6d.
  „   V. Objects of Glass and Pottery, 6d.
  „   VI. Common Objects, 6d.

FREEHAND—SECOND GRADE:

Book I. Various Forms of Anthermion, &c., 1s.
  „   II. Greek, Roman, and Venetian, 1s.
  „   III. Italian Renaissance, 1s.
  „   IV. Roman, Italian, Japanese, &c. 1s.

THE SOUTH KENSINGTON DRAWING CARDS,

Containing the same examples as the books :
Elementary Freehand Cards. Four packets, 9d. each.
First Grade Freehand Cards. Six packets, 1s. each.
Second Grade Freehand Cards. Four packets, 1s. 6d. each

REDGRAVE—

MANUAL AND CATECHISM ON COLOUR. Fifth

Edition. 24mo, sewed, 9d.

ROBSON (GEORGE)—

ELEMENTARY BUILDING CONSTRUCTION. Oblong

folio, sewed, 8s.

WALLIS (GEORGE)—

DRAWING-BOOK. Oblong, sewed, 3s. 6d.; mounted, 8s.

WORNUM (R. N.)—

THE CHARACTERISTICS OF STYLES: An Intro-

duction to the Study of the History of Ornamental Art. Royal 8vo, 8s.

DRAWING FOR YOUNG CHILDREN. Containing 150

Copies. 16mo, cloth, 3s. 6d.

EDUCATIONAL DIVISION OF SOUTH KENSINGTON

MUSEUM: CLASSIFIED CATALOGUE OF. Ninth Edition. 8vo, 7s.

ELEMENTARY DRAWING COPY-BOOKS, for the Use of

Children from four years old and upwards, in Schools and Families. Compiled by a Student certificated by the Science and Art Department as an Art Teacher. Seven Books in 4to, sewed :

Book I. Letters, 8d.	Book IV. Objects, 8d.	
„ II. Ditto, 8d.	„ V. Leaves, 8d.	
„ III. Geometrical and Ornamental	„ VI. Birds, Animals, &c., 8d.	
Forms, 8d.	„ VII. Leaves, Flowers, and Sprays, 8d.	

**** Or in Sets of Seven Books, 4s. 6d.

ENGINEER AND MACHINIST DRAWING-BOOK, 16 Parts,

71 Plates. Folio, £1 12s. ; mounted, £3 4s.

PRINCIPLES OF DECORATIVE ART. Folio, sewed, 1s.

DIAGRAM OF THE COLOURS OF THE SPECTRUM,

with Explanatory Letterpress, on roller, 10s. 6d.

COPIES FOR OUTLINE DRAWING:

DYCE'S ELEMENTARY OUTLINES OF ORNAMENT, 50 Selected Plates, mounted back and front, 18s.; unmounted, sewed, 5s.

WEITBRICHT'S OUTLINES OF ORNAMENT, reproduced by Herman, 12 Plates, mounted back and front, 8s. 6d.; unmounted, 2s.

MORGHEN'S OUTLINES OF THE HUMAN FIGURE, reproduced by Herman, 20 Plates, mounted back and front, 15s.; unmounted, 3s. 4d.

OUTLINES OF TARSIA, from Gruner, Four Plates, mounted, 3s. 6d., unmounted, 7d.

ALBERTOLLI'S FOLIAGE, Four Plates, mounted, 3s. 6d.; unmounted, 5d.

OUTLINE OF TRAJAN FRIEZE, mounted, 1s.

WALLIS'S DRAWING-BOOK, mounted, 8s., unmounted, 3s. 6d.

OUTLINE DRAWINGS OF FLOWERS, Eight Plates, mounted, 3s. 6d.; unmounted, 8d.

COPIES FOR SHADED DRAWING:

COURSE OF DESIGN. By CH. BARGUE (French), 20 Selected Sheets, 11 at 2s. and 9 at 3s. each. £2 9s.

ARCHITECTURAL STUDIES. By J. B. TRIPON. 10 Plates, £1.

MECHANICAL STUDIES. By J. B. TRIPON. 15s. per dozen.

FOLIATED SCROLL FROM THE VATICAN, unmounted, 5d.; mounted, 1s. 3d.

TWELVE HEADS after Holbein, selected from his Drawings in Her Majesty's Collection at Windsor. Reproduced in Autotype. Half imperial, £1 16s.

LESSONS IN SEPIA, 9s. per dozen, or 1s. each.

COLOURED EXAMPLES:

A SMALL DIAGRAM OF COLOUR, mounted, 1s. 6d.; unmounted, 9d.

CAMELLIA, mounted, 3s. 9d.

COTMAN'S PENCIL LANDSCAPES (set of 9), mounted, 15s.

     ,,   SEPIA DRAWINGS (set of 5), mounted, £1.

ALLONGE'S LANDSCAPES IN CHARCOAL (Six), at 4s. each, or the set, £1 4s.

SOLID MODELS, &c.:

*Box of Models, £1 4s.

A Stand with a universal joint, to show the solid models, &c., £1 18s.

*One Wire Quadrangle, with a circle and cross within it, and one straight wire. One solid cube. One Skeleton Wire Cube. One Sphere. One Cone. One Cylinder. One Hexagonal Prism. £2 2s.

Skeleton Cube in wood, 3s. 6d.

18-inch Skeleton Cube in wood, 12s.

*Three objects of *form* in Pottery:
Indian Jar,
Celadon Jar, } 18s. 6d.
Bottle,

*Five selected Vases in Majolica Ware, £2 11s.

*Three selected Vases in Earthenware, 18s.

Imperial Deal Frames, glazed, without sunk rings, 10s. each.

*Davidson's Smaller Solid Models, in Box, £2, containing—

2 Square Slabs.	Octagon Prism.	Triangular Prism
9 Oblong Blocks (steps).	Cylinder.	Pyramid, Equilateral.
2 Cubes.	Cone.	Pyramid, Isosceles.
Square Blocks.	Jointed Cross.	Square Block.

* Models, &c., entered as sets, can only be supplied in sets.

SOLID MODELS, &c.—*Continued.*

* Davidson's Advanced Drawing Models, £9.—The following is a brief description of the Models:—An Obelisk—composed of 2 Octagonal Slabs, 26 and 20 inches across, and each 3 inches high; 1 Cube, 12 inches edge; 1 Monolith (forming the body of the obelisk) 3 feet high; 1 Pyramid, 6 inches base; the complete object is thus nearly 5 feet high. A Market Cross—composed of 3 Slabs, 24, 18, and 12 inches across, and each 3 inches high; 1 Upright, 3 feet high; 2 Cross Arms, united by mortise and tenon joints; complete height, 3 feet 9 inches. A Step-Ladder, 23 inches high. A Kitchen Table, 14½ inches high. A Chair to correspond. A Four-legged Stool, with projecting top and cross rails, height 14 inches. A Tub, with handles and projecting hoops, and the divisions between the staves plainly marked. A strong Trestle, 18 inches high. A Hollow Cylinder, 9 inches in diameter, and 12 inches long, divided lengthwise. A Hollow Sphere, 9 inches in diameter, divided into semi-spheres, one of which is again divided into quarters; the semi-sphere, when placed on the cylinder, gives the form and principles of shading a dome, whilst one of the quarters placed on half the cylinder forms a niche.

*Davidson's Apparatus for Teaching Practical Geometry (22 models), £5.

*Binn's Models for Illustrating the Elementary Principles of Orthographic Projection as applied to Mechanical Drawing, in box, £1 10s.

Miller's Class Drawing Models.—These Models are particularly adapted for teaching large classes; the stand is very strong, and the universal joint will hold the Models in any position. *Wood Models*: Square Prism, 12 inches side, 18 inches high; Hexagonal Prism, 14 inches side, 18 inches high; Cube, 14 inches side: Cylinder, 13 inches diameter, 16 inches high; Hexagon Pyramid, 14 inches diameter, 22½ inches side; Square Pyramid, 14 inches side, 22½ inches side; Cone, 13 inches diameter, 22½ inches side; Skeleton Cube, 19 inches solid wood 1¾ inch square; Intersecting Circles, 19 inches solid wood 2¼ by 1½ inches. *Wire Models*: Triangular Prism, 17 inches side, 22 inches high; Square Prism, 14 inches side, 20 inches high; Hexagonal Prism, 16 inches diameter, 21 inches high; Cylinder, 14 inches diameter, 21 inches high; Hexagon Pyramid, 18 inches diameter, 24 inches high; Square Pyramid, 17 inches side, 24 inches high; Cone, 17 inches side, 24 inches high; Skeleton Cube, 19 inches side; Intersecting Circles 19 inches side; Plain Circle, 19 inches side; Plain Square, 19 inches side. Table, 27 inches by 21½ inches. Stand. The set complete, £14 13s.

Vulcanite Set Square, 5s.

Large Compasses, with chalk-holder, 5s.

*Slip, two set squares and **T** square, 5s.

*Parkes's Case of Instruments, containing 6-inch compasses with pen and pencil leg, 5s.

*Prize Instrument Case, with 6-inch compasses pen and pencil leg, 2 small compasses, pen and scale, 18s.

6-inch Compasses, with shifting pen and point, 4s. 6d.

LARGE DIAGRAMS.

ASTRONOMICAL:

TWELVE SHEETS. By JOHN DREW, Ph. Dr., F.R.S.A. Prepared for the Committee of Council on Education. Sheets, £2 8s.; on rollers and varnished, £4 4s.

BOTANICAL:

NINE SHEETS. Illustrating a Practical Method of Teaching Botany. By Professor HENSLOW, F.L.S. £2; on rollers and varnished, £3 3s.

CLASS.	DIVISION.	SECTION.	DIAGRAM.
		Thalamifloral ..	.. 1
	Angiospermous ..	Calycifloral ..	.. 2 & 3
Dicotyledon		Corollifloral ..	.. 4
		Incomplete ..	.. 5
	Gymnospermous ..	.. .. ..	.. 6
	Petaloid	Superior ..	.. 7
Monocotyledons ..		Inferior	.. 8
	Glumaceous ..	.. .. ..	.. 9

* Models, &c., entered as sets, can only be supplied in sets.

BUILDING CONSTRUCTION:

TEN SHEETS. By WILLIAM J. GLENNY, Professor of Drawing, King's College. In sets, £1 1s.

LAXTON'S EXAMPLES OF BUILDING CONSTRUCTION IN TWO DIVISIONS, containing 32 Imperial Plates, £1.

BUSBRIDGE'S DRAWINGS OF BUILDING CONSTRUCTION. 11 Sheets. 2s. 9d. Mounted, 5s. 6d.

GEOLOGICAL:

DIAGRAM OF BRITISH STRATA. By H. W. BRISTOW, F.R.S., F.G.S. A Sheet, 4s.; on roller and varnished, 7s. 6d.

MECHANICAL:

DIAGRAMS OF THE MECHANICAL POWERS, AND THEIR APPLICATIONS IN MACHINERY AND THE ARTS GENERALLY. By Dr. JOHN ANDERSON.

8 Diagrams, highly coloured on stout paper, 3 feet 6 inches by 2 feet 6 inches. Sheets £1 per set ; mounted on rollers, £2.

DIAGRAMS OF THE STEAM-ENGINE. By Professor GOODEVE and Professor SHELLEY. Stout paper, 40 inches by 27 inches, highly coloured.

Sets of 41 Diagrams (52½ Sheets), £6 6s. ; varnished and mounted on rollers, £11 11s.

MACHINE DETAILS. By Professor UNWIN. 16 Coloured Diagrams. Sheets, £2 2s.; mounted on rollers and varnished, £3 14s.

SELECTED EXAMPLES OF MACHINES, OF IRON AND WOOD (French). By STANISLAS PETTIT. 60 Sheets, £3 5s.; 13s. per dozen.

BUSBRIDGE'S DRAWINGS OF MACHINE CONSTRUCTION. 50 Sheets, 12s. 6d. Mounted, £1 5s.

PHYSIOLOGICAL:

ELEVEN SHEETS. Illustrating Human Physiology, Life Size and Coloured from Nature. Prepared under the direction of JOHN MARSHALL, F.R.S., F.R.C.S., &c. Each Sheet, 12s. 6d. On canvas and rollers, varnished, £1 1s.

1. THE SKELETON AND LIGAMENTS.
2. THE MUSCLES, JOINTS, AND ANIMAL MECHANICS.
3. THE VISCERA IN POSITION.—THE STRUCTURE OF THE LUNGS.
4. THE ORGANS OF CIRCULATION.
5. THE LYMPHATICS OR ABSORBENTS.
6. THE ORGANS OF DIGESTION.
7. THE BRAIN AND NERVES.—THE ORGANS OF THE VOICE.
8. THE ORGANS OF THE SENSES.
9. THE ORGANS OF THE SENSES.
10. THE MICROSCOPIC STRUCTURE OF THE TEXTURES AND ORGANS.
11. THE MICROSCOPIC STRUCTURE OF THE TEXTURES AND ORGANS.

HUMAN BODY, LIFE SIZE. By JOHN MARSHALL, F.R.S., F.R.C.S. Each Sheet, 12s. 6d.; on canvas and rollers, varnished, £1 1s. Explanatory Key, 1s.

1. THE SKELETON, Front View.
2. THE MUSCLES, Front View.
3. THE SKELETON, Back View.
4. THE MUSCLES, Back View
5. THE SKELETON, Side View.
6. THE MUSCLES, Side View.
7. THE FEMALE SKELETON, Front View.

ZOOLOGICAL:

TEN SHEETS. Illustrating the Classification of Animals. By ROBERT PATTERSON. £2 ; on canvas and rollers, varnished, £3 10s. The same, reduced in size on Royal paper, in 9 Sheets, uncoloured, 12s.

PHYSIOLOGY AND ANATOMY OF THE HONEY BEE.

Two Diagrams. 7s. 6d.

A History of Art in Chaldæa & Assyria.

By GEORGES PERROT and CHARLES CHIPIEZ.

Translated by WALTER ARMSTRONG, B.A., Oxon.   With 452 Illustrations.
2 vols. royal 8vo, £2 2s.

"It is profusely illustrated, not merely with representations of the actual remains preserved in the British Museum, the Louvre, and elsewhere, but also with ingenious conjectural representations of the principal buildings from which those remains have been taken. To Englishmen familiar with the magnificent collection of Assyrian antiquities preserved in the British Museum the volume should be especially welcome. We may further mention that an English translation by Mr. Walter Armstrong, with the numerous illustrations of the original, has just been published by Messrs. Chapman and Hall."—*Times*.

"The only dissatisfaction that we can feel in turning over the two beautiful volumes in illustration of Chaldæan and Assyrian Art, by MM. Perrot and Chipiez, is in the reflection, that in this, as in so many other publications of a similar scope and nature, it is a foreign name that we see on the title page, and a translation only which we can lay to our national credit. The predominance of really important works on Archæology which have to be translated for the larger reading public of England, and the comparative scarcity of original English works of a similar calibre, is a reproach to us which we would fain see removed . . . it is most frequently to French and German writers that we are indebted for the best light and the most interesting criticisms on the arts of antiquity. Mr. Armstrong s translation is very well done. '—*Builder*.

"The work is a valuable addition to archæological literature, and the thanks of the whole civilised world are due to the authors who have so carefully compiled the history of the arts of two peoples, often forgotten, but who were in reality the founders of Western civilisation."—*Graphic*.

History of Ancient Egyptian Art.

By GEORGES PERROT and CHARLES CHIPIEZ.

Translated from the French by W. ARMSTRONG. Containing 616 Engravings, drawn after the Original, or from Authentic Documents. 2 vols. imperial 8vo, £2 2s.

"The study of Egyptology is one which grows from day to day, and which has now reached such proportions as to demand arrangement and selection almost more than increased collection of material. The well-known volumes of MM. Perrot and Chipiez supply this requirement to an extent which had never hitherto been attempted, and which, before the latest researches of Mariette and Maspero, would have been impossible. Without waiting for the illustrious authors to complete their great undertaking, Mr. W. Armstrong has very properly seized their first instalment, and has presented to the English public all that has yet appeared of a most useful and fascinating work. To translate such a book, however, is a task that needs the revision of a specialist, and this Mr. Armstrong has felt, for he has not sent out his version to the world without the sanction of Dr. Birch and Mr. Reginald Stuart Poole. The result is in every way satisfactory to his readers. Mr. Armstrong adds, in an appendix, a description of that startling discovery which occurred just after the French original of these volumes left the press—namely, the finding of 38 royal mummies, with their sepulchral furniture, in a subterranean chamber at Thebes. It forms a brilliant ending to a work of great value and beauty."—*Pall Mall Gazette*.

The *Saturday Review*, speaking of the French edition, says : "To say that this magnificent work is the best history of Egyptian art that we possess, is to state one of the least of its titles to the admiration of all lovers of antiquity, Egyptian or other. No previous work can be compared with it for method or completeness. . . . . Not only are the best engravings from the older authorities utilised, but numerous unpublished designs have been inserted. M. Chipiez has added greatly to the value of a work, in which the trained eye of the architect is everywhere visible, by his restorations of various buildings and modes of construction ; and the engravings in colours of the wall paintings are a noticeable feature in a work which is in every way remarkable. This history of Egyptian art is an invaluable treasure-house for the student ; and, we may add, there are few more delightful volumes for the cultivated idle who live at ease to turn over—every page is full of artistic interest."

THE FORTNIGHTLY REVIEW.

Edited by T. H. S. ESCOTT.

THE FORTNIGHTLY REVIEW is published on the 1st of every month, and a Volume is completed every Six Months.

The following are among the Contributors :—

SIR RUTHERFORD ALCOCK.
MATHEW ARNOLD.
PROFESSOR BAIN.
SIR SAMUEL BAKER.
PROFESSOR BEESLY.
PAUL BERT.
BARON GEORGETON BUNSEN.
DR. BRIDGES.
HON. GEORGE C. BRODRICK.
JAMES BRYCE, M.P.
THOMAS BURT, M.P.
SIR GEORGE CAMPBELL, M.P.
THE EARL OF CARNARVON.
EMILIO CASTELAR.
RT. HON. J. CHAMBERLAIN, M.P.
PROFESSOR SIDNEY COLVIN.
MONTAGUE COOKSON, Q.C.
L. H. COURTNEY, M.P.
G. H. DARWIN.
SIR GEORGE W. DASENT.
PROFESSOR A. V. DICEY.
RIGHT HON. H. FAWCETT, M.P.
EDWARD A. FREEMAN.
SIR BARTLE FRERE, BART.
J. A. FROUDE.
MRS. GARRET-ANDERSON.
J. W. L. GLAISHER, F.R.S.
M. E. GRANT DUFF, M.P.
THOMAS HARE.
F. HARRISON.
LORD HOUGHTON.
PROFESSOR HUXLEY.
PROFESSOR R. C. JEBB.
PROFESSOR JEVONS.
ANDREW LANG.
ÉMILE DE LAVELEYE.

T. E. CLIFFE LESLIE
SIR JOHN LUBBOCK, M.P.
THE EARL LYTTON.
SIR H. S. MAINE.
DR. MAUDSLEY.
PROFESSOR MAX MÜLLER.
G. OSBORNE MORGAN, Q.C., M.P.
PROFESSOR HENRY MORLEY.
WILLIAM MORRIS.
PROFESSOR H. N. MOSELEY.
F. W. H. MYERS.
F. W. NEWMAN.
PROFESSOR JOHN NICHOL.
W. G. PALGRAVE.
WALTER H. PATER.
RT. HON. LYON PLAYFAIR, M.P.
DANTE GABRIEL ROSSETTI.
LORD SHERBROOKE.
HERBERT SPENCER.
HON. E. L. STANLEY.
SIR J. FITZJAMES STEPHEN, Q.C.
LESLIE STEPHEN.
J. HUTCHISON STIRLING.
A. C. SWINBURNE.
DR. VON SYBEL.
J. A. SYMONDS.
THE REV. EDWARD F. TALBOT
(WARDEN OF KEBLE COLLEGE).
SIR RICHARD TEMPLE, BART.
W. T. THORNTON.
HON. LIONEL A. TOLLEMACHE.
H. D. TRAILL.
ANTHONY TROLLOPE.
PROFESSOR TYNDALL.
A. J. WILSON.
THE EDITOR.

&c. &c. &c.

THE FORTNIGHTLY REVIEW *is published at* 2s. 6d.

CHAPMAN & HALL, LIMITED, 11, HENRIETTA STREET,
COVENT GARDEN, W.C.